P9-EEM-029

NORMAN'S LETTER

By the Same Author

THE SLIDE AREA

INSIDE DAISY CLOVER

NORMAN'S LETTER

Postscript by Lady D.

GAVIN LAMBERT

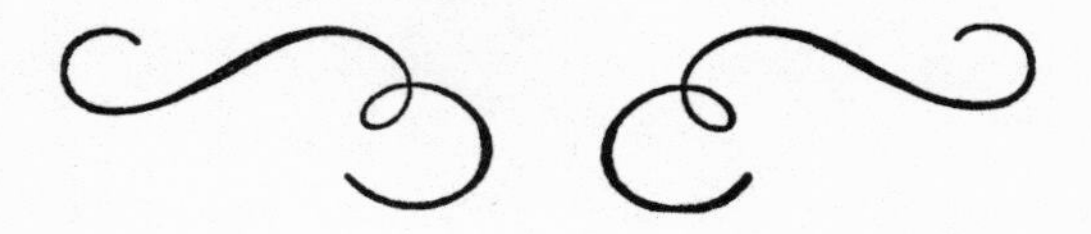

COWARD–McCANN, INC.
New York

First American Edition 1966

Library of Congress Catalog Card Number: 66–20155

PRINTED IN THE UNITED STATES OF AMERICA

To Christopher Isherwood

NORMAN'S LETTER

Casablanca-Bordeaux
3rd of October, 1936

MY DEAR AHMIN,

I WRITE in sorrow; you read, no doubt, in anger. But *can* you read? If not, I humbly believe it might be worth your while to learn, since I have much to tell you—more, perhaps, than I shall ever tell another living soul. Nothing can stop me now, anyway. I'll finish this thing whether or not you begin it. My role is the importunate stranger on the train, the penitent outside the box who doesn't realize midnight struck and the priest dozed off long ago, the madman who buttonholes you in the park, the radio operator, his wireless still intact, stranded on a desert island not on the map. . . . Am I a dodo or a mutation? It depends on your point of view. In any case, I'm a nuisance but not a bore.

Porpoises cause a brace of nuns to exclaim as they rustle past this deck-bench, where I sit with an old typewriter balanced on my knees, heart beating wildly in its usual state of panic and dread! Yearning to be calmed by a calm sea, gazing at the remote, blunt-snouted creatures (porpoises *and* nuns), I wonder if a film can get stuck in a projector and repeat itself maddeningly, like a gramophone needle in a record groove? If so—imagine this person watching, over and over again, images from the most recently foolish and humiliating episode of his life. Suitcase in hand, he sneaks out of a hotel shortly after dawn, and enters a hooded, horse-drawn carriage. Soon he's in a long, dusty snake of a train, chuffing and slithering across the *bled* to Casablanca; he gazes through a squalid window at a desolate treeless world of sand, stones, donkeys and the occasional peasant as white, still and isolated as the occasional cloud in a pitiless sky above his head. Parched and trembling on arrival, he directs a cabdriver to take him like greased lightning to the port, but is stricken on the way with a desire to communicate, and stops at a store to buy a secondhand typewriter, *actually haggling over the price.* Scampers guiltily up the gangway of the *Ziz* just as the final siren blows, loud and clear and rude as the Last Trump.

Empty sky, open sea. Nun glances curiously at me from the deckrail. Do I blush? Small on the horizon passes another ship.

(*Resumed later, after a somewhat greasy lunch.*)

Blue Atlantic, Cape of St. Vincent like a stern, distant finger pointing at me, tincture of oil and salt in the air, lump in the throat, tap tap tap. Despair at making you ever understand. *La chair est triste, hélas, et j'ai lu tous les livres.* Now will the sky please open, will a voice command that solitary passenger to stop being so tiresomely affected? COME OFF IT,

BOY! WHOA! PULL YOURSELF TOGETHER, STAND UP WHEN YOUR MOTHER ENTERS THE ROOM, STOP WEARING HORRIBLE PINK SHIRTS, GET A HAIRCUT, AND MAKE UP YOUR MIND TO DO SOMETHING USEFUL FOR A CHANGE!

So much for the advice I shall never take from the father I never had. Empty sky, open sea, tap tap tap—and my nose twitches suddenly like a sporting retriever's as the Smell of Smells comes back. How delicious it is to arrive in North Africa and be greeted by that insistent yet elusive balm from the filthy, ancient earth. I've wondered before what the recipe is—equal parts of cinnamon, garlic, kif, dung and henna? I first sniffed the classic, all-embracing Fart when I arrived last year in Tripoli, having impulsively decided to visit the Roman city of Leptis Magna. This great ruin stands neglected and solitary on the edge of the Mediterranean, everything—that is to say, the sea itself, the cloudless sky, the occasional scruffy nomad on a donkey—unchanged since legionaries abandoned it centuries ago. Solitary and a bit neglected too, I climbed to the highest row at the back of the amphitheatre and looked down on a vast crumble of steam baths, temples, villas, forum, fountains, stillness. To ghosts and sunlight I recited the only extant line of a verse by my alter ego, the Greek-Egyptian poetess, Oum Salem (1841–1879): *Ah God, dear God, that night when two dark eyes . . .*, and shortly afterward returned to my hotel in a taxi.

Make of this what you can. It was last year, anyway. Now I shall attempt to speak of last night.

The journey was born on a wet autumn afternoon in London, strolling by myself in St. James's Park: damp chill in the air, brown leaves wrinkled on the grass, a tramp truffling for cigarette stubs, a tired sweet toadlike old prostitute roaming the clammy dusk. First a pigeon evacuated on my head, then it started to rain. I dashed into the Ritz bar and ordered a double whisky. "How goes it, sir?" asked the barman with that genial servility of the lower orders, falsely intimate and truly indifferent. "At the moment, not well at all." "And why is that, sir?" I pointed to a window weeping with rain. He smiled oafishly. "If you're only worried about the weather, sir, you're a lucky man." I made no answer, thinking *that's his way of putting you in your place, my sweet,* and retreated to a table in the corner. For a long minute we were silently alone. The barman read an evening paper with a headline about Royal Goats being transferred from Windsor Park to the zoo. Afraid that he might ask my opinion on this controversial matter, I had an answer ready—"Why stop at the Goats?"—but Sir Manfred Barr, an appalling bore, came in. "How goes it, sir?" asked the barman. "Excellent, excellent, thank you, George," Sir Manfred answered, rubbing his hands, ordering a pink gin, nodding as curtly as possible in my direction. Wealth and remote family connections oblige us to acknowledge each other, instinct makes us hate. The bluff fool retreated to another corner, cast a beady eye over the same evening paper. I considered the winter; present company; absent complications like my fiancée, Lily Vail, and my mother, Lady Dorothea; and decided to run for it.

But where? I needed a not too distant place, in order to arrive quickly, yet it had to be exotic and strange, to give a feeling of total escape. Thoughts turned naturally to my guide, comfort and familiar, Oum Salem, and she was on hand as usual, with a particularly exquisite fragment:

Travelers, we came to a dusty crossroads,
Heat, light, date palms, a dark caravan,
King Atlas with snow on his shoulders.
There's mountain chill before desert fever
And the sad lovely Sahara world! . . .

Stepping off the train at Marrakech I saw, like a solemn finger pointing to the sky, the rose-red tower of the Koutoubia. The earth farted silently on all sides. I entered a convenient hooded carriage and a one-eyed Arab whipped his mangy starving horse to the El Bedi hotel. All slanting looks and silent slippered feet, a gracious boy showed me to my room, where I lay immediately on a low hard bed and stared at the courtyard beyond my window. No splash of rain or float of mist, but white walls and blue tiles in the warm late light, and a glistening cypress, another splendid pointing finger, erectly planted in the middle. The effect was simple, uncluttered, hypnotic . . . I closed my eyes and saw nothing but towers, cypresses, fingers, obelisks, lighthouses, skittles—

Then I heard drums!

They were calling me, of course. Like a zombie I arose. Walked. Reached at twilight that huge wild anteroom under the sky, the famous square called Djema el Fnaa. Already it was packed like steerage on a ship, lanterns aloft and figures swaying. Berber youths from the mountains had begun to dance, white robes and sinuous bodies shimmying to the endless whine of music. Kif-smokers squatted in their usual bearded dreams. Outside a tent flying a scarlet flag, a healer with a rotted face waved pieces of live, wriggling snake at me. Past ovens with bread baking and locusts frying in a tornado of steam, past a fat turbaned story-teller spellbinding his circle of listeners cross-legged and unmoving on the ground, I followed the beat of drums. They pounded like thunder as I jostled my way through to a troupe of half-naked Sudanese dancers leaping and cartwheeling in the air, rolling their eyes like epileptics towards a sky with more stars than I'd ever seen. Blank calm faces watched them; pistachio nuts and locusts were stolidly munched; body-spice and tumult closed in; oh thank God, I thought, it's still possible to step from the Ritz bar, and Sir Manfred Barr, and the rain, and complications, to a country where people will tell you that a Negress is imprisoned in the moon because she pissed on a loaf of sacred bread, that you must lower your voice in front of animals—*not servants*—because they understand the language of human beings. I began laughing happily to myself, blessed Oum, noticed snow on the far-away tips of the Atlas mountains. Then I became aware of a dried hedgehog's foot teasingly dangled in front of my face. A scabrous child explained in primitive French that it was a good-luck charm. I bought it, threw it away, and decided I wanted a drink. As I turned, a body collided warmly with mine, a hand touched my arm and didn't let go, a pair of eyes gave me a quick, secretive smile. *Inch'Allah!*

Impossible but unnecessary to speak above the roar of drums. How many dark and winding streets before we reached your shadowy little house, buried in the heart of the medina like treasure in a cave? I know we skirted a puddle with a nauseous stench, and passed a woman crouched against a wall, black veil covering her mouth, eyes rimmed with kohl, hennaed palm waiting for a coin like an art nouveau cup. . . . She whimpered disagreeably, I suppose I didn't give her enough. By now the drums were very faint. You closed the shutters and I couldn't hear them. Beside a flickering lantern on the floor lay a mattress, vast and blatant. I gasped with pleasure at our shivering nakedness when we embraced; I hooted with pain when you came through the back door. And I believe, Ahmin, you enjoyed my pain. Will you be happy to know I still feel it, like a remarkable wine that lingers on the palate, or a very high note of music echoing somewhere in the hills?

Young man on deck-bench gazes at blue Atlantic. Is observed to sigh, fidget, smile at nuns, and ask a passing steward to bring him a cup of tea.

Cavendish Hotel, London
14th of October

The wedding's set for next Thursday so you can imagine I'm fairly busy. This is just a quick paragraph to keep you up-to-date. Arrangements are that Lily will continue her triumphant season at The Dugout until the night before, then she closes for a week and we honeymoon in Venice, at a *palazzo* loaned to us by a friend of Lady D.—who's taken charge of everything, ceremony at the family church and reception (weather permitting) on the lawn at The House afterwards, with champagne, monster cake, marquee, string trio, etc. Roses are doing well but chrysanthemums disappoint this year. Lady D. blames gardener, gardener blames some kind of bug.

Pray for me.

The House, Appleton-on-Waveney
16th of October

Arrived this morning with a dreadful cold and went straight to bed. Lady D. was lying down already, influenza having struck early this year. It rains. We've reclined for hours in separate drafty wings, gazing at high embossed ceilings, ringing bells for breakfast, tea, whisky, and when the fires go out. A performance of *Scheherazade* on the wireless transported me instantly to a secret house, tiled courtyard, huge mattress. . . . Then a bouquet of dahlias arrived from Lily.

Which reminds me. While in London I sent you by special insured and registered mail a gold Swiss watch with more than twenty jewels. It is the first of various gifts you may expect in the future. Since I don't have your address, I sent the package care of the El Bedi Hotel, Marrakech—where this letter will also arrive one day—with instructions to the manager in French and Arabic, on both sides, that it must be surrendered to you and you only. Don't let the sender's name confuse you. I am not George Eliot, which is a convenient alias for use in emergencies and when traveling in the Arab world. You may wonder, all the same, what manner of person you are dealing with; why he flees from you, leaving a light pillow of banknotes beneath your sleeping head, then bares his heart from a distance and vows to overwhelm you with favors . . . ?

Norman Charles Evelyn Lightwood, eleventh baronet, was born the 9th of June, 1910, at the above address—stately home with Tudor markings (31 bed., 3 bath., 4 recep.,

2 din., 2 kit., slave qtrs., etc.)—in the room and bed where he now lies with hot forehead and bloodshot eyes, a coal fire smoking up his nostrils. At the time of birth his sun was in Gemini, his moon in Sagittarius, a "difficult" combination that creates unease, changeableness, and a pronounced tendency to waste time. The Lightwood name claims descent, headlong in my opinion, from that old Duchess of Norfolk mentioned in Shakespeare's (?) *Henry VIII*, and is fairly well known on this particular island. We have produced bishops, generals and madmen, we have accumulated wealth; my grandfather built the Gran Chaco railway, longest line in South America, which I shall own one day, since I'm the end of another long line—infertility having mysteriously afflicted our family in the twentieth century. And yet my position as heir to a name and fortune is odd, not to say fluky. My father was not my father, though he may have been my uncle. I certainly did *not* spring from the loins of Charles Evelyn, tenth baronet, who married Lady D., described in fashionable magazines at the time as "ex-debutante, artist and society beauty." I *may* have sprung from those of his brother Maurice, who left suddenly for Australia. According to Lady D., I *did;* she ought to know but is not the most truthful woman in the world.

Incidentally, the first inkling of a mystery surrounding my birth—I believe that's the correct phrase—was an Object falling from the sky only a few hours before I occurred. Towards dusk, disturbing the languor of that warm windless Sunday, a severe explosion shook Appleton-on-Waveney. No one could agree whether it was a report, or a tremor, or a thud, from above or below the earth itself. It shook the church more than a mile away, overturning a lighted candlestick on the altar and sending the congregation horribly off key in the middle of "How sweet the name of Jesus sounds." All fifty-three rooms of The House shivered; glancing out of her sitting-room window, the cook saw it hurtling through the air and *coming at* the grounds. Following the blast, or bump, an extremely unpleasant odor arose from the middle of the lawn. The cook, like a retriever, tracked it down; gazed, fainted, revived, screamed and gave notice. The rest of the staff calmed her with brandy and complained to Lady D. Although very near her time, to use another correct phrase, her ladyship put on a dressing-gown and waddled to the garden, handkerchief pressed to mouth and pistol clutched in hand.

It was vaguely oval-shaped, Lady D. told me; about two feet long; brownish, clammy, a little warm and apt to give off steam when touched. Feeling it with your eyes closed, you might have been sticking your finger into a fresh custard or sweetbread. The surrounding grass was covered with a delicate ooze, slime or jelly, which soon evaporated. Some said the Object breathed, the cook insisted with a shudder that it wriggled. In her signed statement to the police, Lady D. swore it was inanimate. Asked what it reminded her of, she couldn't say at first, then inclined to a fetus, smiled and murmured dreamily to herself, "It's a boy!" The cook suggested a toad, the chauffeur a turd. But it was too large for any froglike species, and much too large to have been dropped by a British bird. While they were arguing, and waiting for the police, and wondering whether to cover it with an umbrella, the chauffeur's dog came up, ate it, wagged its tail and lived for another twelve years.

So here is something else, Ahmin, to make of what you

will. I have an open mind about *je ne sais quoi* falling from the sky. Are they trying to tell us something, intimidate us, insult us? . . . In any case, I would dearly love to see one of them; if a red or black rain fell on me, if a hairy, rubbery or viscous lump came at me, I should for once in my life experience curiosity without fear.

The mystery of my birth became real, instead of symbolic, when I was ten years old. Lady D. had gone out to dinner and I was woken late in the evening by an owl hooting somewhere. My throat felt dry; I decided to get a glass of milk from the kitchen without asking Nanny Gray, because we were enemies. This young woman (who was murdered some years later, by an odd coincidence, in Casablanca) had red hair, an insolent manner, a nervous giggle and strong communist leanings. All the kitchen lights were out, but I heard laughter and whispering from the servants' quarters as I tiptoed towards the coolers in the larder. Curiosity guided my bare feet to the sitting room door, horror riveted me to the shadows.

She sat as usual on the knee of her paramour, Forbes the chauffeur. A fire sputtered in the grate; his manna-eating dog slept in front of it; the wireless played softly; they drank gin and made lustful sounds. Suddenly Nanny Gray asked in a whining voice, "Did it really say I had a pimple on my neck?" (Yes, I did; and she had; and I'd mentioned it casually to Forbes, just passing the time of day, with no idea he'd betray me.) More heavy breathing, clink of glasses, then— "One day I'll tell the little wretch everything I know!"

"What's that, my duck?" asked Forbes, and she whispered in his ear. Gin, hanky-panky, cruel laughter alternated for a while. "I'll show it the photograph of its Uncle Maurice," she burst out. "You can tell by looking at the eyes! Filthy little bastard, how I loathe that child."

"You can't hold being a bastard against young Norman."

"I'll teach it to spread rumors about my neck." Kiss, grunt. "They're on the way out, anyway." "Who, my duck?" "Rotten rich families, and a good thing too!"

My first reaction to a crisis is always calm. Like the cook, I revive only to scream. I crept away, entered the library, looked up the word *bastard* in a dictionary. *A person born of parents not married to each other. The word is widely and vulgarly used as an indiscriminate term of abuse and sometimes of playful affection.* But Nanny wasn't playing. I climbed the long staircase, ran down a corridor of empty rooms to find and wake my sister, Violet. She wasn't asleep, however; she wasn't there. I climbed a second, narrower flight of stairs. A light burned beyond an open doorway and a voice hissed, *"Don't move!"* She stood in one of the junk-rooms, surrounded by luggage and boxes, wearing a deer-stalker cap and a slim moustache, obviously applied with a piece of burnt cork—you could smell it. The real Violet—pink and ringleted, in a flounced party dress—was by now a blur of memory; after the age of six she was seldom out of disguise. While I told her the appalling news I'd overheard, she up-ended a trunk, climbed on it and examined the ceiling through a magnifying glass. Then she picked up a cane and pointed it sternly at me. "Elementary, my dear Norman. There do not *appear* to be any footprints on the rafters, either. What do you make of that?"

"Tell me what you mean by elementary. I don't want to play."

"I mean it's true." Climbed down, walked to the windows,

glared suspiciously at them, tapping a pane or two, checking latches. They were all closed. "The point is, a gigantic hound got in here somehow. Any suggestions?"

"Is there a trap door? Please tell me how you know it's true."

"I happen to know." She gave me a pitying smile. "Nanny Gray often brings it up over the gin. That woman's tongue is easily loosened."

As usual, she held all the aces. I searched desperately for a trump. "Then you must be a bastard too."

"Won't hold up in court, Norman. We need proof, not hearsay." I got a rap on the shoulder from her cane. "The one who was only *supposed* to be your father really *was* mine. There are documents in the safe." She smiled again. "I found a trap door, of course, but it was much too small for an enormous beast to use."

"Tell me how you know everything."

"It's my profession. And in times like these, it's everyone for himself."

"If you're not really my sister, you don't count—even though you're older."

"I'm half your sister, which is more than enough." The cane trembled. "You're the only bastard here, Norman, so bugger off and let me solve this case." She turned away and began to tap a wall.

In the small cold hours, in the great dark house, a little bastard was weeping. More or less sobered up, Nanny Gray found it huddled on the grand staircase.

"Get up, Norman. What is it now?"

"I wish you were dead."

"You're not to speak to me like that, you little beast."

Night, England and space echo with my screams of rage. She advances on me, then hears the front door open, looks anxious, pretends a smile. "Dear, snookums, petkins. . ." I see her game and roar louder, beating my fists on the paneled wall.

In one of her brilliant velveteen suits, a new fringe to her dark bobbed hair, Lady D. holds a long cigarette wrapped in yellow paper and looks at us with a kind of weary surprise, as if she's entitled to an explanation. I run wailing to her arms. "She told Forbes I'm a filthy little bastard with Uncle Maurice's eyes and Violet said it was true and bugger off."

Drop of ash falls off the cigarette. Heavy eyelids flicker for a moment. Lady D. strokes my head. "And how does Violet know it's true?"

"Nanny Gray always brings it up over the gin."

With a strangled giggle, the creature tries to slink upstairs. Lady D. raises a calm eyebrow. "Well, Miss Gray. The children are evidently out of control. Come and see me in the morning before you leave."

(Frankly, although the newspapers said she had "sunk very low" and was living with a half-caste, and I have no evidence to support my theory, instinct tells me that Nanny Gray's murder was an affair of international espionage.)

Two minutes later I'm warm and snug in Lady D.'s four-poster, watching her undress. Elaborate gleaming rings plop into the jewel box, then she disappears to the bathroom in her corset, winding her watch. The room is suddenly filled with perfume, almost unbearably strong, and she's lying down beside me. Outside, it starts to rain with a lovely sound, patter and drip on roof.

"Dear little Norman." Voice low against the rain. "I didn't

plan for you to know about this, not till you were seventeen." Pause. "Sixteen, possibly." Squeezes my hand. "But forget the rest and remember this. I loved, more than I can ever describe, your wonderful, handsome, glorious, overwhelming Uncle Maurice."

"Then why can't he come back from Australia?"

"It's not done." She gives a long sigh, tickles my neck, and her breath on my face turns the bitter secret into delicious honey. "I've had my great love, you see."

"Is there only one?"

"Alas! But when it's so *absolutely*—" Checks herself. "Only one," she repeats, up to her best trick now, making life into legend, tapping it with a wand of mysterious sadness. "And *you* were the result, my dear little Norman. So you're specially close to me."

"Closer than Violet?"

"In a way."

"Good. But how was I the result?"

"Dearest, I don't know why, your mother is suddenly quite sleepy."

"Tell me."

"It's after midnight. I'll explain tomorrow—it may seem clearer in daylight, anyway."

"I won't sleep till I know."

"I'm afraid, dear little Norman, you won't sleep *after* you know." Lady D. laughs softly to herself, squeezes my hand, starts mumbling about a man and a woman, loving each other, expressing it in *a certain way*, very beautiful. I don't understand. Rain patters on roof, owl hoots again somewhere, I love our secret in the warm scented dark but have to know exactly what it is. "You mean beautiful like Forbes and Nanny Gray?" She tells me not to interrupt, complains she's tired again, but finally switches on a bedside lamp and sits up, looking like a wise statue. I know that look, it means she's about to do something typically startling and extraordinary.

Our voices whisper now, like church. More about love; the moment when people can't help themselves; something to look forward to; *ecstasy*, very beautiful; difficult to follow. Then, cool as you please, she shows me hers and mine, encouraging me to touch. Oddly enough, I drop off to sleep. In the morning I wake and hear it still raining, dull misty light seeps through a gap in the heavy swagged curtains. Lady D. still in the land of Nod. She's the type that always goes very deep into it, takes forever to come out. With her eyes not quite closed, and her mouth slightly open, she reminds me of a Japanese buddha we keep in a glass case in the dining room. I raise the blankets and her nightgown to peep at it again. The dregs of wonder and fear remain, but somehow, in the early morning, it looks disappointing, weedy, adandoned. I hear myself saying loudly to the room, "It's not beautiful and *I don't believe it!*"

Now why do I draw this raffle ticket of memory from the great tub of Time? God knows, it didn't win me anything. Tap tap tap.

Later. Woke up after napping for a couple of hours, found it was dark, remembered part of a long confusing dream in which I rode a mare with a white tulip-shaped marking between her eyes. This must have been India, a present from Lady D. shortly after our little talk in bed. Her forelegs became my favorite place, I lay between them for years, occasionally feeding her sugar and getting a lick. Many silent alone hours passed this way. Sometimes I fell asleep and woke up, just as I did a moment ago, to find night had fallen. Then, walking back across the lawn, I glimpsed Lady D. through windows of a barn she'd converted to a studio, painting a still-life while the yellow cigarette dangled from her mouth and Chopin or Brahms wheezed through the horn of an old-fashioned gramophone. Usually, with a low growl, Violet leaped out at me from the bushes.

Another childhood memory is the disastrous night I spent in the family grotto. This had been built, beyond the lawn, overlooking a stagnant lily pond, for a great-great-granduncle who decided to become an Ornamental Hermit. Lady D. said he was always shown to guests after Sunday luncheon, if the weather was fine; after his death, they found the walls covered with breath-taking graffiti and a mural, extending to the ceiling, of what must have been the longest sex-chain in the world. It exists no longer, of course. The only relic is a plaque above the entrance, dedicated to the Hermit's memory, with the quotation, "Far from the madding crowd's ignoble strife." Violet dared me to pass a night in the place, and I was unable to endure the idea of her taunts if I refused. She gave me a flask of brandy, I wrapped myself in a blanket and fell into a drunken, alarmed sleep. Midwinter; no moon; heavy snowfall during the night. Our tutor cleared the entrance with a shovel after I was missing for breakfast, and found me almost unconscious, stinking of alcohol. I caught pneumonia; Violet told me I might die. Perhaps one thing that attracts me to the desert is its pure, strong, dry air. I never feel snuffly in Islam.

For my seventeenth birthday Lady D. gave me, as well as

a motor car, her latest still-life: haunting little arrangement of three grapefruit, an alarm clock and a length of flesh-colored tube copied (I believe) from an enema kit. Then she lit a yellow cigarette, led me by the hand to a window seat, and said: "Many happy returns, my dear. Charles had gone up to London to see a doctor about some pain in his stomach. Maurice and I fell madly in love that same afternoon. Charles never suspected our tempestuous romance, just as *we* never suspected he had cancer. We were living, I suppose, in different worlds. Unfortunately your aunt Beatrice came upon us in the garage, in the back seat of her Rolls Royce. But please don't think we were careless. The oversight was as rare as it was unwise."

She sighed bravely, as if for a moment the memory had become poignant again, then waved to someone outside. Violet rode slowly down the driveway lined with cedars, on horseback, stiff and alert as she gazed at the sky. She seemed to be expecting another Object—and with a sudden intuition I *understood* my fierce, pathetic sister. From the age of six, the legend of that drastic visitation had haunted her; metaphorically, the Object was still lodged somewhere in her heart, filling it with bile and suspicion, encouraging her fantasy of being Sherlock Holmes. Casting aside all frills and dolls too early, the only security she knew was as a male detective, on the watch for monstrous intruders. . . . Lady D.'s hand rested on my shoulder, her finger stroked my neck, and I realized she was still droning on. "Imagine a horde of Lightwoods arriving by limousine and taxi to harangue, threaten and wheedle your mother. Imagine my showing them to the drawing room, sitting down where I sit now, offering them tea, and informing them I was pregnant again

—by Maurice." She edged closer. "Well, my dear, a treaty was signed over sandwiches and cake. I promised to stay with Charles for the rest of his agony, Maurice promised to stay in Australia, we rang for whiskies and soda and drank to *you,* crossing our fingers for an official male heir. Night fell, the moon came up, the Lightwoods got extremely merry and a few uncles pinched me here and there."

"That's life," I said.

"So it is." She sighed again. "It could have turned out much worse."

"Or much better."

"Really? But how?"

"I don't know. But sometimes I feel all is not as it should be."

"That's rather stern of you, Norman."

"Was it hard, giving up Maurice?"

She appeared to consider the question very carefully. Then she said, "Of course." Getting up, she walked gracefully to the middle of the room and paused in a semicircle of Chippendale chairs. "But I gave up more than Maurice. I gave up everything, except appearances. I became The Lady of Shalott. . . . What are you smiling for, Norman? . . . The pale yellow woods were waning," said Lady D. to the empty chairs, "the mirror cracked from side to side and I began singing my last song. I grew half sick of shadows." Eyelids drooped for a moment. "Then I got used to it. There's much to be said, as I hope you discover, for a convenient, comfortable existence."

At that moment I looked right *through* her, beyond the aura of fatigue and wisdom to a great marble heart, to—

Her footsteps approach along the corridor. *Must hide this!*

17th of October

Five feet, nine inches of body with brown wavy hair and merrily pointed face, alarmed eyes, small hands and feet, still lies in bed recovering from a cold; anticipating with dread and mischief a marriage to Lily Vail; remembering with warm regret a pair of strong Arab limbs. It will now pass an hour or two by telling you how it met Lily—then get up, I suppose, and marry her.

Lady D. and I usually spent a week in London together at least once a year. She bought "amusing," fashionable clothes, a feathered bowler, "Guardsman" suits with epaulettes and army buttons, embroidered silk ties, slave bangles; had her hair bobbed more raggedly than ever; went to morning house parties in Upper Bohemia and danced a fast foxtrot to folk songs; exhibited her still-lifes in a remote gallery, where they were recommended in the gossip column of *The Tatler*—"Lady Dorothea's apples look, as usual, good enough to eat." One evening we went to The Dugout, a nightclub in a cellar near the Thames, and sat drinking beer and eating rather stale sandwiches while a small thin creature sang. Cleverly dressed in rags and a mop of buttery yellow hair, Lily had a knack of appearing innocently shocked at the double meanings she found in old music-hall favorites like "Hold your hand out, naughty boy" and "A little of what yer fancy does yer good." Bawling them out in her slight, hoarse, dockside voice, suitably accompanied by a barrel organ, she clapped a hand over her mouth and looked reproachful when the audience laughed. At the end, she announced she would sing requests. Waving a Russian cigarette, Lady D. called in a commanding Cockney accent, "I'm one of the ruins that Cromwell knocked about a bit." "Ooh, you filthy thing!" said Lily, and obliged. After a sensational version of "Tommy, make room for your Uncle," she came over to our table.

"Well," she said to Lady D., "I'm glad the grand life hasn't knocked all the fun out of you."

Lady D. congratulated her on a charming performance, and introduced me.

"Well," said Lily. It was her way of starting almost every sentence. "How and what do you do?"

"Norman's a poet." Lady D. patted my arm. "He makes brilliant translations from the Egyptian."

"My Lord!" A waiter brought Lily a tankard of beer, and the little thing drank greedily. I was very aware of the contrast between her delicate physical presence—narrow hips, flat chest, white skin, hands even smaller than mine—and the way she winked, rolled her eyes, wiped beer foam off her lips, and nudged me heartily in the ribs. "You ought to take time off from the Egyptian," she said, "and write a song for me."

Lady D. nodded approval. "That would be quite amusing, Norman."

"You've got your Ma's permission," said Lily, "so I won't take no for an answer." She finished her beer, asked me to take her out to dinner the following week, nodded at Lady D., "Be a good girl now, Dotty," and went off to another table.

Lady D. flicked ash off her cigarette. "I met her three days ago, at a swimming party. Strangely appealing, isn't she?"

"Yes. But she frightens me."

"All women frighten you, my dear. It's part of what makes

you enormously attractive." She smiled. "An intelligent, politely scared young man of means, with eyes like yours, is always irresistible. It took only five minutes for Lily Vail to be mad about you."

Naturally I didn't believe her; but the idea, like Lily herself, was strangely appealing. "I hardly said a word to her."

"That was clever."

"Not at all. She frightened me."

Lady D. fixed me with a long, melting, gravely affectionate look.

"That frightens me too."

She reached for my hand, held it softly. Her face a quizzical mask. Lady of Shalott or flirtatious buddha? . . . Sibylline, anyway, with cigarette smoke twisting in the half-light.

"You're up to something. Tell me."

Her perfume became unbearably strong. I thought of our talk in her bed, my early morning peep under the blanket and a tremble of rain on the roof. A line of Oum reeled into my head—*Dark smiling lady, wrapped in your bright cloak, why . . . ?*

"Dearest Norman, I *understand*." Lady D. spoke gently, but it sounded like a warning to me. "And you must always do as you like. But if we're going to be unconventional in private, let's be good sports in public. Otherwise, don't you agree, life's just a little bit awkward?"

I told her she was right, and I was tired, and would she mind if I went to bed? We took a taxi to the hotel, waving Lily goodnight. I relaxed in a hot bath, dressed again, walked to Piccadilly Circus and prowled for an hour or two.

A man with a foreign accent propositioned me outside a church in Soho. I liked the exotic look of him, then felt sudden alarm and rushed away. He called out after me, sounding annoyed, in a language I didn't understand. Roumanian, probably.

After tea. My fear of writing anything under my own name—it's much too compromising—led me to invent, at the age of nineteen, a literary lady named Oum Salem, also known in Greek as Dorkion. I wrote a few gnomic poems and sent them, disguised as translations from the Egyptian via the Greek, to a magazine in America. The editor was enthusiastic and wanted to know all about Oum; my powers of invention were taxed and delighted. I composed a letter telling all I'd been able to discover of this solitary mysterious lady (Lady D, you might say, as she thinks she is and I would like her to be) who spent most of her thirty-eight years in the walled and holy city of Fez. I enclosed a clipping from a defunct French periodical, printed at my own expense, in which she was described as the Emily Dickinson of Islam. Well-born, fastidious, secretive, only child of an Arab merchant and a Greek actress, she never married; convention demanded that her great love remain passionately unrealized. The walled, inward life drove her to a perpetual trance of wisdom and compassion, devious as the cool gray alleys of her medina. Great events, touching in their simplicity, were a trip to Marrakech, an *aouache* (wedding ceremony) in a tiny mountain casbah at night, a camel caravan trailing along the beach at Mogador. . . . Oum died from a stray bullet fired by a Spanish soldier during an outbreak of fighting near Tetouan, and her grave is marked only by a heavy silver bracelet, set with pale red desert stones, in a common cemetery on the edge of the Sahara.

As well as printing copies of the "original" slim volume and a 1901 Greek translation at my own expense, I also made over an old Victorian gown (from a box in one of the junk-rooms) into a *djellabah,* borrowed a picture hat from Lady D., kohled my eyes and hennaed my hands, and then photographed myself in this disguise, slightly out of focus, aging the negative by tinting it with sepia. If you have money, these things are surprisingly easy to arrange, and give the oddest, most secret kind of satisfaction. The best and most lasting lies are always expensive, and the pity is that so few wealthy people have the imagination to indulge in really profound fantasies.

I would scarcely expect, Ahmin, that you heard of the vogue enjoyed by Oum's poems here two years ago, when a British edition followed the American one, both with my photograph on the wrapper. My greatest triumph occurred when they were reissued in Greece, from my faked copy, and translated into other languages. Then, unfortunately, rival English versions of a few poems appeared, and one or two were even pronounced superior to mine. This spurred me to a Moroccan trip, during which I found time to unearth the famous "lost" odes, and regain my ascendancy on the market. (Prudence restrained me from discovering parts of a journal.) Nor would I expect that you've read *Frankenstein* by Mary Shelley; but if I tell you it was the fable of a man who invented a brilliant, imaginative monster and was then dominated by it, you'll understand the allusion. From her modest beginnings—frivolity, revenge, escape—Oum rose to great power. Guide and companion, not to say absolute ruler, she now follows me like a shadow—or do I follow *her,* a shadow myself? These days she tells me what to do before I even ask. She spoke, you know, that fateful morning when I woke beside you on the mattress—she spoke very firmly. I listened, sighed and fled. . . . Last year, by the way, I made a special trip to Vienna to consult a professor of nervous diseases at the university there. After hearing the story of Oum, the great man told me that my problem was very common in the Middle Ages, and classed me among the Higher Masochists, those who glorify and raise to an impossibly high plane the object (Lady D.) of their unnatural worship. I was distinctly not impressed, and said so; but it didn't stop him including me in one of his preposterous volumes—Case 43, sandwiched between a goat-fetishist and a man excited by warts.

However. Oum also developed a habit of *not saying a word* when I needed her most, or putting into my head a line so obscure that it was no help at all. For instance, I knew she would never have agreed to write a song for Lily Vail, let alone propose marriage to her—but on this subject she remained obstinately, cruelly silent.

So, impelled by Lady D., the opposite of silent on this matter, I took Lily to an Italian restaurant in Soho. In a warm little room, ourselves even warmer from the wine, we faced each other across a rickety table. A last carafe stood between us and a voluptuous jet-black mole gleamed darkly above the entrance to her bosom. (She wore an "artistic" smock, cut very low.) This jewel-like growth held me enthralled, like one of those spots you're supposed to concentrate upon before being hypnotized.

"I'll have another friendly drop, please, Norman."

I poured for both of us, drained my glass and found the courage to confess. "I couldn't write a song for you. Nothing seemed good enough."

She looked surprised, but not for the reason I imagined. It was simply that she'd forgotten she ever asked me. "Well! Better confess too, hadn't I? Make me stand in the corner if you want, but it was just a trick."

Alarm coursed through my veins, headier than Chianti. Convinced that she'd found a copy of Oum, studied the photograph, and the jig was up, I stammered that I wasn't a real poet, only a translator, a kind of extension plug for transmitting the current of others. She gave me a generous wink above the rim of her glass. "Stop running yourself down, I don't like it. It was a trick to make sure I'd see you again."

"Really?"

"Posolutely."

"Why?"

Her knee brushed against mine, light and quick as a dragonfly's wings. Damn Lady D. for being right, I thought, it's not like her. And now Lily was staring at me, bewildered, forlorn, on the brink of tears.

"My dear girl, is something the matter?"

"Something's the matter with *you,* my dear boy. You're so wickedly polite, you open doors and stand up and laugh at the right moment, you listen as if you really want to hear and look surprised when people like you—I can't bear it!"

After a moment I burst out laughing. "It's all an act," I said. "To annoy people."

She seemed astonished, then annoyed, then began laughing too and told me she knew it all along. "I've had one over the eight, that's my only problem."

"Mine too, Lily!"

In the silence when we stopped laughing, I concentrated on her mole. She noticed, and touched it. "Some people think I should have it removed."

"Don't listen to them."

"If you say so, Norman." Reflective now, she peered at me again over the rim of her glass. "Dotty," she murmured. "Wonderful old girl, but for a mother . . . no thank you." She clapped a hand over her mouth. "Make me stand in the corner?"

I shook my head. "Go to the top of the class."

"That's a relief. Had to say it. Been on my mind. Lovely to get it off. Got a sister too, haven't you?"

"Violet, a bully. But she disappeared."

"Who did it?"

"She walked out last summer and failed to get in touch. Lady D. says she'll come back if she needs us."

"What a mother."

"Then there was Nanny Gray." I gulped the rest of the wine. "The unspeakable terror. Pushed me in the closet with the family skeleton . . . Lily, I feel I can confide in you. Am I right?"

She nodded and stubbed out a cigarette. I noticed the ashtray was stolen goods—*Royal Hotel Edinburgh* printed across the middle, under a coat of arms. Dipping my finger in Chianti, I drew a crimson line across it, slanting from upper right to lower left.

"Now what's that?" Lily asked, as I'd intended.

"A bend sinister. I was born, hushed up, on the wrong side of the blanket."

Her eyes gaped. "You're not Dotty's then?"

"Not Sir Charles's."

"I'll be jiggered. Now who got into old Dotty's bed?"

"Possibly my uncle Maurice. They sent him to Australia but I wouldn't describe the case as open and shut."

"What a mother. Never mind." A friendly nudge. "How do you do, Sir Norman, child of love? They're always exceptional, you know."

An attractive waiter (Italian, but with a musky hint of Saracen forebears, probably from Naples) handed me the bill.

"In my case, Lily, I'm afraid it would be difficult to tell. Exceptions have surrounded me from birth, to say the least. When I was a child, people used to find me sitting by myself, talking to myself. 'How odd,' I was always remarking. 'How very odd.' " Saracen or not, the waiter's addition was incorrect; he'd overcharged me one and sixpence. But when I complained, his charming smile vanished. I made it up on the tip.

"Can't say I blame you." Lily's voice was growing louder. "Take their money away and most rich people would find themselves in the booby hatch today. Some's amusing, like old Dotty, but they're all touched. I mean it, Norman, and if you read Lawrence you'd know how and where the rot started." To my amazement, the little thing beat the table with her fist. "At the top and in the blood!"

Indignant spots burned on her cheeks. Like a concealed mine suddenly stepped upon, she asked the restaurant (empty now but for ourselves and the waiter, who probably didn't understand, since he looked bored) whether it knew there'd been three hundred years of syphilis in the Royal Family. "It began with the Tudors, the Virgin Queen never had eyebrows and all her teeth fell out. They passed it around like the latest news, Norman, till finally they had to bring in Germans to clean it up, and even then . . . Well! It's no surprise the upper classes are what they are. The ones who weren't dripping with it were terrified they soon would be—which explains America, you know. The Puritans piled into the Mayflower, trying to get away from it, but someone on board had it already, because . . . We all know the rest, and I think you'd better take me home."

In the taxi I couldn't help thinking of uncles and aunts, all mysteriously unmarried or sterile or barren. "Very interesting, Lily, but I'm not sure exactly where *I* fit in."

"You don't, I hope. So take my advice and stop worrying." (Strange advice after what she'd just told me.) "Time to strike out on your own, my boy." Her hand snuggled into mine. "Over twenty-five and still living at home's not right."

"Lady D. and I inhabit separate wings. I make trips, and translations, without her."

"You could be saying that till you die." Taxi stopped. She put an arm round my neck. "Funny sweet Norman, thanks for a wonderful evening." Warm, vintage breath on my mouth. "Kiss me goodnight . . . Mmmm. Put your tongue inside . . . Oooh, mmmm. See again soon." She opened the door. "Don't get out, I hate it when you're polite." She lurched to the pavement, turned back, winking at me through the window. "And it's time they stopped holding you back."

"Who?"

"All those strong women. Make a start by clearing them out of your life."

A week later, on Hampstead Heath, I asked her to marry me. Sunset stroll beside a large gray pond, mothers and nannies watching children sail toy boats. From time to time they sound anxious tribal cries—"Toby, dear!" "Come *along,* Marjorie!" Lily imitates them, then her voice slides obstinately into something the vicar's wife at Appleton calls *See-oh-em,* meaning Common. As she tells me about her family, it's like being read to from a novel on how the other half lives. *The Brass Tack* in Limehouse, perched on stilts above the Thames: father owned it, mother served behind the bar, Doreen the hunchback helped on weekends and tried to interest rough customers in meetings of the Theosophical Institute. While luckier babies sleep or howl in hooded carriages, I have a vision of Lily opening her eyes to foul language, sailors bellowing for beer, fights, tattoos, a mystic cripple and fog from the sluggish river. . . . No sign of this, however, in the mischievous, chattering girl who takes my arm as we walk to the edge of the Heath, and tells how at sixteen she fell in love with a Communist.

"Name of Jack. He was a dish but much too serious. I only joined the Party because he made such a fuss. We went on rambles, carried silly placards that said Down with the Means Test and the Ruling Class. But you weren't supposed to laugh about anything, and I couldn't stand it. He's married now, I saw them last year getting off a bus. She wore glasses." Lily's face became wistful. "Isn't it a pity when people with the right ideas are awful bores?"

The sun slipped away, it was suddenly dusk. "Am I to take it, Lily, that you disapprove of capitalism?"

"Oh yes, it's unfair."

"Then you disapprove of *me?*"

"Oh no, it's nothing personal."

"You don't think I should give it all away?"

"Not yours to give yet, is it?"

"Only part of an enormous income at present. But unlimited credit, which comes to the same thing."

"Well, then." Her eyes twinkled. "Sit back and let everything take its course. It'll all be swept away in the end."

"Don't be ridiculous, Lily."

"Don't be obsolete." She sounded fierce. "Look around for once, open those nice eyes wide and admit it's a changing world."

"I admit it. But why do you talk about change as if it's disagreeable, and means I'll lose all my money?"

She giggled. "Well, when we take over, we'll spare a few of the Lightwood millions, if you behave yourself."

"There's only a few to spare. Some property and holdings here, the Gran Chaco railway, a good deal of Malayan rubber—"

"Don't boast, it's vulgar. And a minute ago you said even a part of the income was enormous. Besides, if you don't believe in socialism, what's left? God?"

"When I was fifteen, I'd go into churches, if they smelt nice, sink to my knees in front of the altar and pray. Just for faith. I thought if I had it, it might help."

"That's pathetic."

"No, it wasn't serious enough."

"Then *be* serious and tell me what you really believe in."

After a pause I said: "The Loch Ness Monster."

"Sometimes I wonder why I bother with you."

"That's what all my nannies said. I wanted to believe in Doctor Abram's Box as well, but according to *The Times* it's been totally discredited."

"You mean the piece of rubbish that looks like a gramophone? How could you even *want* to fall for it?"

"It was supposed to diagnose any ailment through one's handwriting, and I like the idea of plugging in a little gadget to solve everything."

"Every joke you make is really a cry for help."

"And are you going to help?"

Almost without realizing it—speaking for myself, anyway—we had walked into a little hollow screened by tall shrubbery. Lily put her arms around me and bit my ear. The pain was a delicious surprise. It thrilled and terrified me, unmistakable sign that I'm going to be deeply involved. Soon we were on the ground, Lily burrowing into me like a mole. I suppose she was the first person I met who wouldn't take no for an answer. Oum was desperately needed, I begged her to speak, incomprehensible or not, but the voice I heard belonged to Lady D. "Dearest Norman, I hoped for this but I never expected it." Damn her! The rest was fear of pneumonia and the police arriving, and a leaping, glorious sense of doing something unavoidably wrong.

When I asked Lily to be my wife, she seemed surprised and drew away. "All right," she said. "If you're sure you really want me."

Palazzo Steblechi, Venice
25th of October

We arrived here last night, not speaking.

At least the wedding itself was quite amusing. Lady D.'s

preparations had included "bringing around" the Lightwoods, since our distinguished family might have been expected to disapprove of my marriage to a publican's daughter. "I shall point out there's a pleasant Edwardian touch to it, like a Duke carrying off a chorus girl. Also, my dear, from their point of view it's the first really spunky thing you've ever done."

Seventeen uncles, aunts and cousins arrived, and all the absentees sent spoons, silver teapots, tureens, etc., regretting that age or disease prevented them from making the journey. Aunt Beatrice was among the missing, due to a recent attack of gout, but her sister arrived in that famous Rolls Royce upon whose back seat Lady D. enjoyed her one great love. (I intercepted her nostalgic glance at the finely preserved, classic limousine. Later she told me it had been reupholstered.) To the Lightwoods, a wedding was rather like a hunt. They'd have picked Lily up by her brush, if she had one. Noisy throughout the ceremony, they drank endless toasts afterwards on the lawn. There was a good deal of stock market talk between uncles, and the aunts investigated flowerbeds, begging Lady D. for cuttings. Dog-keeping aunts, I noticed, had a tendency to look like their pets—you could tell by her large, watery eyes that Aunt Hester was fond of spaniels, while frizzy and snappish Aunt Madge obviously preferred chows. The bride's family, less numerous but just as colorful in its way, was represented by Mr. and Mrs. Vail "and friend." They'd asked if they might bring Doreen, and the hunchback sat between them in church, holding a hand of each. I remember she wore a mauve teagown; Mrs. Vail was gaunt in lace, her husband had a bushy moustache and a pair of large scarlet ears. (Unspeakable *menage a trois?* I don't think so—people say that the English look drab and are really extraordinary, but I find the opposite equally true.) Lady D., very much the star of the show—"look what I've brought off," she seemed to be saying—offered them a tour of The House. Vail asked jovially where she kept the ghosts.

By late afternoon the sun rested low and huge in the sky, like a red-hot dinner gong, but the air was chilly. The Lightwoods had moved indoors for serious drinking, and the garden lay abandoned in a blurred hazy light. A wind ruffled the marquee, which reminded me for a long aching moment of an emir's tent. . . . Then Lily and I were driving to Dover.

A travel agent engaged by Lady D. met us at the customs house. Wearing a black suit and bowler hat, he looked more like an undertaker. After he'd instructed a porter to be careful of Lady Lightwood's baggage and offered his best wishes for a smooth crossing, the happy pair fled up the gangway to a stateroom jammed with flowers and champagne. Lily patted my hand and suggested we start drinking. Did I explain that after our sunset performance on Hampstead Heath she'd said, "Not again, love, till we're legal"—imagining, I suppose, that to withhold her priceless favors would strengthen her position? In fact it strengthened *mine,* since I doubted I could ever take the stage with her again, unless a moment of truly soul-stirring panic occurred. So the cork popped, the siren blew, the engines shuddered and we drifted out to sea! At last Lily retired to the w.c., and as soon as she locked the door I shouted "Back in ten minutes!" and went up on deck. Dark sky, cold sea. Naturally, Ahmin, I thought of another boat, the *Ziz* that took me away from you and back to Lily; in retrospect, those nuns seemed symbolic. . . . I wanted to continue this letter, which I'd packed in a suitcase, but it wasn't of course the time or the place. Leaning over the deck-rail, I tried once more to summon Oum—but my old companion was still cloaked in a treacherous silence, a falling tide, a lodestar that refused to shine. So I was forced for a giddy interval to communicate with *myself,* began to understand my situation and felt much worse. Perhaps you've guessed that I'm romantically a timid person (in action, that is, not feeling), but do you know why? *You and Lily were both my first,* because for a long time I thought life held only two alternatives, one horrid and the other against the rules. Now, realizing which way the cat had jumped, I saw a third: the English Channel. After a brief, hopeless, enjoyable fantasy of leaping into the swell, hearing cries of "Man overboard!", I returned to the nuptial cabin—where Lily greeted me with a rather tight-lipped smile. When I asked if anything was wrong, she accused me of abandoning her. My excuse of feeling a little seasick and needing fresh air apparently satisfied her.

At Calais we boarded the Orient Express, and rattled through Normandy while the bride undressed in our sleeper. Smoking furiously, I sat on the edge of the bunk and watched. Thin and wiry in the buff, she came to sit on my knee, removed my cigarette and bit my ear again. I switched out the light at once, and in a whirl of champagne, regret, speed, terror and general inconvenience everything went quite swimmingly, the narrow bunk became a vast mattress, there were gasps of "funny sweet Norman," bony hips and sharp nails digging into the base of my spine. At last I lay back in a mild sweat and asked her to light me another cigarette. A flame lit up the darkness as she leaned over me, watching me inhale with the same tight-lipped smile and letting the match burn down almost to her fingers. She blew it out and I gave a startled cry. The hot charred end had dropped—deliberately, I was convinced—right below my navel. She clambered swiftly off me, switched on a harsh bluish light. Dazed, blinking, I looked around the compartment and found it empty. I sat up and bumped my head on the bunk above. Her laugh came from somewhere, sharp as a knife, while I felt two centers of pain, the burn and the bump, in my body. As I got to my feet, I saw her huddled in the top bunk, wrapped in a blanket with *Chemin de Fer* across it. Too astonished even to cover my nakedness (another correct phrase), I merely gaped at her while she glowered back, transformed from minx to fury, and the train surged through the night at sixty miles an hour.

"Well!" Her voice was cutting now, like the laugh. "That was an unexpected bonus, Norman—but it won't work!"

I could only stare at her, helpless in the altogether.

"For God's sake cover yourself up." She threw me another blanket. I threw it back and put on a dressing-gown, trying to appear calm. "What did you want me for?" she asked loudly. "Hostess or camouflage? Were you going to tell me or let me find out for myself? How did you think I'd feel? Did it even matter to you?"

"Goodness, Lily." I was beginning to recover composure. "What a lot of questions."

"I'm waiting for a lot of answers, my boy." Then: "I read it. Well, ten minutes of it. While you needed air."

In a flat cold voice she pronounced your name. She made it sound quite ugly, like "Aymin." I corrected her: "Hahmeen." A long, crucial silence followed, during which I had a wry memory of being ten years old, in the library at Appleton, searching a dictionary for the word *bastard.* I felt peculiarly reassured, and began to dress.

"Where are you going?"

"I need air again."

"Not till I've finished with you."

"You had no right to read that letter and I refuse to discuss it."

"Ooh, aren't we grand?"

"We are disgusted and have nothing further to say."

She threw everything available at me, which fortunately wasn't much: a pillow, *The Undying Fire* by H. G. Wells and a bottle of perfume that broke, filling the compartment with a rich, heady aroma. I left to pace the corridor for a while, then asked the conductor if he had a *couchette* to spare. Nothing. The train lurched through darkened countryside as if it would never stop. I found a suitcase and sat on it; an image came to me of Lady D. in moonlight, peacefully asleep with her mouth not quite closed; I returned to the honeymoon compartment, but Lily had locked the door. Since she obviously expected me not to make a scene, I beat on it with all my force. She opened up, her face bright and smiling as if nothing had happened.

"Sorry, love, didn't think you were coming back and didn't want any strange Frenchmen barging in."

The scent was still overpowering. I climbed to the upper bunk and lay down in my clothes, exhausted. When she switched out the light, her voice came soft and wheedling from the darkness: "Give me that letter, of your own free will—give it to me and never ask what I've done with it—and I swear I'll never mention it again."

"It would be like giving you my soul."

"Norman, I'm feeling better now and trying to make a go of it after all." Her voice hardened. "Won't you meet me halfway?"

"It seems to me I already have. Leave me alone and let me sleep."

Mercifully, she did. I awoke late and saw Alps outside the window. Lily had gone. It suddenly occurred to me that she'd made off with this letter, I opened my suitcase with a wildly beating heart and found the pages still safely clipped together in their large manila envelope. However, my passport was missing. As I entered the dining car I saw Lily at the far end, sipping coffee and munching a croissant. She looked up as I approached, her face elaborately impassive now.

"Sleep well, Norman? Have some eggs, you look peckish."

"My passport has vanished."

She didn't bat an eyelid. "My word! Are you sure? Have you looked properly?"

"Everywhere."

"Well, that's a nuisance for you. You'll have to see the British consul when we get to Venice."

"There's the Italian border first. They may not let me through."

"Try a handsome bribe, love, it usually works." She got up, handing me her breakfast bill. "Someone got off the train at Lyon and now there's an extra single sleeper, so I've taken it. We need time for ourselves to think things out, don't we? See you in Venice."

She walked off calmly, giving me a little tap on the shoulder. Of course I knew she'd taken my passport, she suspected me of planning to jump the train. Of course she waited till the last moment to rescue me—an Italian official was practically dragging me out of the compartment when she appeared in the doorway.

"Would you believe it? You must have put it in my luggage by mistake!" She sat down beside me on the bunk, thumb between her teeth in the childish gesture she sometimes affected. "You *do* get into a lot of trouble," she said, eyes smiling, "I suppose that's why you married me, to have someone to get you out of it?"

She stayed with me, chattering brightly, until we steamed out of Milan, the last stop before Venice. She gave me a nudge as she left—"I'll never forgive you, you know"—and I didn't see her for the rest of the journey.

By mistake, Countess Marguerite Osterberg-Steblechi was still in residence at her *palazzo*. She was supposed to be going to Paris, but at the last moment couldn't remember why. "Under the circumstances, dear child, I couldn't face it," she said.

Undoubtedly she's still depressed by the death of her husband three years ago. The Count was scandalously unfaithful, but she adored him. I remember meeting them both as a child, when Lady D. took me to tea at their house in Curzon Street. Slim and handsome in her late forties, poised between bewilderment and boredom on the edge of a wing chair, she looked then like an illustration from a furniture-and-antique magazine—"Notice the Biedermeyer console on her left, the Bokhara rug and the Count himself standing in front of the Adam fireplace with its unusually fine arabesques. . . ." Now she shuffled across the flagstones of her enormous, drafty salon like an exhausted drudge, stout and wheezing, her mouth smudged with the remnants of (I think) chocolate cake. She apologized for her distracted mood; a Hungarian couple who claimed to be cousins of her late husband had been staying with her, and after they left two nights ago she discovered a set of Persian miniatures was missing.

"They seemed charming and certainly knew everybody. Who would have guessed it?" The Countess sank to a sofa with springs that creaked like a sigh. Beyond the window I saw Venice on the edge of winter, splendid and melancholy. The room stretched away on all sides, a sparse yet extravagant landscape: the red plush sofa, some spindly Gothic chairs with legs and arms like skeletons, a chandelier pockmarked by flies, a great stone male nude presiding over a card table, and a harpsichord decorated with tender gods and goddesses in the style of Botticelli. The Countess turned to Lily and began asking whom she knew in London, reeling off improbable names like ex-King Manoel of Portugal, Lord Kinnoull the racing motorist, Somerset Maugham and the Mitford girls. Lily said she knew them all and even had the insolence to imply that the ex-King made a pass at her in the royal enclosure at Ascot, which amused the old thing greatly. "Lady Lightwood is charming, really charming," she informed me. "Happy young couples are so rare these days; one is always hearing of marriages that don't even last a week."

Lily asked if she might have a drink.

"You may have anything you want!" The Countess

beamed at her and pulled a bell cord that obviously didn't work. I went out to the hall on the pretext of finding a servant, and discovered no less than four, playing cards in the dining room. "*Scusi*," I opened with deliberate irony, then told them the ladies were thirsty, sneaked out of the *palazzo* and found myself on the edge of a small, evil-smelling canal. Fortunately Marguerite's gondolier was waiting, almost as if he expected me; I felt he was Charon piloting a black bark with rich purple cushions as we glided down to the Piazza San Marco on a chilly, empty, silent journey. I stepped out to the square, where pigeons outnumbered people, dusk was falling and time tolled out suddenly from the Clock Tower, its bell sounding like the crack of doom when those giant blackamoor marionettes struck it. Outside Florian's were nothing but deserted tables, I chose one, ordered a grog and wondered about Lily's game. Her brightness now was much worse than her anger, it had the radiance of absolute hatred. In fact her behavior since discovering this letter to you seemed overwhelmingly fishy—if she'd decided never to forgive me, why come to Venice and ingratiate herself with old Marguerite? There was only one answer, and it unnerved me: to gain her confidence and spill terrible beans. . . . I rushed back to the *palazzo* in the gondola, if that's not a contradiction in terms, and found them side by side, cocktails in hand, the Countess showing Lily her scrapbooks, Lily crowing with unlikely enthusiasm over photographs of yachts and dowagers, the Count being decorated with some obscure order by an exiled monarch, and—"Look at this one, Norman, isn't she lovely?" Lily called out, handing me a page from a society paper of the 20's. It showed the Countess wearing a ball gown and tiara to endorse a patent medicine, a glass of which she held in her hand like champagne, saying that she knew from a Bonaparte that Napoleon attributed his vitality to a daily dose of its chief ingredient. "You never told me Marguerite was so fascinating!" said Lily, and the Countess actually shot me a disapproving glance, then turned back to her admirer with a smile. "Not everyone appreciates me as you do, I'm afraid." Not to lose face, I was obliged to sing her praises at length, but this only drew another veiled rebuke from my wife: "You don't have to convince *me*, Norman, I can see she's wonderful." The nightmare continued through dinner, with three servants waiting on us, placing meager food on crested china and pouring cheap wine into priceless goblets, while Lily regaled the old thing with her account of our courtship. "You've no idea how shy he was! Really a blushing bridegroom! I've got Dotty to thank for bringing the whole thing off, always there to encourage me when I'd just about given up hope. . . ." The Countess dozed off, however, over zabaglione. When she began to snore, I decided it was time to put a stop to everything.

"Lily, the situation is absurd and humiliating."

She put a finger to her lips, jerking her head. A servant watched us from the doorway, no doubt wondering if we were going to steal an heirloom. I glared at him but he didn't move.

"Don't make a scene, you silly; he doesn't understand English and it doesn't matter what we say as long as you keep calm."

Marguerite's head drooped lower over the table, chin dangerously close to her glass of zabaglione, which Lily moved away and replaced with a napkin. "There, now she can slump without getting messy."

I started to get up. "Wouldn't it be better to talk in private?"

"No, I want more wine." Holding the empty decanter aloft, she snapped her fingers at the servant. "*Pronto!*" she said.

"You are behaving like a fiend."

"I don't believe I understand you." Lily's eyes grew enormous with astonishment. "Are you accusing *me* of behaving badly towards *you?*"

"Your indiscreet curiosity may have given you a shock, for which I'm sorry, but that doesn't excuse you dropping a hot match on my bare stomach, throwing books and bottles at me, stealing my passport, trying to make me feel ridiculous and uncomfortable in front of countesses and servants—"

"You're free to go, Norman, any time you like."

"I'm aware of that. I'm leaving tomorrow."

"Oh, I hoped you'd leave tonight." She gave me a pitiless smile. "I'm staying on for a bit, it's interesting to get a glimpse of this frightful meaningless world, though I suppose you're used to it."

"Your real motive, I'm sure, is to blacken my name in this place."

"It's black enough already. Everything's fallen beautifully into place. Of course I guessed about you from the start, Norman, I can always spot one, but I didn't expect that letter to drop in my lap on our first night together. In fact I was afraid you'd go to bed with me again and again, just to prove something to yourself."

"Then what are you after now?"

The servant brought back the decanter, filled with less than two inches of wine. "My God, the rich!" said Lily. She poured, then raised her glass to me. "I'm going to make you hoot with another kind of pain, my boy. Nothing romantic about it this time. Just the cry of a Lightwood when he has to part with an awful lot of money."

Magically, the word caused Marguerite to wake up. She gave us both a vague, alarmed look and asked who was losing money, and how much, and why.

"Ex-King Manoel," my wife answered promptly. "I heard someone took him all the way to Queer Street."

I excused myself abruptly, leaving them to lies and candlelight and the dregs of rotten wine.

When I said goodby, the Countess was having breakfast in her canopied bed: tea with a spoonful of honey, and a single rose laid on the crested tray.

"Dear child, I don't understand. Why have you decided to abandon this charming young person?"

"She's not charming, she's dreadful. Last night she admitted she's only after my money. Beware of her!"

A veil of confusion slipped over the deep, small eyes. "Why? She's not after *my* money too, is she?"

"She told me she intends to stay on here. I suggest the servants watch her every move."

"She'll be bored, I'm afraid. There's no opera at the moment."

As I entered the gondola, I heard the harpsichord jingling away in the salon: Lily accompanying herself while she sang, "Yes, we have no Bananas!"

Orient Express
27th of October

Nuit blanche. Shortly before dawn, as I lay drugged and drunken but still conscious, the miracle happened. Oum spoke, she is back! I took down her utterance like dictation from the sky. Then I had a wild thought of leaving the train at Paris and returning to you, Ahmin—but everything must be explained before we meet again, and this letter is far from finished. Instead, I telegraphed Lady D. to expect me—something I'd forgotten in the despair of Venice—and hurtled on toward the cold north, kippers for breakfast and a view of Canterbury Cathedral in the fog, through the streaked and murky window. Meanwhile—

And still no rain.
Air has stopped breathing,
Earth turns to stone,
Lovers to statues.
I walk in the hills,
Wait like the earth,
Harden into stone—

Yet, at my feet, a cactus
With a purple flower in bud!

The House, Appleton-on-Waveney
11th of March, 1937

I have to break this long silence; it's too uncharacteristic! Much time has been spent, Ahmin, gazing at the view from my bedroom window, the same view to which I opened my eyes, upside down and bawling with rage, slapped by the midwife's hand. The countryside refuses to change; flat and empty it remains, with a dead serpent river, clumps of twisted trees and flocks of clouds driven across the sky like endless sheep. Sometimes I take the car, and a flask of brandy, and an umbrella, to park by the North Sea, then walk all alone, buffeted by the winds of March, by the shore of the salty deep. No wonder I'm drawn to this melancholy symbol of the unconscious, afraid yet longing to plunge into it, flirting with the tide as I wander close to the edge, oddly affected by its detritus of weeds, stones, shells, something dead. . . . In the solitude of grayish beach, heaving sea and hungry swooping gulls, something malevolent and disturbing seems to breathe down my neck from the past. Wasn't that crack in the face of the cliff about to open further, weren't my footprints stretching away along the sand really those of an invisible stranger? Later, I put this down to the old Celtic blood stirring in my veins—Lady D.'s ancestors crossed the Irish sea, coming from that strange land of potatoes and hallucination; but Lady D. herself tells me rather sharply to be practical, and realize the threat I feel is coming from the future. She has a point, but I admit it grudgingly—our relations are more strained than in the old, happy, carefree days.

Two trips on the Orient Express having made me weary of trains, I hired a chauffeur and car in London to take me home, and went straight to bed. I drugged myself to sleep until early evening, and woke to see Lady D. sitting opposite me in an armchair, face wreathed in cigarette smoke but clearly expressing more displeasure than sympathy. Handing me a glass of whisky, she demanded an explanation. At the end of it, she walked to the window and gave a long sigh.

"Norman, how *could* you be so careless? If one writes wildly incriminating documents, the least one can do is lock them up."

"I know that now. I bought a strongbox when I got off the train."

"Then may I have the key?"

I stared at her.

"Naturally I want to read what you've written."

I shook my head.

"Not for your Arabian Nights, I promise. I want to know what you say about *me*."

When I demurred, she sat on the edge of the bed, took my hand, dropped it again, and gave me a long, amused, third degree look. "Is the portrait so unflattering?"

"I'm afraid you might think so."

Eyelids flickered for a moment. "Dear little Norman, what can I do to make you trust me?"

"I honestly don't know."

"So we're moving away from each other." Lady D. moved away. "How sad. At a moment like this, I thought you'd need my help. But if you feel you can manage alone, I can only say . . . it's time you did."

And the door clicked softly closed. I lay flat on my stomach, face buried in pillow, hand clutching key underneath it.

Next day, Lily fired the first shot. The London gutterpress had headlines, BARONET ABANDONS BRIDE!, etc., with a photograph of her posed forlornly against male nude and harpsichord in the salon of the Palazzo Steblechi, and an interview in which she explained how she woke up in the morning, found me gone, felt completely bewildered and hurt, and was consulting lawyers. (The Countess, having apparently remembered after all why she was going to Paris, had gone there.) It seemed advisable for me to consult lawyers too, so I told Lady D. I would take care of everything, telephoned the family firm of Parkinson and Parkinson, reserved a suite at the Ritz and found myself once more alone in the bar, replying to George's "How goes it, sir?" with a firm "Very well!" Sipping my whisky while the rain pelted down outside, I was startled by sounds of a commotion in the corridor. "Where is he? I want to see him!" a man's voice called loudly, and then the door swung open and a large, choleric-looking person of about sixty entered, wearing a mackintosh cape like a policeman's and waving a heavy stick. For a wild alarmed moment I braced myself to face arrest, then recognized my uncle Hector, the racehorse owner. To my astonishment, his flushed and angry features beamed with approval at the sight of me. Roaring at the barman for a round of drinks, he shook me warmly by the hand, then pulled me to a chair beside him, almost sitting me on his knee.

"So the little nag is trying to bilk you? She'll be cut up root and branch! She'll be roasted alive!" Then a bone-shivering slap on the back. "Hope you rode her good and hard while it lasted, eh?" His laughter rattled glasses above the bar. I noticed the Hon. Dorothy Fielding come in, and felt myself blushing all over; but she gave us a cheerful nod and sat calmly by herself at the other end. "We'll settle that trollop's hash!" My uncle scarcely paused for breath. "We'll cook that whore's goose!" At the wedding, he continued, he'd cast an eye over Lily and judged her a good but risky mount—like that wicked little stepper who once tried to sue him for assault, battery and siring her colt. "I scuttled that bitch! Sent her crawling back to her sty!" This memory, and the prospect of doing Lily to a turn, made him purple with excitement—but when I asked for practical advice he only uttered more threats, obscenely mixing metaphors of stable, farmyard and kitchen, finished his drink, shook my hand again and staggered out.

The barman said it was nice to see Mr. Hector so healthy. The Hon. Dorothy Fielding nodded, very friendly and agreeable. I retired immediately to my room, where another surprise awaited me. A man wearing a hat and tinted glasses stood in my bedroom; the chest-of-drawers was open. Claiming to be the hotel detective, he made a quick obsequious exit down the fire escape. I knew he must be one of Lily's agents, engaged in that sordid profession of stealing "evidence," and rushed to my strongbox. The lock had been forced! *Three pages of this letter were (and are) missing!* They contained a further allusion to our encounter, and a description of a young Arab prince I happened to see getting out of a taxi at Harrod's, with a breath-taking entourage. The situation was not only frightful and hideous, but a bitter farce—the theft had occurred while my uncle Hector shouted his revolting threats in the bar downstairs. Utterly humiliated, I decided to leave the country—but then realized, since Lily was pursuing me like the fiend incarnate, that I'd be followed. To be seized by the law, with one foot on the gangway of a transatlantic liner, would simply heighten the scandal. So I telephoned the Hon. Dorothy instead, remembering that she was famous for playing almost continuous bridge, pausing only to sleep a few hours and munch a few sandwiches. After saying how delighted I was to run into her again, I wondered if we could make up a four. She was completely overwhelmed, the Hon. Rachel having gone to the country for a week, leaving the Hons. Clare and Evelyn desperate for a replacement.

So, in a Kensington house clotted with oriental porcelain, hunting prints and floral cretonne, the hours pass like Olympic runners over a green baize table. My nerves are soothed by talk of the ace that wasn't trumped and the six of hearts that made a trick; I relish the occasional halt for tea, sherry, veal-and-ham pie, the 6 P.M. news on the wireless. Nazi troops have just occupied the Rhineland, and the Hon. Clare remarks jokingly that what with Spain and Abyssinia we should think twice before cutting gas mask drill again. I strike my only wrong note by suggesting it would be more practical to join the Peace Pledge Union. Hon. Evelyn earns general approval by condemning it as much too extreme. We change partners and deal again. Apart from a casual reference to Lily's bad taste in discussing her marriage with the newspapers, the innocent ladies show their breeding by asking no questions about my recent unhappy experience. They are more interested in my game, anyway, which is not quite equal to their own. I've lost three hundred pounds by the time Lily's lawyer summons me to his office, but have slept well and feel surprisingly confident.

Tarnished nameplate on door, waiting room with copies of *Country Life*, dark leather upholstery, trusted spinsterish secretary announcing I may go in now, stout legal encyclopedias in glass-fronted bookcases, and the great jowl and stomach of Montagu Legg himself behind a desk, his frump of a wife smiling from a photograph—on the surface, nothing but respectability! Legg shuffles a few documents in pudgy hands, and with cool effrontery offers me a cigar. I refuse it. He polishes his spectacles with a small black cloth. Another door opens and Lily enters, looking brave and hurt. I make a point of not standing up while Legg heaves and fusses round her. When he sits down again, I attack—wishing it to be placed on record that I regard the pair of them as thieves and conspirators, guilty of hiring a man with tinted glasses to enter my suite at the Ritz Hotel and bag a section of my personal correspondence.

Lily cries out that I've insulted her. Tapping on desk with silver pencil, Legg advises me not to make groundless accusations. The pages in question were found by Lady Lightwood in Stateroom I of the S. S. *Caledonia,* night of October 23rd. No doubt they fell out of my luggage. I roar with laughter. Disconcerted, Legg inquires the cause of my merriment. I tell him I expected a slightly less farcical lie.

The partners in crime now exchange quick, alert glances. Legg's blandness gives way to a smirk of triumph, Lily's mouth sets cruel and hard. A suspicion is born that my approach has been too hasty. With a clearing of the throat, Legg confirms it.

"Hrrm, a lie must be proved, Sir Norman. Otherwise, it's the truth. Now have you any evidence of this fantastic assertion?"

"Not until I find your agent and make him confess."

"I see." Smirk broadens. "When may we expect this dramatic denouement?"

"Probably never. Haven't you already spirited him out of the country?"

"Oh, come, come." Polite glaze appears on face of Legg,

expression of someone who believes he's dealing with a harmless madman. "We shall get nowhere unless we confine ourselves to reality."

But what, Ahmin, at this moment, *is* reality? No more and no less than Lady Lightwood sticking out her tongue at me! And then Legg glancing at her over his spectacles. "I know, dear lady, that a certain amount of bitterness is inevitable in a case of this nature. But I must ask you to try and control it." Blatant pretense of rebuking his client in order to appear impartial, which he repeats by turning on me with the same benevolent disapproval. "I wouldn't be representing your wife, Sir Norman, if I had any reason to believe her a thief."

"Are you sure? I have the impression it wouldn't deter you at all."

He brushes this aside like a fly that threatens to alight on his nose. "I regret to say your impressions don't impress me. They have no basis in fact." Shuffles documents. "My own impressions, on the other hand, can be checked and verified. *One!* You deserted Lady Lightwood in Venice."

"Her behavior forced me to leave."

"If you left, you deserted her."

"I see now that was her intention. To make me leave in order to claim I deserted her."

Another fly is brushed aside. "*Two!* Lady Lightwood has in her possession some pages from a letter in which you describe sexual contact with an Arab youth. In other words, perversion. You also express the hope of repeating same with same—or with various other members of, broadly speaking, same ethnic group."

"Legg! I'm afraid we have different views of perversion." Since a grisly game is now being played and I'm bound to lose it, all I can do is beat a disgraceful retreat. "To me, the only times I've committed it were once on Hampstead Heath and once on the Orient Express with that creature sitting powdering her nose over there."

Lily utters a loud, filthy word. Face of Legg registers mild earthquake shock. Then—

"Hrrm, that remark may not go unquoted in court, Sir Norman. And may I remind you that most civilized countries of the world support *my* view? *Three!* The same letter contains a sentence suggesting you've committed a literary fraud involving forgery and female impersonation."

Face of Norman registers strong earthquake shock. I'd forgotten entirely that the purloined pages also mentioned Oum!

"My client and I consider this a minor matter, but I've told Lady Lightwood that no one could blame her if she feels morally obliged to inform the reading public of your deception."

"I disagree." (Recovering.) "It's the first important matter you've brought up. Buggery is neither here nor there, but I won't have Oum brought into this."

Lily bursts out laughing. "He's off his head!"

Hands shaking but voice firm, I point a finger at her. "I'm of sound mind and will prove it by telling you exactly what's going to happen next." My accusing finger moves to Legg. "In your language, you wish to discuss the terms of a settlement. In mine, the wheels of blackmail begin to turn. I can't stop them, so let's get it over quickly. How much?"

Without hesitation, Legg mentions an enormous sum. After haggling, he and Lily reduce it by two thousand a year. Legg rings for trusted spinsterish secretary and dictates in the usual jargon that I admit desertion and adultery, and promise to atone for it by parting with a thick slice of my annual income. I sign the typed document, the missing pages are handed back to me, Legg becomes almost obsequious as he suggests a meeting with Parkinson and Parkinson to arrange a time, hotel, female person and witness for my act of legal infidelity. And I'm back in my suite at the Ritz in the sad aching light of dusk.

Because the pages have been soiled for ever by prying eyes, rude snickers and vast expense, I tear them into little pieces and flush them down the toilet. Outside my window, the curtain of night falls on St. James's Park. I lie on the bed and wait for Oum.

12th of March

There might have been more than a useless fragment, only the telephone rang.

"Norman, my dear, there's something I want you to know before you see Lily's lawyer."

I told Lady D. that I'd just returned from an interview with the monster, and how much it was going to cost me. No answer at first—but a sound like a muffled report at the other end of the line. Presumably she struck a match and lit a cigarette.

"Why will you always try and manage alone? I've had a private detective following Lily ever since she came back from Venice." She sounded almost apologetic. "I felt it couldn't do any harm, you know."

"But why didn't you tell me?"

"You're so indiscreet. You couldn't have resisted letting

her know she was being spied on. Anyway, I got a full report this afternoon. She's committed adultery thirteen times in six weeks."

"Is that good or bad?"

"Of course I realize her charges against you are rather more sensational, even though you only did it once. But when there's dirty linen on the market I feel we should be cut in."

"It's too late. Besides, if we brought it up, she'd bring *me* up. I'd be blackened in public forever."

"That doesn't follow, my dear." I heard a long, maddeningly wise sigh. "Anything truly sordid—forgive me!—is always settled out of court. The law's like politics: they decide the fate of nations at a conference table and the fate of individuals in an office. And no one's any the wiser, till the guns go off or the papers are signed."

"You make everything sound so sinister."

"Because it is. We are creatures struggling in the dark," said Lady D. "And what a pity there's no chink of light this time. There *could* have been—we had bargaining power, and since your wife is only after money, it was important." Another sigh. "However, let's look on the bright side."

"Is there one?"

"Certainly. We can afford it." Pause. "When are you coming home?"

"There's just one little final job I have to do. They want me to pretend to commit what Lily obviously enjoys committing—so she'll have grounds for divorcing *me*."

Lady D. remarked that the situation was so ironic it was almost French. Then I asked who Lily had done it with; she didn't think there'd be anyone I knew.

21st of March

She was waiting outside the front door to greet me when I arrived, looking more than ever like a piece of statuary in the pale afternoon light, against the huge gray house. As I slammed the taxi door, black crows flew off the roof and shot like arrows into the sky. Our purple Clematis was famous. It covered more of the house's face each year, and was trained to creep round windows. It was coming into bloom now, and buds seemed to open directly out of stone. We walked together through the hall, which smelt of floor polish and roses. We entered the drawing room as a grandfather clock struck five, and a thick, unpleasant mist drifted toward us. A coal fire burned smokily in the grate; a strong draft of air blew in from the French windows, which were open.

"Nothing works," said Lady D. "But it will in time. Let's have some whisky." She poured, then stood sipping in the semicircle of Chippendale chairs. As the room faced east, and it was almost sunset, everything glimmered. We were silhouettes until I switched on a lamp.

"Yes, that makes it more cheerful," said Lady D. "But why do houses die? I'm excluding disasters like fire and earthquake, anything called an act of God. And I know they die when they're closed and empty too long, which doesn't apply to this one."

"They die when the wrong people live in them."

"Yes, and when the wrong things happen in them." She walked slowly towards me, took my hand, gave me her mysterious inquiring look. "Norman, do you suppose I owe you an apology?"

"For anything in particular? Or just generally?"

"Please don't mock me now, my dear." She sat beside me on the window-seat. "I'm offering to take the blame for your marriage. And yet I truly believed it could work! I thought you and Lily had interests that might coincide without ever having actually to meet. I wanted you to have the best of both worlds." She sighed. "After all, it's been done."

Another grandfather clock struck four.

"But you're such an innocent boy. You give yourself away so quickly." Her head rested against my shoulder. "Now tell me what you think of this. Since we're both so unlucky in marriage, would it be a good idea to start traveling together?"

*Lady D. and myself at the Inghilterra in Rome; at Monte Carlo; at a villa for the summer on Lake Garda. I carry her easel, open her umbrella, put the wrong stamps on her letters. We give a cocktail party on our host's yacht, we regretfully decline an invitation from the Marquise de la Merde because we're off to Biarritz—Athens—*TUNIS . . . *Good heavens!*

Open window is supposed to clear the air, but I feel stifled. Lady D. stares at me in an odd, almost frightened way. . . .

In three months I'll have passed my 27th birthday. That's still very young. And after all, I have a reputation as discoverer and translator of Oum, I am rich and not totally unattractive, what I lack in courage I make up for in wit—can't I do what I like?—

The next thing I remember is opening my eyes to see Lady D. standing anxiously over me. I'm lying down on the window-seat. It's almost dark outside.

"Don't worry. The doctor's on his way."

"Did I faint?"

"You seemed to lose consciousness."

"How Victorian."

"I think it best not to talk till he comes." Pats my hand. "You're so pale!"

After the examination, Lady D. and the doctor leave the room. They return in five minutes, looking cheerful. The doctor tells me I need never have another heart attack as long as I'm sensible. "I'm putting you on a diet, young man!" Winks. "Cut out all strain and shock. You'll have to go without a care in the world. But you're allowed all the leisure and relaxation you can take." Then he nods at Lady D. "These little upsets are sent just to warn us, you know."

"I agree," said Lady D. when he'd gone. "You've been overdoing it lately, that's all."

Ritz Hotel, London
17th of April

In London again, on my diet—the specialist approved of it, and I find it easier to keep to without Lady D. I've started translating a *very long* poem by Oum, on the subject of St. Simeon Stylites, which "occurred" to me as I left the consulting-room in Harley Street. The word *anchorite* entered my mind for no apparent reason, followed by *anchor*. I at once took a taxi to the nearest public library, excited by the idea that both words had the same linguistic source. No luck! Anchor comes from the Greek *ancora,* a hook, and anchorite from *anachoretes,* a retired person. All the same, I persist in finding an emotional link between the two, because if one decides to live on top of a pillar like St. Simeon, or inside a tub like Diogenes, or behind a wall like Oum herself, one certainly ceases drifting out to sea. This is the starting-point of her new masterwork. I have no idea where it will end, and it was interrupted, anyway, by an astonishing event that occurred last night.

The Hon. Dorothy had been very anxious to see a new drawing room comedy at the St. George's Theatre, so I bought two excellent seats and invited her as my guest for the evening. During the first scene, a butler appeared on the stage. He had only to announce "Dinner is served, madam," and exit immediately, but it was time enough to recognise him. VIOLET! I burst out laughing, which astonished everyone nearby, since there was nothing comic in the line itself. Lighting a match to study the program, I found the actor called herself George Holmes, which started me off again. The Hon. Dorothy wondered if I was all right, or would prefer to go outside, and I invented a story that Holmes reminded me uncannily of a former member of our household. During the third act Violet made another brief appearance, asking "Will that be all, madam?" I emitted a wild shriek, was indignantly shushed on all sides, and Violet herself glared suspiciously over her shoulder as she disappeared to the wings. When the curtain fell, I told the Hon. Dorothy that a sudden attack of fatigue would unfortunately prevent my taking her on to dinner. She looked relieved, said, "Of course, you've got to be careful," and put me in a taxi. I made it drive round the theatre once, then stop outside the stage door.

In a squalid dressing room, shared with another minor actor, I found Violet calmly removing her tails. She looked up, saw me in the doorway and gave a deep, angry frown. "I thought that hyena was you."

"I'm sorry, Violet," I began, at which the other actor quickly closed the door and said, "For Christ's sake hold it down." Her disguise was so effective that he had no suspicion of it, so I was obliged to refer to my sister publicly as George, which didn't suit her. She was more a Rupert or a Neville; cropped, brilliantined hair with sideburns, a sporty tweed jacket with leather patches on the elbows and twilled sailor-blue trousers gave her the air of a slightly unearthly man-about-town. She accepted my invitation to dinner rather grudgingly, asking me to wait while she fetched Kitty. In a minute she returned with a pretty, fair-haired little thing who played the ingenue lead.

"I regret to say this is my brother. We're having dinner."

She insisted on being taken to a dingy basement cafe in Bloomsbury, where the habitués were all shabby Indians who displayed no interest in us. A waiter wearing a turban and a dirty apron said, "Good evening, Mr. George. Your usual table?" Violet nodded curtly and we retired to an alcove behind a bead curtain. She put her arm round Kitty, then leaned accusingly toward me.

"You look as if you don't get enough exercise." A faint grin. "Not the right kind, anyway. I read about your escapades in the papers. Pretty ridiculous, Norman."

I sneezed suddenly. Violet jumped to her feet.

"If you've got a cold, we're leaving! It's so selfish to spread germs in public."

"I'm not," I said. "It's something peculiar in the air. Can they be smoking hemp?"

Mollified, Violet shook her head and sat down again. "Curry. The best in London."

"George has an instinct for finding wonderful cheap places," said Kitty. They kissed passionately, and for a moment I was afraid they might lose control. Then Kitty gave a contented little sigh and took out a cigarette. Violet lit it for her. I began to think they were the most devoted couple I'd ever seen.

"Violet—"

Immediately Kitty tapped me on the wrist, like a teacher reproving a forgetful pupil. *"George,"* she said.

"George," I said to Violet, "how long can you get away with this?"

They only gazed deep into each other's eyes. Then Kitty laughed. "I'm sorry for him. He sounds as bourgeois as my parents." She gave me a condescending smile. "When I took George to meet them, they thought he was odd. I've never spoken to them again."

Violet looked anxious. "You've never regretted it, have you, my darling?"

"You know I haven't. It was a small price to pay for such overwhelming happiness."

"You misunderstand me," I said. "I'm not shocked. I only thought, considering the life you've chosen to lead, it's quite chancy to flaunt it by appearing on the stage together."

Violet seemed completely astonished. "That never even occurred to me."

"Or to me." Kitty stroked her hand. "Don't worry about it."

"He may have a point. The theatre's a hotbed of gossip, my darling."

"What can they do? We're not hurting anybody." Kitty glanced reproachfully at me. "You've upset him."

"I am not upset!" Violet sounded fierce. "What do you take me for?"

"I didn't mean it like that. Don't let him come between us. I know you're the bravest person in the world."

"Yes," said Violet, and kissed her again. "There's nothing you can do," she said to me. "The day I walked out of Appleton, I had no plans. I only knew I had to escape and find a better world somewhere. So I bought a suit and moustache, walked into a pub and met Kitty. It was love at first sight."

"Though I didn't like his moustache." Kitty giggled. "For a moment it nearly came between us."

"I tore it off on the spot," said Violet. "Her slightest wish became my command. It was Kitty who launched my theatrical career. I owe her everything. She's the one with real talent, of course—wait till you hear her sing. For me the stage is just a means of bringing home the bacon, I've no ambition to be a leading man."

"You could if you wanted," said Kitty with absolute conviction.

"I'm quite happy to go on playing butlers. It's a way of staying together." Then her voice went bitter. "*I* have to think of things like that, Norman! Though I'm the legitimate heir, I'm obliged to work. It's the meek bastards who inherit the earth."

I flinched from the memory of a cane rapping me on the shoulder. "But I'm sure Lady D. would give you an allowance. Have you asked her?"

"I don't want charity. I want my rights or nothing."

"We'll get that little house, George!" Kitty turned to me.

"Our fondest dream is to retire to a villa on the Mediterranean. We've opened a savings account."

"I've told you before," said Violet, "that talent like yours must never be allowed to retire. It's too rare. The world needs it."

"But I want children."

Violet kissed her again, and steaming curry arrived. As we left, she gave me a half affectionate, half ironic punch in the chest. "I remember him as a child," she told Kitty. "He hasn't changed much." She looked me over critically, shook her head. "You never learned the first lesson, did you? *Nothing venture, nothing lose.*"

"But I have to be careful," I said. "I'm not as strong as you. I had a slight heart attack last month."

"You poor bastard. Now promise me something." She moved close. "Not a word to Mother. If you tell . . ."

Her face went very tense as she reached into a pocket and brought out a pair of knuckle-dusters. They gleamed for a moment in the darkness; then she put them away again.

"Good night now."

"Do we have to see him again?" asked Kitty. "I don't trust him."

"He won't bother us, my darling. We'll leave orders at the stage door."

They walked off arm in arm down the empty street, then suddenly sprinted to catch a bus.

Hotel Crillon, Paris
19th of April

When I'm feeling confident, the streak of oddness in our family strikes me as close to genius; when I'm depressed, it looks like madness. My reunion with Violet provoked a sleepless night, during which I pondered this question—and finally, an hour or so before dawn, lost consciousness without having answered it. I woke late, with the distinct sensation that a voice had just said in my ear: "Bat's milk." Naturally I have no idea what this means, but in view of the appalling event that occurred shortly afterwards I interpret it as a kind of warning.

I ordered breakfast and wrote a few lines of the St. Simeon poem before the waiter arrived with my tray. Two letters were placed beside the teapot, one with the royal seal, inviting myself and Lady D. to the coronation of George VI; the other, in a cheap and slightly soiled blue envelope, had been delivered by hand. It was addressed in block capitals to SIR NORMAN LIGHTWOOD (HA-HA!). Opening it, I discovered in the same block capitals, on a sheet of coarse toilet paper, the following:

WE ARE WAITING FOR THE GREAT ONES TO EMERGE FROM THE HOLLOWS! KINGS WILL GO FORTH FROM THE CENTER!! ICE WILL BE BROKEN BY THE CONQUERING FIRE!!!

THE MAJOR

Though obscure, the message was clearly threatening. My heart beat wildly, but didn't fail me. When a degree of calm returned, I examined envelope and paper for clues, but found nothing except the watermark of a well-known brand of sanitary products. Wondering who the sender could be, I wrote down a list of my enemies, from Lily through most of my family, but instinct told me to look further afield. The

Ha-Ha! after my name on the envelope appears to contradict this, since it looks like a reference to my illegitimacy, and yet I have to admit that Lady D.'s indiscretion is quite widely known. Polite circles, though I'm sure they discuss it behind my back, never mention it to my face; but I'm not dealing with polite circles now. This twisted thing comes from the underworld of the criminal or crank, some stranger or chance acquaintance who's decided to torment me because he imagines himself slighted (that waiter in the Italian restaurant who tried to overcharge me?), or rejected (the man who propositioned me outside a church in Soho?), or bears a social grudge (the sly barman downstairs?). The knowledge that I'm an innocent, helpless victim is an immense relief, but naturally I ask myself *what they're after,* whether the final motive is to terrorize, kill, or bleed me dry. . . .

I telephoned the hotel manager to explain that I'd received an unspeakable anonymous threat, and asked him to find out who was on duty in the lobby when the blue envelope came. A night porter, roused from sleep in the basement, remembered a man wearing some kind of military uniform (The Major, obviously!) handing it to him about five o'clock in the morning. Foreigner, he thought; strange, guttural accent; regimentals did not belong to any of the British armed services. The manager advised me to turn the matter over to Scotland Yard, but I informed him I was in no mood to deal with the Flatfoots—police, law and Church being, in my opinion, different faces of the same blind authority that invented the idea of sin. Instead, I packed a suitcase and hired a private aeroplane to fly me to Paris. It's not one of my favorite cities, even in spring, but I felt absolutely obliged to leave the country.

20th of April

Registered at the hotel as George Eliot and haven't left since I arrived. My suite is a litter of red plush, the new Oum manuscript, meal trays and British newspapers. *The Times, Daily Mail* and gutterpress are sent up to me; I search them for any mention of my disappearance, any hint that *they're on the lookout.* So far, not a word. Most of the news is gossip about the coronation, which I would like to attend, but daren't run the risk of appalling humiliation in the Abbey. The rest is a trunk murder, blackshirts demonstrating in Hyde Park, elderly laundress winning a fortune in the football pools, controversy about women wearing slacks, another bluffing speech by Hitler, my Malayan Rubber Rises Sharply again—nothing out of the ordinary.

22nd of April

Looking cautiously to right, left and rear, I ventured out for the first time this morning. No one followed. Chestnut trees leafing, delicious fragrance of brioches in bakery window, of *Gauloises* smoked by a handsome youth at a pavement cafe. Then, outside the offices of Thomas Cook and Son, a leering, disreputable person approached me, holding a small blue envelope in his hand! Curiosity overcame dread; I stopped to examine my tormentor, disguised now in slouch hat, crumpled Panama suit with open-necked shirt, flashy black and white shoes. Pale as ashes, I took the envelope and drew out a colored photograph of a woman kneeling in front of a man with penis erect.

He was only a tout trying to sell me obscene postcards.

23rd of April

An item in *The Times* caught my eye this morning. Convinced that socialists, pacifists and intellectuals are turning the British Lion into a neutered tabby, *Sir Manfred Barr* has offered our government an enormous sum for the manufacture of guns and bombs. Furthermore, he's built a structure of neon signs on his Daimler, which he drives through the main thoroughfares of London every night. They light up alternately with DOWN WITH GENEVA and SAVE THE EMPIRE.

Now, this deranged jingoist has hated me for years. As a poet and intellectual I stand for everything he considers effete. And since I once spoke favorably of the Peace Pledge Union to the Hons. Dorothy, Evelyn and Clare, the remark may well have reached his ears. Is it possible . . . ?

24th of April

I took a stroll along the *quais,* browsing among those useless bookstalls: detective stories, engravings on Notre Dame, *Confessions of a Monk* sealed in cellophane, etc. No one followed. For a while I thought someone was watching me from a barge moored in the Seine; but he turned out to be waiting for a young woman, who went aboard. . . . My suspicions of Sir Manfred grow stronger every moment. I would like to set a trap for him, but it must be foolproof, because people of his kind turn violent when cornered.

The House, Appleton-on-Waveney
1st of May

Sir Manfred is innocent!—mad, deplorable, but innocent. The mystery has now been solved with dreadful unexpected-ness, but at least it confirms the old theory that misfortunes come in pairs.

Last week *The Times* printed another story of aberration in noble families. Walking down Piccadilly, a young blackshirt passed a man handing out anti-Franco leaflets, shouted that he was a notorious Communist Jew and attacked him with knuckle-dusters. The assailant was arrested, taken to prison, stripped of his uniform and pronounced a woman. Although he insisted his name was George Holmes, it was of course Violet Eunice Lightwood. Transferred to Holloway, she seemed dazed but stern, ordering the wardresses to salute and call her Major—an honorary title she'd apparently been given after joining the British Union of Fascists. Lady D. stood bail for her at once, and she was released yesterday. A group of journalists waited outside the prison gates; Violet gave them the command *At Ease!*, under the impression they were loyal household troops, then made a very truculent speech. She reviled Jews, blacks, yellows, gypsies, demanded a Strong Hand in India and a moral clean-up in the theatre. She revealed that she also belonged to a secret society, founded in Berlin, called the Luminous Lodge, whose members believe that a superior Aryan race existed before the First Moon fell and wiped almost everybody out. A few survivors, who fled to caves in the bowels of the earth, continued to live and breed there; as Lady D. hustled her into a limousine, Violet announced that these unpolluted giants were now ready to emerge with tongues of fire, melt the stars (which are only blocks of ice) and take over the universe. You can imagine what a bad impression all this made. The press is full of allusions to the Mad Major, facetious jokes about Unshrinking Violet and the Storm-

Trouper and reminders of my "sensational" forthcoming divorce, which the Palace must have overlooked—but has now taken into account, since we've just received a note explaining that our tickets to the coronation were sent by mistake.

3rd of May

Returning home for what was, I suppose, our first family reunion since Violet disappeared in search of a better world, I found Lady D. in the drawing room, lacing a cup of tea with whisky. My sister sprawled on the sofa in her storm-trooper uniform, empty bottle of beer on the floor near her boots.

Lady D. put a finger to her lips. "She's sleeping now." Taking my arm, she walked me to the garden; after spring rains, it lay fresh and luminous in sunlight. "The roses will be spectacular this year, I think." Then her face went haggard. "Where have you been? I'm at the end of my rope."

I could only stare at her in astonishment, feeling that everything must be more wrong than usual if Lady D. couldn't go on, resourceful and wise, for ever.

"Don't you see it's extremely painful for me? My own daughter, in the house where she played so happily as a child, now strides up and down in that vicious outfit, telling me the earth is going to split open, giants are on the march and I'd better look out."

"She tells that to everyone. I don't think you should take it so personally." I described our meeting in London, and Violet swearing me to secrecy.

"Then you know about Kitty," said Lady D. "I gather it's

all her fault. They had a quarrel that morning. Violet got dressed up and went out for a walk. When that man gave her an anti-Franco leaflet, something inside her snapped." She smiled sadly. "*Cherchez la femme,* as usual . . . I really have to lie down. Please don't disturb me unless it's absolutely necessary."

She wandered off in the direction of her studio. I returned to the drawing room. Violet now sat on a low stool, head in hands. She looked up at me through interlaced fingers. "There you are, you little bastard." I thought I detected a note of gruff affection in her voice.

"You really frightened me," I said.

She got up, walked towards me. Her eyes were vague and clouded. "How?"

"That horrible note."

"Oh . . . It was Kitty's idea. She didn't trust you, she wanted you out of the way. I only wrote it to please Kitty." Her voice ached. "Oh, Kitty, Kitty! You wicked, heartless girl!" She tried to pull herself together, gave me a sheepish grin. "Women . . ." she said. "They twist us around their little fingers." She sank to a chair. "I saw them together. Locked in a passionate embrace." And a tear glistened in the corner of one eye.

"Kitty and who?"

"Her understudy. I surprised them in the dressing room. Oh Kitty, oh my faithless darling."

With an abrupt change of mood, she jumped to her feet. "They want to throw me in a filthy polluted jail, they'll force me to mingle with sheeny scum and nigger garbage!" With a thrill of fear I heard the old ringing, bullying tones resound across the drawing room. "But I've seen it coming, I've laid plans against the day. It's time to press the button." She clapped a hand on my shoulder. "You're going to help me. Is that understood?"

"I'd like to," I said. "But in my present situation I can't afford anything that involves a brush with the law."

"There's no risk, as long as you follow my instructions. We shall begin by telephoning Berlin from the library. No one'll disturb us there." I hesitated, and she gave me a push. "Wheels are turning that your puny strength is powerless against. You're involved in this whether you like it or not."

Realizing that she'd gone over the edge, I decided to humor her. I sprang to attention, saluted smartly. "Very good, Major. Shall we proceed?"

"That's better. Hand me my boots."

In the library, Violet took a piece of paper from her pocket, asked for the European operator and gave a number. Then she placed a hand over the receiver and said to me, "We are about to speak with the most powerful woman in Germany. I met Ilse von Knoop in London last year. She has connections you wouldn't dream of. She knows the monk with the green gloves and the Lords of Thule. She has masterminded—DON'T COME IT WITH ME!" she broke off loudly, into the receiver. "There *can't* be a delay of three hours!"

I advised her not to insult telephone operators; it might arouse suspicion.

"You're right, Norman. Thank you. Oh my dear," Violet said in a low, intimate tone to the operator, "I'm so extremely sorry. The last thing in the world I intended was to insult you. It's just that the matter is of some urgency and my nerves are slightly frayed. I do appreciate your charming efforts and if you can possibly hurry things up, I'll be your eternal slave. Thank you—Elsie, is it? You're very nice." She replaced the receiver. "I shall tell them of your excellent advice in Berlin. And they'll show their gratitude, when the time comes."

I turned to go, but she grabbed hold of me. "We have a long, desperate wait ahead of us—but we mustn't let it show. Try and behave as if nothing has happened."

It was, for the moment, her last attempt at bravado. Like a crumpled doll she subsided in her chair, beginning again, "Oh Kitty, Kitty, see what you've driven me to, my dark angel. . . ."

I crept up to my bedroom, stared at the view from the window; flat and empty the countryside stretched away, clouds raced across a darkening sky. With Violet descending to the abyss, Lady D. prostrated and my own series of ordeals that began after marrying Lily, I felt the stars were locked in unfavorable conjunction. I tried hard to summon Oum, to fix my thoughts on St. Simeon, refuge, sanctuary, the blessings of withdrawal—but the voice that spoke said only *Mektoub!*, *Inch'Allah!*, *It is written!*, etc., which seemed a little facile under the circumstances. I went downstairs to fortify resignation with a stiff drink, then looked into the library to see how Violet was doing.

She sat very rigid in the chair, gazing in concentration at half an orange suspended by a string from the ceiling. "What's up now?" I couldn't help exclaiming, and she jumped up blazing with anger, telling me that I'd interrupted her gymnasium of the interior. Apparently this was a Luminous Lodge exercise to gain inner strength. Ironically enough, it was a better remedy than I could find; she seemed full of energy again, rudely dismissing my apology and saying I'd nearly ruined everything. Trying still to humor her, and also curious just to know what she thought she was up to, I asked her to finish the story of Ilse von Knoop and the monk with the green gloves.

"You ask too many questions." A basilisk glare. "And you're not ready for the answers yet."

We dined alone by candelight, Lady D. having sent word that she was too tired to join us. Violet sat at one end of the long, gleaming table, myself at the other, and Ellen the maid served roast beef and claret. My sister was alternately brooding and jovial. Once she pinched Ellen in the buttocks, but when the girl left the room, gave a heavy sigh. "Probably polluted. Better not risk it." A glance at the army watch on her wrist. "Why doesn't that call to Berlin come through?" Then she stood up, removed her tunic, opened a disguised flap in the lining and took out a small box. She rolled it down the length of the table, past silver candlesticks, a bowl of roses and elegant Spode, and it came to rest at my brandy snifter.

"A gift?"

She nodded.

"Thank you. Shall I open it now?"

"Only if anything goes wrong. It's cyanide."

Before I could recover, the phone rang. Violet leapt to her feet, closed the doors, picked up the receiver and gave a smile of triumph. *"Ilse!"* She began talking in German, which I don't understand. I heard the words *liebchen* and *Heil Hitler!* several times; then Violet went into a long monologue, eyes dilating with horror, and I presumed she was explaining her situation. After that it was von Knoop's turn, Violet listening tensely, occasionally nodding and rapping out *"Ja!"* At last she put down the phone, returned to the table, and rested her chin on a clenched fist.

"They'll have a submarine waiting off the coast at dawn."

"Thank God," I said.

"You're driving me. Rendezvous on the beach four miles north of Aldeburgh. Longitude one point seven degrees east, latitude fifty-two point three. The password is *Agarthi.*"

(*Resumed later, after a visit from Scotland Yard.*)

A sickle moon hung in the sky as my car moved through hushed, suspended countryside. We hardly spoke. Violet stared straight ahead, almost in a trance, insignia and buttons glittering in the dark. For the first fifteen minutes I had an attack of nervous hiccups; do you know that feeling when, at the end of a ludicrous and demented charade, the mask is lowered, the cloak parts and reality stares you in the face? I was, to put it simply, gasping with terror. Violet cured me in her usual drastic way; when I wasn't looking, she pressed a burning cigarette against my ear. We narrowly missed going into a ditch, but the hiccups stopped.

The rest of the journey was uneventful. Once Violet muttered, "Damn her!"—referring, I supposed, to Kitty, and once, "When we take over, she'll be on the list." And a rabbit streaked in front of the car.

The moon was down when we reached the North Sea. With a shock I recognized the strip of beach—I've already described my solitary walks along it while convalescing from my honeymoon. Now, by the shore, were two silhouettes: of a dinghy, and a man standing on a rock, apparently pointing at us with one hand. Violet ordered me to stop the car. She lowered the window, cupped her hands over her mouth and called in a sepulchral voice:

"*A-garth-i.*"

The man's hand dropped to his side. I realized he was holding a revolver, and hiccuped again. With a flicker of irritation, Violet got out. When I started to follow, she gripped my arm. "You've seen enough, you poor frightened bastard. Don't come any further."

I tried to compose a suitable goodby. "Well, Violet, I suppose this is what you always wanted."

Her answer was a stinging blow on the face.

"So long, Major," I said, and gave a trembling salute.

"That's better." She glanced suspiciously at the sky; satisfied that no Object threatened, she strode towards the beach. A faint silvery ribbon of light appeared on the horizon, and somewhere a cock crew. "*Ultima Thule!*" I head her cry. The man stepped off the rock to meet her. They embarked. She sat erect and motionless as the dinghy moved out to sea. Soon it was swallowed in the murky dawn. I was left with a single vile memento of my unhappy sister, took the deadly capsule from my pocket, buried it in the sand, and drove home past gentle fields and farmhouses already stirring.

Later. "I really think you should have consulted me," said Lady D. "A mother likes to know when her own daughter is carried off these shores by a foreign power."

"I suppose I did the wrong thing again, but there didn't seem any alternative at the time."

"I'm sure there wasn't, my dear. It's just the principle of the thing. Of course, if you hadn't been so frightened . . ."

She sighed, kissed me, moved briskly towards the telephone. "Now let's be practical and inform the police. We'll just say we woke up and found Violet gone. But let *me* do the talking."

Across a tea-table, laden with her best china and silver, Lady D. received an Inspector from Scotland Yard. He placed his hat on a chair, she rang for a servant to remove it, then gave him a gracious smile.

"How do you like your tea, Inspector?"

"Milk and sugar, thank you."

"Not at all. One lump or two?"

"Two."

"Really . . . ? Shall we have our usual lemon, Norman?" Another smile for her visitor, to make him feel at ease, and extremely privileged to be here at all. "Now, you may ask me—within reason—whatever questions you consider necessary, but please remember I've been under a terrible strain."

When I compare Lady D.'s handling of the authorities to my own encounter with Montagu Legg, I feel like an amateur. Of course, it takes a marble heart to behave like that. Lady D. has never blamed herself for anything, including her daughter's emotional difficulties. No matter what happens, she is maddeningly right, and if only her advice had been sought, it would never have happened anyway.

"Have you any idea, ma'am, where Miss Lightwood might have gone?"

"How could I? I'm afraid I find that question tactless and insulting. I've already told your people on the phone that she disappeared once before without a word, and my son discovered her whereabouts by pure coincidence."

"I certainly didn't intend the question that way, ma'am.

That would be when she was playing a butler on the London stage?"

In a stage whisper, Lady D. remarked to me: "One has to tell them everything twice."

"Take my tip, Inspector," I said, gaining confidence. "Forget about Violet Lightwood and start looking for George Holmes."

It didn't work. His eyes went cold and unfriendly. "Frankly, sir, I believe I know more about my job than you."

Lady D. pressed my foot under the table. Humiliating! No matter what happens, I am maddeningly wrong.

"My son was trying to be helpful." After this gentle reproach, Lady D. offered him more tea; he accepted with a deferential smile. Now they seemed in league against me. "I have complete confidence in your ability, Inspector. I made inquiries, and heard nothing but good reports of you and the Yard."

"Thank you, ma'am. I appreciate your cooperation."

"Does it strike you that way? I'm so glad. I'm just doing what I feel to be right."

"Doing it very well, ma'am."

She waved this aside. "I believe you're trying to flatter me. Now, in small return for all the help I've given you, I must ask you something. When you find my little daughter, don't be too hard on her. She's . . ." Lady D's voice trembled. "Help me, Norman. Explain what I mean."

"When Violet was six years old," I said, "an Object fell from the sky. The local police probably still have a report on it, although the thing itself was eaten by a dog. Anyway, it landed on the lawn out there, all dark and warm, and my sister has never been the same since. You understand?"

"Not exactly, sir." I didn't like the expression on his face. "You mean it hit her, or it brought her bad luck?"

Lady D.'s hand rested firmly on my shoulder. "My son is tired and upset, too. And it's not easy for him to admit that the sister he grew up with was never quite like other children." She moved away. "Excuse me, I would like to lie down now. If there's anything more you need to know, you're welcome to be our guest for dinner. Pot luck, of course."

The Inspector thought he had all the information he needed for the moment. As for what might happen to Violet, he now understood that Lady D. was referring to her state of mind. He regretted that unless medically extenuating circumstances could be proved, the law had to take its course.

"I see." Lady D. paused in the doorway. "The Machine has no feelings, has it? Sometimes one almost envies It. It was a little dishonest of you, you know, not to admit that sooner. Norman, would you ring for the Inspector's hat?" A last, hesitant smile for the visitor. "I hope we can meet again under happier circumstances."

She's gone. The Inspector gives her an admiring but puzzled look. I decide to offer him more tea, but meet with a curt refusal.

"No thanks. *I've* got work to do."

Rejected again. That awful feeling George the barman gives me. Just a member of the idle rich in *their* eyes . . . I am left with an abandoned tea-table and a draft from the unclosed door. I feel a plateau of depression ahead. There seems no end to this life of being brushed aside, outwitted, intimidated. I'm ashamed to introduce a note of self-pity at this point; but what *are* we, dear Ahmin—and when I remember your gift of innocent lust, you're the exception that proves my rule—what are we, except what we know and what happens to us?

29th of July

Today
Because the view of a desert
is not exactly restricted
but monotonous as truth
(discounting periods of cold and invisibility)
I shall be Apis
Sacred bull beloved by Ptah
In a thousand years
possibly a little longer
they will uncover my tomb
without disturbing my sleep
Tomorrow
Because the view of a desert
is monotonous as love
and not exactly restricted
I shall probably be Thoth
God of moon, of letters and Time . . .

This morning I came down as usual from my pillar and found Lady D. at breakfast on the terrace. Opposite her sat a lean, sunburnt man of about fifty, smelling of expensive leather and reading *The Times*.

"Isn't it a beautiful day?" said Lady D. "Norman, I'd like you to meet your father."

I stared at a pair of deep blue eyes, a full and friendly

mouth, crammed with superb teeth. His hand moved up suddenly to scratch an immaculate little moustache.

"Uncle Maurice?"

"That's my other title." His eyes flickered for a moment. "How do you do?"

"He arrived very late last night." Lady D. poured my coffee. "We decided not to wake you."

"Did you know he was coming?"

"Of course. He wrote to me a month ago."

"You never said a word."

"I've never asked my children to tell me anything they don't want to," said Lady D. to her great love. "And I encourage them to expect the same from me. It doesn't always work, and has caused some painful surprises on both sides, but in the long run I feel it's the only way for us to get along." She got up and kissed him on the cheek. "I'm going to leave you two alone together for a while." A whiff of perfume drifted towards me. "You'll have so much to talk about. He knows everything."

She kissed him again, and then stood looking at him; an extraordinary warmth and softness crept over her face, sloughing off twenty years; she'd been let *into* Shanghri-La, not turned out of it. Obviously reluctant to lose sight of him, she walked backwards into the drawing room, graceful and dreamlike, a figure from a film run in reverse motion. She closed the French windows, vanished into shadow. I wanted to rub my eyes, then noticed my presumed father as spellbound as myself.

"Dorothea is still the only woman in my life." He coughed, poured more coffee, glanced at *The Times* and pushed it away.

A long, uncomfortable silence.

"Sorry to hear about the business with Lily," he said politely at last.

I agreed that it was unfortunate. I would be relieved when the divorce proceedings were over. And I wanted to know how long he was staying.

"That depends on your mother." He grinned almost boyishly. "I want her to come back to Australia with me."

After the shock, I felt a rising tide of rage and jealousy. It was partly being left out of things again. And, for some reason, being absolutely scandalized that he could admit his passion in front of me, drinking coffee, glancing again with blatant infatuation towards the French windows. I sat pursing my lips. I picked up *The Times,* saw headings of BIRTHS, DEATHS, PERSONAL, SITUATIONS.

"You could come with us if you want," he said.

"I shall have to think it over."

"Naturally we'll make it legal this time."

"Oh, don't feel obliged to. Scandals to this family are like coals to Newcastle."

He laughed. "But they're not so plentiful in Australia. Please think it over. I know Dorothea wants you to come."

"Then she *has* agreed to go back with you?"

"Not yet. But she will." He stretched his legs, insolently assured of his powers of sexual persuasion. I was unable to resist a quick look at his crotch. After all, it was a historical relic. Without its magic powers, would I be sitting opposite him at this moment?

I knew his blue eyes watched me, very steely and intent, made a clumsy panicked movement and overturned my coffee cup. Fortunately it was empty. "So how does the old country seem to you," I asked, "after all these years?"

He didn't answer at once, but continued watching me, back of sunburnt hand across his mouth. He spoke through it. "I've had a strange feeling of returning to the past. Well, not so strange, really—this *is* the past, here. But I keep wanting more room to move about in." Another stretch. Had I misinterpreted the gesture? "You see, Norman, if I were having breakfast at home this morning, I'd be a thousand feet up in the Blue Mountains. Miles from anywhere. Open spaces . . ."

"It sounds grand but lonely."

"Dorothea will cure the loneliness."

"Oh, then it'll be just grand."

Fingers of the hand twitched. When he lowered it, I saw he was smiling. "Not getting on too well, are we?"

"It's difficult to accept a man as one's father simply on hearsay."

He laughed again. "I'd call Dorothea's evidence more than hearsay."

"I don't know why it's never entirely convinced me. I'm sure it's my own fault."

"No, it's mine. I often thought of writing to you," he said with disarming sincerity and ease, "but what's the use of phrases like 'I wish to God it had happened differently' and 'there seemed no other way out at the time'—especially when I understood from Dorothea that my son was quite an ink-slinger himself?"

So they'd been secretly corresponding about me all these years! I made a rushed, awkward exit through the French windows—laughable opposite of Lady D., no doubt—and ran upstairs to my room. *In Australia. Every moment the moment when people can't help themselves. Miles from anywhere, in all the open spaces, I'd find them doing it!*

And then, no longer looking quite so young, Lady D. stands over me.

"Norman?"

"It's all right. I've been Victorian again."

"Taken your medicine, my dear?"

"Quite a dose." Turning my face to the wall, I advised her to go to Australia with her great love.

"I'd like you to come with us."

"You used to recommend the convenient comfortable life rather strongly. I believe I prefer it."

She left the room and I experienced a succession of violent thrills, betrayal, shame, rage, an erection. Drifted into sleep and woke up with the impression a voice had just remarked in my ear, "Nun's fiddle." These messages are beginning to annoy me. Then I found that more than two hours had passed, and wondered if Lady D. and my presumed father were too alarmed or too busy to come near me.

Stateroom C, S.S. Queen Mary
21st of October

On my way to the station yesterday afternoon, the taxi was held up in Piccadilly by dozens of men lying flat on their backs in the street. They had apparently taken up this position a few minutes ago, in front of a crossing with traffic lights that blinked from red to green and back again while they remained motionless, like beggars sleeping at night in the Orient. Posters demanding a Square Deal for the Unemployed were spread on their empty stomachs. Crowds watched silently, traffic piled up unable to move, half an hour of this peculiar stalemate went by; meanwhile Oum spoke to me, and I jotted down some lines about my Syrian hermit. The sound of singing ("Onward Christian Soldiers") interrupted me. I looked out of the window and saw squads of police dragging the men away by force. Some of the crowd joined in the singing, and it all seemed remarkably good-humored. Then a member of the Unemployed peered in my window as he scuffled past, all stubbly chin and amazed eyes. I reached in my pocket for a sixpence, but he blew two scorching raspberries right in my face and shouted "And the same to you!" before being hauled away.

Still feeling outraged and vaguely guilty, I hurried towards the barrier beyond which the boat train waited. Among a row of newspaper placards one headline caught my eye: MAD MAJOR'S BROTHER CALLED MORAL MENACE! This was the umpteenth reference I'd seen to my divorce case of the previous day. The judge, a pot-bellied fiend of the Montagu Legg kidney, had granted a decree *nisi* (with costs) to Lady Lightwood, and my shaking hand recorded his words:

"We can feel only dismay when a man as privileged and educated as Sir Norman Lightwood contributes to the general decline of human decency. A mere settlement (*but I pay through the nose!–N. L.*) can hardly compensate this young lady for the humiliation of being abandoned in a foreign country on her honeymoon because her husband had a secret rendezvous of passion at a hotel in South Kensington." A thin little voice cried, "Hear, hear!" and I saw Doreen the hunchback shake her fist before I fled from row after row of stony faces to the Ritz bar—where Sir Manfred cut me and the barman smirked. "But you don't know the half of it," I wanted to tell the imperialist fool. "I loved an Arab youth in Marrekech and helped my sister to escape from British justice in a German submarine!" I was stopped by the thought that my visa to the United States might be canceled.

So, to the world, a rich, young, eccentric baronet chooses expatriation and exile; sits, luxurious but alone, in his stateroom on a great ocean liner. The peninsula beyond his porthole window, already blurred by distance and gray weather, is known as Land's End. Soon he will see nothing, appropriately enough, but the Atlantic with its blank horizon and its birds. Very well. May the rum customer explain how it looks to him? If he could turn an imaginary globe, his hand would stop it for a moment at four different places. First an island that contains, notably, a vast, empty house with dust-sheets shrouding the Chippendale, and a place of entertainment where an attractive but merciless creature with yellow hair charms old friends as well as new by singing, "Ooh, what a loverly bunch of coconuts!" directly towards the fly-buttons of a sailor in the front row. (It's a sign of the times, by the way, that the house is abandoned and unwanted, while the singer is very popular; but we don't complain, since we dislike both equally.) The next stop is Nuremberg, Germany. The Nazi Party struts on parade at a spectacular convention, and in whatever's the equivalent of the royal box, he glimpses Miss Violet Lightwood, visibly swelling with power and pride. Then his finger touches Islam, a little house in a medina, his spiritual home, with a lantern that he likes to imagine always flickering in the darkness; and lastly the Blue Mountains of Australia, where

Lady D. and her love lie sleeping and satisfied in each other's arms.

I am going somewhere off the map of my world now, choosing the unknown instead of *you,* Ahmin, for a reason I hope you'll understand. In a voice of grave authority and power, Oum advised it. She's been pointing out for some time that my St. Simeon ode is far from finished; she considers me not even halfway up the pillar. Of course her advice is not disinterested, since you and she are rivals, but I shall only be free of this old companion and scourge when the peak of my solitary meditation is reached.

In the meantime, clear sky and open sea. Tap tap tap. I shall continue to let you know how things go.

First day at sea, 22nd of October

Forgot to add that before leaving, I sent you further gifts. They are only toilet accessories, prosaic but stylish considering their nature. Hairbrush; combs; a razor in a case; a few handkerchiefs, and so on. My instinct is to bombard you with luxuries, but I feel that in the circumstances these useful practical items may fill an important gap.

Rather pointedly, I have *not* been invited to cocktails with the captain, nor to dine at his table. However, an enemy I know slightly has been granted this favor. I encountered on deck a large, plain woman in a cartwheel hat whom I recognized as Mrs. Florence Lovejoy, sister of the abominable Sir Manfred Barr. Naturally I prepared to cut her, but she cut me first. When I entered the dining room, I saw her seated at the captain's right, guzzling champagne. She glanced up, saw me, whispered something in her host's ear. They nodded and smirked. I took my solitary place, ordered a cocktail, and pointed her out to my waiter, wondering casually if he knew she had recently been acquitted of murdering her maid.

Third day at sea, 24th of October

A long time ago I stopped wondering whether the fates had picked on me. I know they have, but continue to wonder what they're trying to prove.

This morning I was wakened by the sound of snoring. Somewhere to the southwest of me lay the Azores; on the spare bunk opposite me lay a handsome young man wearing only a jockstrap. He had a classical face and body, like one of those athletic fashion plates turned out by ancient Greek sculptors, and a dark bruise on his forehead. The skin was tawny with sun, the hair midnight black and wavy, the eyes were closed, of course, but I remembered them as green—recognizing him, after the first shock, as the companion or husband of a tallish blonde with blue sunglasses and a Southern accent. My table in the dining room was close to theirs, and they were always in either the middle or the sullen aftermath of a passionate quarrel. The previous evening, when things were clearly more tense than ever, he'd got up and left the table. He hesitated for a moment as he passed me, and I felt I should say something friendly and polite. So I bade him good evening and hoped he'd chosen the *vol au vent,* which was excellent. He ignored this and strode away. I could tell he'd been drinking.

Now, as he slumbered and snored without explanation in my stateroom, I felt the need to say something again. First, however, I picked up his clothes, which were strewn over the floor, and put them on a hanger. Curiosity made me examine his linings, and I saw his suit had been bought on Fifth Avenue. I was about to peek at his wallet when he muttered something under his breath, and I spun round quickly as he stirred.

"Perhaps," I suggested, "you would care for some breakfast?"

The eyes opened, fixing me with a long green stare. He hugged his knees to his chin, tilting his head to one side; his nose wrinkled slightly, like a panther's, when he smiled. Then he belched and confessed he had a terrible hangover. I offered to ring immediately for coffee, but he said he wanted a drink.

"There's some scotch and a bottle of *framboise* on the table, but I hardly think—"

"Hair of the dog," he said. Got up, gave a vast contented stretch, rested his hand on my shoulder for a moment, then yawned his way to the table. "Let's have some scotch." He poured two large ones, handed me a glass and chinked his own against it.

"Cheers."

"Cheers," I repeated and sat down, feeling nonplussed. He walked towards me and I began playing nervously with the cord of my dressing-gown. He stood over me and watched this for a while, his eyes fixing me with an intent, darkly mysterious look. My throat went dry. He put his hand on the cord. I couldn't tell whether he wanted to hold it still or strangle me.

"Hey, my name's Scotty Drake and I had a row with my wife." I received a dazzling smile. "You were there!"

"Yes." I wanted to move away, but felt frozen. "I saw it."

"I saw you seeing it. And I recognized a buddy. I spotted a very present help in time of trouble." He was still smiling. "I'm good at that. I get vibrations. I can be swimming around in a sea of strange faces, nothing friendly, nothing that vibrates—then I spot a buddy."

Now there was something imploring in his eyes; I interpreted it as an appeal not to let him down, nor to shatter his ideal, and decided that a return compliment would be in order. "Well, how good of you to say so. I believe I *am* a sympathetic person. One doesn't like to witness two charming young people—"

"My wife is not charming."

"Really?"

"That's what I said. Charlotte is not a charming woman." He sprawled back on the bunk and scratched his head again. "I'll tell you one reason why I knew you'd understand. You've had wife trouble yourself."

I stared at him. "Now that's uncanny. It's more than vibration, it's positively telepathic—"

"Hey!" He laughed and held up his hand. "Charlotte saw your picture in the paper and pointed you out. That's all."

A warning signal flashed through my mind—*they know I'm rich and are concocting a plot!* Then I looked at Scotty and dismissed the thought as unworthy.

"Well, the good God invented them so I guess they have their place," he said.

"Who?"

"Broads."

I raised my glass. "The ladies, God bless them!"

"Listen, Norman. I want no part of that broad. I'm leaving her."

"For good?"

"For very good. Will you call her up and tell her?"

Naturally I was astonished at this, but managed to remain calm. Possibly the two of them were playing a very dangerous version of the badger game. One hears of such things. "You're not serious," I said, hoping to pass it off as a joke. "I hardly know you!"

Scotty seemed very disappointed. He turned over and lay on his stomach, face buried in a pillow. His voice sounded muffled and morose. "Does that matter, if you like me? Or maybe you *don't* like me?"

"Of course I like you. I think I do. But please be reasonable. Think of the impression it might create if I telephone a strange woman on the *Queen Mary* to say that her husband, at present drinking whisky on the spare bunk in my stateroom, wishes me to inform her that he wants no part of her. Think of that and please be reasonable."

"You British certainly stand on ceremony." He rolled on his back now, one leg dangling over the edge of the bunk, and studied me warily, like a child uncertain whether to wheedle or sulk. "I'd certainly do it for a buddy. All you got to do is call Charlotte on that phone, say 'this is Sir Norman Lightwood,' or however you like to introduce yourself, 'Scotty's right here with me now and wants you to know he's calling it quits.' Then hang up before she can answer."

I didn't answer. Scotty got up, slapped me on the shoulder again and poured us both another drink.

"Cheers anyway." He chinked his glass against mine.

"Cheers. Now, suppose I *did* telephone your wife—"

"Then you will?"

"*Please,* Scotty. I said, *suppose* I made this telephone call and hung up quickly as you instructed. What do you think will happen? She will go to the purser's office and discover the number of my stateroom. She will come in here, probably accompanied by a steward—"

"And throw something at me again." Scotty touched the bruise on his forehead. "That's okay. It's worth it."

"She'd probably throw something at me, too."

"If she did that, I'd slap her!" He looked indignant. "I like slapping broads, even Charlotte, but if she asks for it, she'll get it. I promise you, Norm, if she harms a hair of your head—"

"And what will you do when you get to New York?" I asked, hoping to change the subject.

Scotty said he hadn't decided yet. He proposed "bunking down" with me for the rest of the voyage, then playing it by ear. With a glint in his eye, he handed me the telephone.

I stared groggily at it. "Won't there be a scene? I simply can't afford any more scenes or scandals."

He took the receiver off the hook and placed it tenderly against my ear.

Two scotches before breakfast were inducing dizziness but a certain bravado. Seizing the instrument, I asked boldly for Mrs. Drake's cabin.

"Scotty?" The voice sounded anxious.

"No, this is Sir Manfred Barr speaking. Your husband has decided to bunk down in my stateroom. He doesn't wish to see you any more."

I was amazed to hear her laugh. "Well, ah'm just so relieved someone's lookin' after him. Scotty's a very sweet boy, Sir Manfred, but a handful—a real handful!"

She hung up. The Adonis winked, then pulled a suitcase

from under the spare bunk. Evidently he felt so sure of me that he'd packed his shaving kit and some clothes before arriving here to sleep. I was intrigued and deeply alarmed. You know by now what that combination of feelings does to me.

Later. Scotty repaired to the bathroom and I heard the sound of running water for almost an hour. This seemed excessive at first, then I remembered having been told that Americans, like the Romans, took a voluptuous delight in hygiene. I tried to concentrate on St. Simeon, but felt too disturbed. Oum was in one of her cryptic fragmentary moods, she refused to say anything beyond *"Voyages are dreams, you must know the signs, or . . ."*; I resent this trick of hers more and more, since she always breaks off in a way that strikes me as ominous or teasing. To pass the time satisfactorily I was reduced to investigating Scotty's clothes and wallet. His papers revealed that he was twenty-six years old, born in Los Angeles, and belonged to some trade union for photographer's models. He had been to Hawaii. In case of Death or Accident notify Mrs. Amy Basoalto, 33f Calle Rio Neva, Mexico D.F. (Deduction: his mother divorced his father and married a Latin.) There was $137.17 in his account at the Fidelity Bank.

When he returned from the bathroom I saw that he'd taken the whisky bottle with him. It was more than half-empty now, but Scotty wasn't visibly drunk. He chucked me jovially under the chin, asked how I was doing and began to dress. I watched this closely—whole personal dossiers can be compiled from observing people at their rituals of wardrobe and toilette, and as a child I'd been deeply impressed with Lady D.'s mascara routine. (She stuck a magnifying glass in one eye to make sure the strokes were perfectly even. The painter in her, I suppose.) Scotty rigged himself out with pride, not to say vanity. He admired my best set of cufflinks, which I impulsively offered to him, and chose my favorite silk tie. He brushed and combed his hair with extreme concentration to achieve a casual, ruffled effect. Then he poured himself another drink, which moved me to protest that I was in need of food.

"Okay." He nodded, surprisingly affable. "Let's go eat."

I breathed a secret sigh of relief. The last thing I wanted was for Scotty to feel I might be a nag, but I'd been afraid his drinking habits could create a barrier between us.

(*Resumed later, in the small hours. He lies snoring on the spare bunk, in a drunken sleep.*)

"Hello there!" said Charlotte brightly as we entered the dining room. She sat alone at their table. Scotty ignored her, putting his hand on my arm to guide us to my own table, where he picked up the menu and buried his face in it. Slightly taken aback, I did the same. After a minute or so I glanced over the top and met Charlotte's blue sunglasses over the top of *hers*. With a friendly wave she got up and walked over. She wasn't a pretty girl, but she had chic; she reminded me of a well-bred Lily. There was the same instant friendliness and androgynous charm, the same mocking mouth and bony figure.

"Now you just know you're not Sir Manfred Barr!" she remarked, sitting down between us. "You know you're not." Her lips bunched up with amusement, becoming a Cupid's bow, then she glanced at Scotty. He refused to emerge from behind the menu.

"Ah believe he's nearly ready to come home now," she said. "When he just sits there without bein' rude, he's nearly ready."

"Ready to sock you to dreamland, bitch," came from behind the menu.

"Mercy, he's been drinkin'. Gets so mean when he's been drinkin'."

Still in hiding, Scotty snapped his fingers at a waiter and ordered scotch on the rocks. At the same moment Charlotte gave an odd little squeak of pain. She recovered herself quickly, asking if I felt like roast beef or fish, then gave another squeak. Scuffling sounds occurred under the table. I looked down and saw that Scotty had ground his heel into the toe of her shoe, and was keeping it there.

With a smile and an occasional wriggle that tried and failed to release her foot, Charlotte began prattling about England and what a wonderful trip they'd had. "We went crazy about everythin'. We loved havin' tea in the afternoon. There's nothin' like your knitted sweaters." Impossible to interrupt her; she interrupted herself once, to order filet of Dover sole, and began recommending hotels in New York. "Takin' it all in all, you'll like the Plaza best. It's a convenient location with a kind of old-world charm." Squeak. "If there's any little thing ah can do for you, you just give me a call at *Man*. That's the gentleman's fashion magazine and ah work for it." Squeak. "Mah column is called 'Fine Feathers' and it recommends styles and accessories—like how wide they should wear their ties this year and the new color for daytime shirts is ecru!"

"They sent the bitch to photograph me in jockey shorts." Scotty laid down the menu. "Next thing I knew, we were married." He stared at her in sullen disgust and she squeaked again.

"Scotty," I said, "please take your heel off Mrs. Drake's toe."

"The bitch likes pain."

"Please, Scotty. It's embarrassing."

He obliged. "But you're too good to her," he said.

"Ah've told him and told him it's wrong to involve other people in a private quarrel." Charlotte took a delicate sip of water. "But he keeps on doin' it, all the time."

"I recognized a buddy," Scotty said.

She laid a hand on my arm. "Every time we have a silly little quarrel about nothin' at all, he finds a pal. Ah just hate that. And ah agree it's embarrassin'."

"It's impossible," I said. "People don't keep on quarreling about nothing at all."

"You're right, but we do. Scotty's a sweet boy who gets mean when he's liquored up, and starts callin' me names."

"Bitch," said Scotty.

Charlotte smiled triumphantly. "What did ah tell you?" A thud came from under the table. The smile left her face, she squeaked again and emptied the glass of water over his head. It was done with the swift art born of experience. Any other woman would have created a scene, but Charlotte carried it off with such tact that no one noticed.

Scotty stood up. "She's getting hysterical. Let's go."

I complained that I'd had nothing to eat yet, but he said we could call room service, and walked away. Since it was clearly impossible for me to be left alone with Charlotte, I hoped she'd do me the honor of being my guest for lunch, told the waiter to put everything on my bill, thanked her for her advice about New York hotels and followed Scotty out of the dining room. Back in my quarters, I tried to explain that I felt neither of them could go on like this, but Scotty only laughed, advised me not to take life so seriously, poured himself a drink, sprawled in his favorite insolent position on the spare bunk and was soon in a happy stupor.

I lunched sadly while he muttered from time to time in his sleep. Later in the day I tried to wake him, but received only discouraging grunts, so took a stroll on deck and encountered Charlotte talking gaily to a middle-aged military man about the charms of afternoon tea. She broke off to exclaim, "Hello there, Sir Norman!" and moved on.

Fourth day at sea, 25th of October

Mrs. Amy Basoalto is, as I suspected, Scotty's mother—but she didn't divorce his father. She married Senor Basoalto ("a Mexican doctor, and a bastard") after Mr. Drake died.

Mr. Drake was a lawyer (and a bastard) in Los Angeles.

A buddy was of the opinion that Scotty was handsome enough to be in motion pictures. A test was arranged but Scotty never made it, being drunk that day ("with a stupid broad") in the border town of Tijuana.

Buddy never spoke to Scotty again and it was all a load of crap, anyway.

New buddy took Scotty to New York, where he became a photographer's model and married Charlotte.

New buddy never spoke to Scotty again.

Scotty wishes he'd met me earlier, then he could have left Charlotte sooner. I'm the greatest buddy of them all.

These facts and incidental opinions have been gleaned from desultory conversation with the baffling Adonis, who rests in an armchair this morning, wearing my pajama trousers. He says he doesn't feel like getting up or moving around right now; and neither do I, since I slept badly and he makes me drink too much. The status in fact remains quo, which is to say deeply unsatisfactory.

"Scotty, I don't care about Charlotte—"

"Leave the bitch out of it."

"Very well. But in or out of it, *we* can't go on like this."

"Why?"

"You can't just leave her and sit here making no further plans."

"I told you, let's play it by ear."

This seems unanswerable, or not worth answering. I sit in silence, gazing out of the porthole and pursing my lips.

"Hey, you don't look right. What's up?"

"I am thinking things over."

"You mean you want me to go?"

"No, Scotty, I didn't say that."

Gets up, grinning at me. "Then do me a favor. Relax. Take it easy. Let it happen." Lifts my hand, kisses it—I detect a note of mock respect—and declaims unexpectedly:

In summer when the days are long
Perhaps you'll understand the song—

and retires indefinitely to the bathroom. For sheer mystification, it was worthy of Oum.

Last day at sea, 29th of October

Without pity, passion or visible purpose, the Adonis has kept me confined to quarters. When I try to leave, he objects; when I stay, he picks up a magazine or a drink. To remain calm and even optimistic, I drug myself to sleep at night and write down by day (since Oum has abandoned me once again) any quotations suitable to my predicament that come to mind. These range from tiresome folk wisdom such as "More haste, less speed," etc., to specific consolation from profound thinkers and artists—"Beauty is its own excuse for being" (Emerson), "Personal beauty is a greater recommendation than any letter of introduction" (Aristotle), "None but the brave deserve the fair" (Dryden) and "Satisfaction is death" (George Bernard Shaw)—and have boosted me to a state of Olympian confusion. However, gazing out of the porthole this morning while he was in the bathroom, I sighted land; and knew it had to be established as *terra incognita* or *terra firma*.

"Scotty," I said when he emerged with tousled hair and a towel draped round his waist, "look out there and tell me what you see." Rather surprised, he did so. "The voyage will soon be at an end," I went on, "and before that happens, I'd like to understand you a little better."

"Yes, sir. Anything you say, sir. What's on your mind?"

"When you step ashore, what will you do? Where will you go?"

He looked even more surprised. "What will *you* do, old bean? Where will *you* go?" His ingenuous cunning disconcerted me again and I made no answer. "You're a secretive bird, you never tell me anything. Are you planning to buy North Dakota—I hear it's back on the market—or put in a bid for New York?"

"That, Scotty, is one of the things I wanted to ask you about. Would you consider New York a sound investment?"

"Oh, blue chip, definitely." (Mocks my English accent, but with affection.) "But it depends what you're after."

Is he extremely clever, or simple-minded? I took a deep breath. "You'd be there, Scotty. That's a very large point in its favor." I received another dazzling smile and closed my eyes. "The largest, in fact. Practically the be-all and the end-all."

When I opened my eyes, Scotty was not only still there but showed no sign of becoming violent. Do you realize, Ahmin, that such a declaration doesn't always go down very well in our western world? Not the least charm of your neck of the woods is that no one there could ever be offended by any kind of proposition—if he doesn't care to accept, he either smirks politely or offers to find you someone else. Puritans, those bondslaves of police, law and Church, find this corrupt, but I regard it as a sign of maturity!

"Put it there." I was startled for a moment, then realized that Scotty referred to my hand, which he wished to shake. "I'll get you settled in a hotel," he said, "and then find myself a place to live."

"But I've been thinking of taking a house. You can stay in it if you like."

"Okay. You're the boss."

I was puzzled for a moment by his lack of gratitude; then the expression inspired me to take a bold step. "Furthermore, I've been thinking of engaging a secretary. Something tells me I shall need one in New York. Would you like the job?"

"Hell, I can't type or anything like that."

"*I* can, so it's not important. You have a career, I know, but I can offer you a much better salary."

"How much?" he asked calmly.

"A thousand a month."

"You're kidding."

"Cross my heart and hope to die, Scotty."

His eyes danced. "But will I have to call you Sir?"

"Definitely not."

"Old bean, you're a dream come true. Let's have a drink on it."

"I was coming to that," I said. "My only condition—and I don't think it's unfair, under the circumstances—is no boozing on the job."

"The job starts when we land." Scotty winked, and poured out two scotches. "Listen, we won't want to stick around the city all summer. We ought to travel. Jamaica? The islands?" I looked blank. "Hawaii," he explained, and went through the motions of a hula-hula, using the towel like a skirt. Then he chinked his glass against mine. "Cheers."

"Cheers." My heart beat wildly. "By the way, I find it rather odd that Charlotte hasn't kept in touch. Don't you think we should speak to her?"

"You speak to her if you want."

"Very well. I'll have lunch in the dining room today, if you don't object."

He gave me a blank look. "Sometimes I don't get you at

all—you asking *my* permission to leave your own stateroom?"

"To have lunch with your wife," I replied rather pertly.

"Tell her to get my bags sent over here right away."

Charlotte sat alone at her table, back to the room, peering grimly through blue glasses at a copy of *Punch.* I invited her to join me and she agreed with enthusiasm. She looked a little pale, I thought, but her style was glittery and unremitting as ever. "Let's stay at mah little table, Sir Norman, it's cozier than yours. You're a knight in shinin' armor, you know, rescuin' me from this weird little magazine that's supposed to contain the cream of British humor and makes me feel like Queen Victoria herself. We ain't amused. We just ain't amused at all. Isn't that terrible? Some day you must explain it all, but in the meantime it's so good to see you again—ah was wonderin' where you'd been."

I offered her a drink, not wishing to plunge into business until she'd downed something stiff. She decided on a martini, then reeled off titles she'd encountered in London, wondering which of them I knew. After that she commented on the distant skyline of New York, which lay in a gray, dreamlike, misty, overcast light and might as well have been the moon, or Iceland, as far as I was concerned. At last she drained her glass, paused for breath and to munch the olive; like a driver securing a parking space I slipped in nimbly and broke the news that Scotty was definitely leaving her to become my secretary and had requested his bags.

Charlotte didn't reply immediately, but glanced at the menu and thought she'd like an omelette. No, maybe a veal cutlet. No, an omelette after all. And another martini. The first one, she told the waiter, hadn't been dry enough; would he kindly ask the barman to mix five parts of gin to one of vermouth? "Ah hope you won't consider me an ungracious guest, Sir Norman, but we're kind of finickin' about our martinis, just like you with your tea." Then, without a break, "It's very kind of you to offer Scotty a steady job. The modelin' field is up and down and in and out, you know, and in three or four years Scotty'll be too old for it, anyway. There *is* a future for older models, but only for the tweedy and business type of man, the mature type, you know? Scotty will never be that, ah'm afraid."

And the subject was laughingly dismissed. "Aren't you excited about landin'? Doesn't it feel like the New World is your oyster? You know it does. Ah hope it is." Etc., etc. After an hour I was exhausted with not saying a word and called for the bill. I got up to leave; Charlotte thanked me for a delicious lunch, then laid a hand on my arm as I turned away. "Please sit down for one more minute. It's important."

Reluctantly I did so. She remained unexpectedly silent, drawing on long, black gloves over long, white hands and regarding me with a crooked little smile. The action struck me as sinister. I had a thrilling fantasy of myself on the operating table, Charlotte the surgeon delicately laying a chloroform-soaked handkerchief on my mouth. "You just know you'll never wake up," was the last thing I heard. . . . The hand was again on my arm. "It's embarrassin'," she said, "but it's important. Life with Scotty hasn't been a bed of roses, though he's a sweet boy in many ways. Ah don't truly regret that he's asked for his bags, but there's something else that really makes me want to cry. Ah'm mortified, chagrined and provoked, Sir Norman, that life never gave *us* a chance! Together—you know? you and ah!" Voice dropped to low, urgent throb. "You're the most strangely attractive and unusual man."

She removed her blue glasses. Her eyes were huge, dark and sad, like a basset-hound's in a chihuahua's face. As I gazed at them, they swelled with tears. "They're for you," Charlotte said quietly. "Not for Scotty . . . Well, maybe just one or two for him." She dabbed at her cheeks with a handkerchief and put on her glasses again. "That's all. Forgive me, please."

I kissed her gloved hand, wondering what she'd say if she knew Scotty had kissed my naked one.

Plaza Hotel, New York
5th of November

We are installed here in a spacious suite that reminds me of an anteroom in Versailles, and will move into my new house shortly. I've seen nothing of New York yet, because on the first night here I began to feel unwell, and by morning knew I'd been struck by influenza. It doesn't surprise me, since it's a fairly common reaction I have to arriving anywhere.

The Adonis has at least found me a large, odd brownstone with thirteen rooms, which I rose from my sickbed to inspect. From the room he's selected for my study I shall look out on a huge fan-shaped elm planted in the back. A few branches brush against the bow windows, creating an atmosphere of subtly filtered light and almost Moorish seclusion. Scotty was very pleased that I liked it; he felt it was right for me, and also hoped I'd appreciate the Englishness of a butler's pantry. Sometimes he's uncannily perceptive. A housekeeper, butler and maid were lined up for my approval when I got there; I gave it, feeling rather like a monarch handing out court appointments. The house is four stories high, with dramatic but very steep stairs. My staff assisted me up and down, but at the end of tapping walls, looking under rugs and rummaging generally, I felt exhausted, signed a year's lease on the spot and lay on an impressive red sofa in the living room, gazing up at a row of Tiffany chandeliers. Scotty made drinks and I noticed the bar had already been lavishly stocked. Then, cool as you please, he said he had an appointment and the butler would put me in a taxi.

Since I've already paid him a month's salary in advance, and on his suggestion bought a car so that he can chauffeur me, I was mildly displeased. I pointed out this was the first time I'd asked him to drive me anywhere. He answered that if I cared to wait for two or three hours he'd come back and drive me home. "But, Scotty," I said, "I am unwell, my temperature is one hundred point six. And I've asked very little of you—and *seen* very little of you, incidentally, since most of the time you're off in the car somewhere. Furthermore, when I *have* asked you to do something simple but important, like checking the Public Library to see how many copies of Oum they bought, you forgot."

To my astonishment he roared with laughter and called me fantastic. It was only common sense, he suggested, since I now had four servants including himself, to ask a second for whatever I needed if the first was busy. Also, he'd kept away from me because he didn't want to catch the flu. Before I could protest, he tweaked my ear lightly and walked out of the house.

On the basic circuit of human feeling, I begin to suspect that Scotty has a faulty connection somewhere.

Later. Having no choice, I returned to the hotel by taxi, felt better after a nap, called room service to bring me tea and composed two exceptional St. Simeon stanzas. (Oum has been in fine, insistent form since influenza struck.) Scotty came back before dinner and behaved as if nothing had happened—that is to say, poured himself a drink and sprawled on the sitting-room couch. Then, apparently remembering my existence, he asked how I felt.

"I shall be all right. But my temperature's two points higher."

"It always goes up in the evening. Just take it easy, old bean." He got up and lounged in the doorway to my bedroom, holding his glass in one hand and unknotting his tie with the other. He gave me an amused, intent green stare. "Angry with me, aren't you?"

"No, but you hurt my feelings."

He seemed surprised. "I did?"

"I don't think of you as a servant, Scotty. It was unkind and unjust to imply that I treat you like a cook or butler."

After a moment, he came and sat on the edge of the bed. He hugged his knees and tilted his head to one side, still staring at me.

"I don't want you to catch influenza, either."

He didn't answer, but leaned over me, removing his tie and placing it round my neck. "Wrap up well," he said, and knotted it rather tightly. Then he walked out, and a minute later I heard the shower running. I felt a sharp pang, half sigh and half tingle, reflecting that once again I seemed to be on the edge of something, rather than over it.

7th of November

Yesterday, feeling better, I decided to get up. Rather annoyed to discover that Scotty was off somewhere in the car, I walked out of the hotel lobby and was delighted to find a row of horse-cabs waiting immediately outside. For a moment I stared at them, entranced with thoughts of Marrakech and even sniffing the air for a remembered draft of warm henna, kif and dung. All I got, however, was a capful of cold, frowzy, unseasoned city ether, and a smut in my eye. Undaunted, I stepped into the first cab and told the driver to give me a ride through Central Park. As we jogged down 57th Street, a peculiar unnerving sensation attacked me; as a result, I suppose, of being conveyed by obsolete carriage through a canyon of high, sheer, looming concrete and glass while cars and trucks growled past, I felt suddenly and terrifyingly *out of it!* It was a journey down a corridor of machine-ridden dread: lights flashed colored warnings that came too late, horns blew unspeakable raspberries and two masked creatures emerged from a steaming manhole. . . . I believe I almost fainted. At any rate there was a black, uncertain interval, then we turned a corner; I was greeted by rocks, grass, trees, a mile or two of sky; and everything seemed quite friendly and cheerful again.

When I returned to my suite, Scotty was waiting. "Where have you been?" he asked. "I was worried." I told him, and he reproached me for not leaving a note. This struck me as ironic and touching; I laughed merrily and asked him to mix me a martini. I've decided to acquire a taste for them. Then

I suggested moving into the house after lunch, if he could spare the time, and going out on the town later. "I have recovered, and am taking up residence—doesn't that make a celebration in order, Scotty?"

"Okay. Shall I run up the Union Jack on the roof?"

"The Stars and Stripes, too. It's hands across the sea."

No doubt the wine went to my head—but I attribute my almost immediate tipsiness at the restaurant to something more fundamental: being out in the world again, and the Adonis across a candlelit table. After the first sip, anyway, I felt sealed in an envelope of warmth and promise, snug in a bed of voluptuous ease. Yet something seemed deviously wrong from the start. Knowing that Scotty was still a little shaken by my complaints of the other day (though they weren't unreasonable), I wanted to make clear that all was forgiven. "Let bygones be bygones!" I said and he answered, rather surprised, that he thought they were. I dropped the subject instantly and began regaling him with stories of my life, Lady D., the monstrous treachery of Lily Vail, the strange case of the Mad Major, even the mystery surrounding my birth and the invention of Oum. (No mention of *us*, however, Ahmin; naturally we remain a secret as deep and revered as the Eleusinian mysteries.) I was in excellent form and told these little anecdotes very entertainingly, yet I had the impression that Scotty thought I exaggerated. He also advised me not to speak so loudly, and I admit I noticed people at nearby tables staring anxiously at me. Changing the subject again, I inquired if he'd heard anything from Charlotte.

"Hell, no. I don't want to speak to the bitch."

I wondered whether to tell that she'd confessed her love

for me, and decided against it; he might think I was exaggerating again. "Have you thought about getting a divorce?" I asked, and Scotty shook his head. "But won't she demand money anyway?" Scotty said that if she did he'd let me know, and suggested we go somewhere for a drink.

He drove me to a place in the region of Times Square. Heavy shutters across the windows gave it a boarded-up look, but he pushed open a door with iron studs; I followed him inside and was reminded immediately of Marseilles, although I've never been there. A gross red-headed man wearing an open checked shirt and a medallion round his neck came up and greeted Scotty, who turned to me and said, "This is Skipper, he runs the joint." Joint's the word, I thought. It was bleak and uncomfortable, rather like a church hall, with booths as hard as pews and a dim if irreligious light, and large enough to seem empty with about thirty people in it—all men except for a couple of haggard, disreputable-looking females. Most of the customers were seamen or, I judged, waterfront types. The others, mainly lined up on stools at the bar, were as incongruously well-dressed as myself. My entrance provoked curious, not altogether friendly stares from the riffraff. The room was un-unnaturally silent, hardly anyone spoke and I sensed an atmosphere of conspiracy and waiting.

"Now what's all this?" I asked Scotty as we sat down at a booth, but he only snapped his fingers at a hawk-eyed brute in a cap and black sweater, whom I'd have placed as a burglar but who turned out to be the waiter. I ordered brandy, which he seemed never to have heard of, and was about to repeat my question when I noticed something at the bar. An elegant man with silver hair was engaged in low, earnest conversation with a young roughneck; one of the females stood by, a predatory sneer on her crimson lips; the silver-haired man smiled, the other nodded and followed him out of the bar, with a wink at the harpy and a promise he'd see her later.

Though I lack experience in this kind of world, I knew instinctively that a deal had been made. My throat went dry and I asked Scotty what on earth possessed him to bring me here. His response was cool, almost hostile. "I thought you ought to know about it." A shrug and a contemptuous flicker of the eyes before he looked away and the improbable waiter returned with our drinks. I drained my brandy at a gulp and ordered another, knowing we were on the edge of a volcano.

"*Why*, Scotty?"

I spoke more loudly than I intended, it startled him and the corners of his mouth turned sullenly down. When he faced me again, I saw an expression that reminded me of Lily's as she perched on the top bunk on the Orient Express. It wasn't hatred, nothing as simple or bracing as that; I'd underestimated my wife, indeed, when I believed that was all she felt for me. *Malevolence,* nourished by God knows what pain and loss of heart, confronted me again across this squalid table.

"If you put the Old Adam on the market," I said, "you lose half the poetry of life. Even St. Paul, that stiff-necked old prude, admitted that love is the fulfilling of the law! But this joint, as you call it, Scotty, this dingy little bazaar demeans a lover to a mere client, it assumes he can only attain his beloved if the price is right, and the beloved responds only for the same reason. What a world of calculated insult that conjures up! Do you really want to be part of it?"

I was holding forth again, I realized, but this time nothing was going to stop me—not even two arrogant, devastating young ruffians at the next booth, listening in with the same contempt as Scotty. "Ever since we met so oddly at sea, I've been wondering just how innocent you were. And even now, Scotty, at this not exactly reassuring moment, I refuse to admit you're lost." A guffaw from somewhere. "You think I'm absurdly ineffectual and romantic, I suppose? Well, I am—but I'd be a successful romantic if I weren't, through some loading of the cosmic dice, always scared to death! I wish you knew me better. Then you'd understand that even my weakest actions are the result of strong beliefs."

"Pip-pip." Scotty shrugged again. "Listen, you pay a doctor and a lawyer—and a secretary. So what's the difference?"

"As great," I answered grandly, "as that between heaven and hell." Then I announced I was tired (which was true, what with baring my heart so soon after influenza) and wished to be driven home. He obliged me in a dangerous silence.

(*Resumed later, in my brownstone study.*)

I drew out the key to my new house and unlocked the front door. Scotty went upstairs without a word, and a door slammed, in more senses than one, I thought. The small, cold hours were on their way; sitting on the stairs, I remembered the night when I was ten years old and Nanny Gray let the cat out of the bag. This time there'd be no Lady D. to appear in the hall with a puff of smoke from her long cigarette. *Voyages are dreams, you must know the signs,* said Oum.

Quite irritably I told her to shut up, made the long climb to my bedroom, took a double sedative, undressed and lay down between fresh, stiff sheets.

There was a dream I couldn't remember but felt sure was unpleasant, and the sound of footsteps coming nearer woke me up. My bedroom door opened; Scotty's silhouette loomed forward; I heard him breathing heavily, jerkily, but couldn't tell in the darkness whether he carried a weapon or not. Rigid with terror, eyes open and fists clenched, I feigned sleep. He lurched to the bed, swaying and belching a whiff of alcohol. Then, without a word, he lay down on his back beside me. The mattress springs vibrated like distant thunder. I remained motionless, praying not to gasp, choke or hiccup. Scotty muttered something to himself. After that, for several minutes, silence except for his impassioned breathing and a curiously heart-rending sigh.

When he got up and stumbled out, I think I heard him say: "Let's have some scotch."

227 east 61st Street, New York
8th of November

At first I wasn't unduly worried, realizing after the episode in the night that poor Scotty was fighting a battle with himself, strongly drawn to his understanding rescuer and as strongly gripped by the old bitter habits and despair. He'd gone off to think things over, and I resolved to be patient and tactful on his return. Although bursting with questions, I would ask none; his exact relation to the world of Skipper, his motive in flaunting it to me, his whole course of singling me out only to baffle and torment me, would remain mysteries until he cared to solve them.

However, when there was no sign of him all day and I'd walked several blocks to make sure the car was gone, I felt a twinge of alarm. In the past he'd never stayed away for more than a few hours. Night fell, but I remained in darkness on the red sofa, waiting for the sound of a key in a lock. The maid entered to switch on lights and shrieked with surprise when she found me there. The formality of dining alone had to be endured, staff hovering in expectation of my compliments. Immediately afterward I rushed out and took a cab to the bar. It was difficult to locate, even more difficult to enter; almost shaking with dread I pushed at the iron-studded door, looked in, was looked at, spied the thuggish waiter and the bull-necked Skipper, who told me curtly he hadn't seen Scotty and turned an indifferent back. I left under the scrutiny of coldly hopeful eyes, to write this in my study, opposite the fan-shaped elm, its branches groping like tentacles outside the window.

9th of November

Nuit blanche, not unexpectedly. A snatch of exhausted sleep before dawn, and a dream of Violet in lion-tamer's costume; a listless breakfast and a deluge of rain. Then the telephone rang.

"Sir Norman Lightwood?" Brisk, rather loud female voice. "Hold the line, please." Click, silence and a distant announcement, "Sir Norman's on one." Somebody's office, obviously: *hospital?* I thought wildly, then—

"Hello there, Sir Norman! How are you this mornin'? Don't you hate it when a day starts bright and lovely and then it comes on to rain darnin' needles?"

"Yes. I hate it."

"So do ah. You just know it's depressin'. Sir Norman, dear, ah'm callin' you on behalf of that naughty Scotty."

I felt stunned. "You've seen him? Where?"

"At home, of course. Isn't that where a wife's in the habit of seein' her husband?" Blob of laughter. "We have our ins and outs, and ups and downs, but right now everythin's in and up. He's a sweet boy really, and ah appreciate all your care and interest in him. But he's thought it over and decided to return to the modelin' field."

"You mentioned something about a message," I said crisply.

"That's right. Scotty wants his bags sent over right away."

Charlotte gave me the address of her office, hoped I hadn't wasted too much time and trouble, and rang off. I sat listening to the rain for a while. Finally a thought struck me and I telephoned *Man*. "Sorry to bother you, Charlotte," I said politely, "but although I'm willing to forego the salary I paid Scotty in advance, to say nothing of a year's lease on a large and expensive establishment, *I want my car back*."

After a moment, Charlotte admitted that she saw my point and wished she could do something to help.

"I don't need help. Just my car."

"Ah know, but ah wonder if it's wise for you to brave another storm of scandal?"

"Charlotte, what are you talking about?"

"Ah truly don't know exactly what ah'm talking about, but Scotty said he'd like to keep the car. And then he said, if you tried to get it back there *might* be trouble. Ah'm afraid he means it, though ah don't know *what* he means."

So, with a familiar whir, the wheels of blackmail turn again. *In summer when the days are long,* I think grimly, *perhaps you'll understand the song.* How does the next verse go? *In autumn,* I believe, *when the leaves are brown, take pen and ink and write it down.* For several autumns this is precisely what I've done. And where, to coin a phrase, has it got me? Another empty, otiose house on my hands. Fleeced of a thousand or two. No car. That awful feeling of . . . Shall I place a long-distance call to Australia, announce my impending arrival? No. That would be abject surrender. All the same, I feel a need to disappear, to vanish rather drastically from sight. *Aysha, a plump dusky woman with one wall- and one cross-eye atop her veil, managed the rundown little hotel usually patronized only by natives, and remembered the Englishman quite well. Lying on a mattress in his cell-like room, he seemed in good health and was always immaculately dressed; yet even the casual stranger noticed a strange, remote, glazed expression in his eyes. As a servant entered and with silent expert hands prepared the* narghilye, *one understood . . .*

Forgive me then if I put this aside for a while.

S.S. La Perla
26th of November

Waiting to cross the Equator, I remember something I wished to place on record and overlooked in the chaos of departure. From New York I sent you *two packages* of clothing and cigarettes, registered, insured and addressed to the El Bedi hotel. Your devoted servant signed himself, as usual, George Eliot.

Again, farewell.

Bahia Quemu, Brazil
4th of March, 1938

It's no good—now that I'm more alone than ever, I must keep in touch to feel you haven't gone completely away. Think of this, and others that follow from God knows where, as a Very signal, a sudden raging flare fired from the pistol of my heart, across the night of my solitude!

Here, rivers with lovely names—the Beni, the Miranda, the Madre de Dios—wind their way through dreadful swamps and ancient forests. Yesterday, in the strange green dusk, I boarded a steamer and sipped gin for hours as it crept downstream; animals howled from the Bongo trees and a blind Negro strummed his guitar. This morning we stopped at a steamy inland port and I went ashore, walked down the quay, dodging huge bales of something-or-other loaded by half-naked creatures bright and wild-eyed with sweat, rested on a bench in the dusty plaza, picking two fleas off my right leg and listening to a sour flute played in the distance. Beggars, children and a wandering cow watched me with a kind of grim stupefaction. After a breakfast of figs and sardines—one takes what comes in these parts—I pondered, as Oum must surely have done, on a ghastly fact of life: the romantic and the sinister are always entwined, in an attitude somewhere between a struggle and an embrace. Beyond the fatal thrill is a child screaming its head off in the dark, an act of monstrous vengeance on a hurtling train, a madwoman disappearing into a submarine at dawn, a door that opens to a world of pimps and pitiless roughnecks. . . . Against these, all I can set is a single exception that proves the rule—welcoming limbs of your sturdy naked body, nightlong skirmishes on a vast mattress. You have an idea, now, of my present mood.

So, consoled by a memory of joy but grieved because it's only a memory, I tossed a few coins to beggars and children, returned to the steamer and lay back in my deck-chair. With a shudder the engines started up again; the journey continued.

Buenos Aires, Argentina
30th of August

Limbo of a half-empty cosmopolitan hotel: air heavy with boredom, rum, perfume; gypsy band plays a brisk yet mournful tango. Couple passes my table to take the floor: stout middle-aged businessman with a rakish sombrero, giggling young Jewess trying to look Spanish with a rose behind her ear. Through half-closed eyes I watch them advance and twirl; she bends dizzily backwards in his arms, he leans over her, black sombrero touches crimson rose. . . . Oum whispers in my ear (after her longest, most sullen absence), *if the clock has stopped, why does the music play?*—and I decide, quite suddenly, to ignore her, to put a stop once and for all to her jealous taunts and wheedling promises! From now on, we shall do better to lead entirely separate lives. Caught up in the tango's relentless rhythm, I snap my fingers at the waiter and order another *porto blanco.*

Guayaquil, Ecuador
25th of April, 1939

Furthest end of a cobbled waterfront; sundown; orange and purple sky; no breeze; long shadows. I watch silhouettes of ships at anchor, feeling becalmed as they, then become aware of a human silhouette, fifty feet down the waterfront, watching *me*. Smoke from our cigarettes drifts in each other's direction, but dissolves before it can meet. Trembling, I sense an invitation—but neither accept nor reject it, since I can see nothing but a hard, intent shadow, immovably waiting. At last it stirs—approaches barefoot with a lithe, provocative, deliberate saunter—its hoarse voice calls out in Spanish for a match. As I comply, the face moves close to mine, emerging from deep shadow into golden light. I reel back from the dreadful, mincing, knowing, gold- and gap-toothed smile of a timeworn *tapette*, DOLORES tattooed on his arm.

9th (?) of September

How typical that the moment I'm brought to my senses is the moment I'm utterly trapped. Having set off almost two years ago in a mood of glamorous despair, compass pointing resolutely off the beaten track; having lost myself in a world of pampas and orchid jungles, gasped for breath in ruined cities high in the Andes, and been cruelly disappointed on a promising waterfront; having seen ant-eaters, flamingoes, crocodiles; ridden mules and my Gran Chaco railway—I am now stranded in a small South American seaport with a name I can neither spell nor pronounce, because war has broken out miles away in Europe.

Week of steaming tropical heat, lurid food, ancient fans that turn too slowly, and I'm unable to leave my room, relapsing into total flux.

11th of September

This morning a mulatto captain entered and offered to take me, at great cost, on his boat. I agreed, after failing to persuade him to lower his price. It sails tomorrow. Hotel servant tells me it's laden with copra, twenty-eight years old and notoriously unseaworthy. But there's no turning back.

St. Johns Hotel, Jacksonville
Florida, U.S.A.
2nd of January, 1940

The shave, at moments, has been terrifyingly close. First of all, my villainous mulatto dumped me without explanation in Costa Rica during the rainy season. There, worst horrors of all awaited me. Since I needed funds, I telegraphed various banks—even, in desperation, Lady D. in Australia. Obviously my urgent pleas never arrived, and I found myself down to my last *colón*. The hotel manager, a typical Hun, wouldn't listen to my explanations and had me sent in a wagon to the local jail. A night behind bars with primitive desperadoes, and my fantasy of a mysterious disappearance threatened to become hideously real. . . . Then a guard showed signs of friendliness. I gritted my teeth, threw myself on his mercy and he agreed to telephone the British consul in San José. The tide at last had turned, for Oliver ("Finnan") Haddock responded with immediate sympathy to my name, having once been engaged to old Aunt Madge. (When he asked after her, I refrained from mentioning how she now resembled her numerous chows.) I was quickly released, loaned money, put on a respectable boat, and stepped ashore at Jacksonville, Florida on New Year's Day, almost unrecognizably thin.

Bluewater Inn, Kuola, New Mexico
10th of June

The landscape here reminds me of yours, which is why I fell instantly in love with it. Same sweep of desolate eroded ranges, same exhilarating distances filled with nobody—and the Indian population provides that touch of the exotic without which no game is worth the candle. (Even a chunky silver bracelet, however poorly worked and set with gaudy, worthless stones, makes my nomadic heart beat faster.) Yesterday I awoke with a feeling of acute dread, an imagined knocking on my door; realized I was thirty; drove up into the mountains, under a frowning sky, in a rented Cadillac; had a flat tire miles from anywhere and skidded to the edge of the road, above a terrifyingly sheer drop. A thunderstorm broke immediately. I sat behind blurred and streaming windows, unable to move, vertiginously trapped, alone with the wrath of Oum. She'd been fled, like the Hound of Heaven, for much too long—and hadn't she warned me, when I left England, that I'd never be free until our work was done? Lightning flashed dangerously near, the sky gave another roar. I agreed to put the wanderyears and false alarms behind me, stop drifting, settle down, honor our ancient pact of solitude. . . .

As the rain stopped, brightness flooded the air. Glancing at snow-tipped mountains, thinking quite suddenly of *you*, I resolved to cast anchor as an Ornamental Hermit—no hole in the ground but an appropriately oriental villa or chateau above it, sanctuary for concentration and surprise, peaceful walls to guard me, walks to soothe, views to startle, a courtyard, fountains, clouds . . . Two hours later a huge gasoline truck, lumbering like a dinosaur, came to my rescue.

29th of July

After pricing various mountain slopes and backwoods, I bought last week a thousand acres of heroic untamed land, part brown and empty desert, part canyon with blue-tinged balsam pines and a foaming stream, part grassy meadows, dotted with wild roses and pack-rats. Eight miles away is Kuola, in a valley of adobe church, motel, pueblo, ranchers; far up in the highlands live a flagellant religious sect, the Penitentes, all hoods and thongs, who fortunately keep to themselves except on Good Friday, when they grimly crucify one of the order and parade him in the village square.

15th of August

No architect has yet been found, perhaps none exists, who understands my need for a dome here, a minaret there. When I explain that, in order to complete Oum's finest work, I wish to re-create her world, they seem confused. When I try another tack, and point out that, since reality has even less than usual to offer me at the moment, I'm willing to spend a fortune on a very profound fantasy, their eyes positively dilate with alarm.

Discouraging . . .

8th of September

In desperation, I added a few frills to a *National Geographic* photograph of a Mameluke house in Cairo, and took it to a construction company. They agree to draw up plans, but decline the responsibility of building. No matter; I shall pick my own team; forged by the simple hands and rough tools of native craftsmen, the result should be even finer. Meanwhile, I take up residence in a convenient disused log cabin. Most of my luggage remains stored in a Santa Fe warehouse, and I content myself with bare necessities—bed, table, oil stove, books, dungarees, whisky, typewriter, Cadillac. For decoration, a bowl of wild roses and the Oum *djellabah,* hung on the wall.

26th of December

None of the workmen arrived yesterday. This morning I got up early to wait for them, and ask why. Under the impression I'd made a joke, they laughed. I repeated the question rather angrily; after a long silence, one of them wondered if I'd forgotten about Christmas. I admitted it, and we all laughed for about ten minutes.

24th of January, 1941

There have been days, since I first gave myself the green light, when things seemed to move with intolerable slowness and confusion. Organized labor, though one's willing and able to pay through the nose for it, is a contradiction in terms here; my battalion of thirty Indian workmen is never present in full strength, and outbreaks of drunkenness are not infrequent; my mind, rushing ahead to minarets, balconies, etc., is constantly wrenched back to consider electricity and water, those mundane staples. (For electricity I'm installing my own power-house, and for water have traced my mountain stream to a spring seven miles away, and begun to pipe it down.) But gradually I became reconciled to the longer, larger view. My lawyers Parkinson and Parkinson recently pleaded from their beleaguered island for a return on my swelling investments, for a "little something coming in" now that my Malayan rubber is a dead duck with Japanese swarming over south-east Asia. I reminded them that time is a dream, tomorrow another maddening day.

5th of February

Yesterday a station wagon drew up near my cabin. A small, trim woman with a tiny waist and long reddish hair got out and strode energetically towards me. She wore jeans, cowboy shirt, sungoggles; heavy Indian bracelets and earrings swung in perfect coordination with her admirable haunches. A tall Navajo followed her, also in cowboy costume. His limber, slightly rolling walk and a vivid bandana tied round his blue-black hair gave him a piratical look.

"Good morning. Denna Marx." She held out an authoritative hand, implying that she not only expected me to shake it, but to know who she was. Having seen and admired her paintings, this was possible. At close quarters she looked older—the firm and springy body was twenty-five, the skin with its faintly tired lines and dusty freckles, nearer forty.

"My husband, Freddy." With a glitter of bracelets, she touched his arm. The word *squaw* flared through my mind. The Navajo didn't shake my hand but clasped it gently, as if examining a strange and fragile object. I was uncertain whether to withdraw it or let him weigh it in the balance for as long as he wished.

"He could hold it for ever, you know." The woman calmly read my thoughts. "The time depends on how long it is since they last saw you, and as Freddy's never met you before . . ." She turned away, raising her sungoggles to inspect my territory. "We heard you were getting in pretty deep around here, and I see it's true. Roughing it in the cabin, I suppose, till the roof goes over your head? Well, I did the same thing. One gets slightly desperate in the final months; in fact I sat them out on a beach in California. . . . Now what exactly are you building, anyway?"

Freddy released my hand and gave me a mysterious look, which puzzled me until I saw it was his natural expression. He had the Indian face at its most handsomely stylized and masklike: almond-shaped eyes under heavy, enigmatic brows, strong cheekbones, wide and sensual mouth with an extremely full lower lip. Without a word he walked back towards the station wagon, and the secrecy of the gesture somehow thrilled me.

"He's probably brought you a present." She raised her sungoggles again briefly. "Don't be put out if it's a ring. Turquoise is the great symbol here; they call it the eye of God watching over you. But you haven't told me what you're building!"

"A surprise." I described its general inspiration, and she gave an approving nod. "It sounds," she said, "as if we may expect more translations," and obviously enjoyed my flash of astonishment.

"You know the work of Oum Salem? I'm dazed and flattered."

"Please don't be. I took it for granted you knew my paintings. They are very great poems, anyway, and the highest compliment I can pay the translator is that he conveys their greatness."

Which encouraged me to tell her that I'd been at work for several years on Oum's tremendously long *The Crowns of Seclusion,* a poem of Homeric proportions, an Odyssey of the interior, with which others had tried but failed to grapple. "I've been through a period of discouragement myself," I went on. "But here, I feel, a solitude as epic as hers may turn the trick."

Freddy now returned with a small package wrapped in wax paper, and opened it. No jewelry, but something oblong and yellowish, which reminded me of a small Object.

"Taste it," Denna said.

Under her husband's inscrutable scrutiny I did so bravely, and found it delicious.

"Goat cheese." These were Freddy's first words to me, spoken in a quiet husky voice. "The Mexicans in Rio Arriba make it. But not for much longer."

When I asked why, he shrugged fatalistically. So I nodded back wisely and remarked that it seemed a shame.

"Yes." He broke off another piece, handed it to me. "We think so."

"But sometimes you feel a strange, obstinate indifference in this country," Denna said. "As if the gods have gone, and they know it." She gave a little shiver. "And yet, in a way, that's good. Puts you on your mettle, leaves you entirely on your own. You'll find that out, I'm sure."

Freddy gave me the last piece of cheese, and watched while I ate it.

"Quite remarkable," I said.

"You really like it?"

"Of course."

"Then why not make it?"

I stared at him. "How?"

"Buy goats." His eyes waited, steady and dark and patient. "The cheese is made from the milk of Angoras."

Somehow it seemed a crucial moment between us, as if I were being tested. "How many?"

"Five hundred at least," said Denna, "if you're going to put it on the market."

For a moment I was totally disconcerted; then thought of a little something coming in for Parkinson and Parkinson. "In for a penny, in for a pound—let's make it seven hundred."

Neither of them seemed surprised, or congratulated me. I was slightly disappointed. "You could build the corral down there, where it's green," Denna said. Then her hand rested on my arm. "If we're going to be friends, and I feel we are, you'll have to accept the fact I'm a bit bossy. Here's one more suggestion. Buy another thousand acres and you'll be absolutely safe."

I felt alarmed. "From what?"

"Someone else buying them. And those goats will take up space, you know." She glanced at a bracelet that turned out to be a watch, tiny dial set in elaborate silver and lucky turquoise. "Freddy, we have to be going." Shook my hand again. "We're on our way to Santa Fe. I need paints, for canvas *and* face. Now please drive over and eat with us any time you feel like it, beginning tonight. Freddy's a wonderful cook."

It was difficult to decide which had overwhelmed me most: the invitation, the prospect of becoming a goat-owner, or the drama of our encounter. She seemed surprised when I told her so. "But I'm sure we'll find it all in your horoscope." Freddy moved off again in fascinating silence, and almost before I could feel a pang at his not saying goodby, she explained, "They never do. They think it, though," and followed him briskly to the station wagon. It disappeared, at considerable speed, round a sheer, rocky curve.

In the hard, fading light of dusk, two grinning sculptured hippogriffs, colored lights gleaming in the slots for eye and jaw, look down on me from wrought-iron gates; the driveway is like a tunnel beneath arching trees, densely foliaged, trunked in red, and I switch on my headlights. Then a sudden brilliance of massed tulip trees, like huge butterflies against the dying sun. They surround a severe, flat-roofed adobe house, built on a raised mound, terraced with vines. I climb the steps and a carved front door swings slowly open, Denna greets me in long purple skirt and white peasant blouse. I follow her to the L-shaped living room and am immediately confronted, on one bare spotlit wall, by a larger than lifesize painting of somebody half-woman, half-spider. (Goddess of weaving, she tells me.) Arrangement of Mexican ranch furniture in golden leather and dark pine, lanterns of tinted glass, Navajo rugs patterned with broken black lines like Morse-code signals; vista of twilit mountain peaks through a bay of windows; and round the L, a dining room with a long refectory table and a bar at which stands Freddy, rattling cocktails in a silver shaker. One final magic touch and I almost swoon—photograph of an Arab woman stares up at me, somehow familiar behind veil and *djellabah.* It is myself as Oum, on the dust jacket of my book, artfully set on the coffee table.

"Waiting to be signed . . ." Denna smiles and hands it to me. After the usual panic of seeing myself in that outfit, I write impulsively on the flyleaf, "*Voyages are dreams . . .*", etc., and then, "*to my dear Denna, in her castle on the ground.*" She's pleased, I can tell; skirt flares triumphantly as she sits on a cushioned wooden bench, and Freddy (who doesn't say hello, they never do) serves me a perfect, ice-cold martini.

Denna flicks over a few pages of Oum, closes the book with a snap. "Do you agree," she asks rather sharply, "there's no resemblance at all to Emily Dickinson? Reviewers' rubbish, wouldn't you say?"

I nod. "The resemblance is superficial, the polarities deep."

"Quite so. If one can label her anything, I'd say a female Cavafy. No doubt she was lesbian, is there?"

"We are led to that conclusion." And I ask to be shown her studio. We pass the Spider Goddess, whose combination of beauty and monstrousness I admire again, cross a patio, enter an adobe outhouse. Pressing a switch, Denna floods her world with light. Since the only way to describe painting is to say what meets the eye, not the mind, I will remark that, in a strict and definite manner very like her gestures and speech, this artist shows us women—or perhaps, one woman, since she is always naked, unruffled and red-haired—in some fairly unusual situations. In a lonely, moonlit field, she receives the embraces of a black steer with glittering ruby horns. Seated in a wicker chair on a colonnaded terrace, she has taken out her heart and hands it, with the polite air of a maidservant offering a departing guest his hat, to an imperious jaguar. She stands knee-deep in the ocean, patiently breast-feeding a salamander crouched by the shore, his tail extending in a vast suggestive curve beyond her, all the way to a tropical horizon. These images, at once menacing and erotic, I found extremely powerful;

and their after-effect was almost stronger, for as we turned to leave, Denna switched the room back to darkness, the moon poured in through a skylight and a coyote howled somewhere in the mountains.

At dinner, for which Freddy had cooked a savory *pot au feu,* Denna returned to the subject of my house. "From everything you describe, I feel you must be Sagittarius, like me."

"Only Gemini, I'm afraid."

"So was Queen Victoria. How strange. But with all that fantasy, there has to be Sagittarius aspected in you somewhere."

"Aspected somewhere in *you* there have to be magic powers."

"There are." She nodded calmly. "If Jupiter presides in one's fifth house, the place of dreams and visions, one is inevitably off to the races. But what made you say so?"

"My moon's in Sagittarius."

"Oh dear, that's the one place I hoped *not* to find it. The nature of Gemini, as I'm sure you know, is basically dual. Add to it that particular combination, and one's liable to be in at least eight places—metaphorically—at once. Freddy, darling, pour him more wine." Her eyes gave me a long, bright, approving look. "It's the darkness in your chart, of course, that makes you so cheerful. You'll be a fascinating horoscope to make."

"Freddy," I said. "I want to know your sign."

"Capricorn." A faint smile. "The Goat."

I raised my glass to him.

"We have the compatibility of fire and earth," said Denna. "You being air, Norman, would mix best with water."

I secretly damned my sun and moon, thinking that water and air sounded much less exciting than the more substantial elements, feeling astrologically blighted. Then I saw Freddy was watching me.

"Is the food not good?"

"Delicious!"

"But you looked," he said, "as if something displeased you."

With that uncanny primitive instinct, he'd guessed that a shadow had fallen. Since all instinct (when it's correct) is sympathy, it was like being handed a rose, a sweet, reviving balm, after Denna's brilliant vinegar and thorns. I felt more cheerful again, and told Denna that her sculptures at the entrance to the driveway had given me an idea. "I know you could design some beautiful things for my house."

"I know I could." Nodded again. "But let's wait till everything's finished. Fantasy, I need hardly tell you, is a very practical thing. It only works when the foundations are firm, we must never put in the poetry till we're sure it won't interfere with the plumbing. I'm not ashamed to admit I need hot and cold running water, central heating, good food and wine, and . . ." As Freddy offered her more of both, she touched his hand. "Then the juices, so to speak, begin to flow."

"How right you are," I said. "I've never understood why people expect artists to starve, and mistrust them if they've made or inherited money."

"Having done both, I agree with you." And began to recount her childhood. "My father, with whom I was deeply in love, was a consul general attached usually to minor but exotic islands: Haiti, Iceland, Sumatra. . . . I grew up everywhere, speaking so many languages I sometimes wondered which was my own. They say I was a formidable child, with access to all kinds of rare experience—voodoo, revolution outside my bedroom window, the midnight sun. Yet, because of my infatuation, I was deeply shy and unhappy. *J'ai été encore vierge à vingt-six ans, mon cher!* Only at his death was there a kind of indirect sexual release. My colors grew bolder, the galleries got interested, and finally, in a quest for peace and independence not unlike yours, but helped by a remarkable *guru,* I arrived (in every sense of the word) in the southwest. Yet I've always had my detractors, believe it or not, those who say 'striking but cold,' 'colorful and intriguing, no more and no less,' 'fashionable but somehow intrinsically dated surrealism,' and so on and so forth—all of which, in my opinion, is the kind of puritanical downgrading that anyone endures in this country unless he's impoverished, Jewish, Ben Shahn or Grandma Moses. The last two, anyway, are different versions of the same thing."

"Don't you mean the last three?" I asked.

"Well, yes, of course, but I didn't wish to appear . . ." She stood up suddenly, fragile and defiant, like a red-haired priestess about to signal for the rites to begin. "On the other hand, why not say it? How I detest the Old Testament for inventing that idea, and contaminating the Western world with it throughout the centuries, of a chosen people, a common destiny, a superior purpose. It has encouraged people who love humanity to think themselves superior on that account, when in fact they're incapable of genuinely loving anybody. It has encouraged them to complain that an artist's world is too private, when *we* should complain that *their* world is too public. For I believe, Norman, with the early Chinese and de Sade, that we are born not brothers, not equals, not chosen, not humanity in the abstract, but solitary and isolated, individually split atoms—and perhaps instinctively enemies. And across this glorious separateness of terror and despair, we build bridges of love, singly and personally, joining us to each other, and—if it exists—to eternity."

"Bravo!" I said, and Freddy suggested we move back to the living room for brandy.

"Or chartreuse, if you prefer it." Denna led the way. "I wonder why I tell you this? I suppose because I guessed that you would understand, and perhaps had to emerge from the cocoon of an impossible love yourself."

"Yes. But which one do you mean?" Alcohol was beginning to fuddle me. "Oh, I know—my mother. It's certainly true that she gave me access, as a child, to at least one rare experience." And heard myself relating, for the first time outside these pages, Lady D.'s behavior in the four-poster when I was ten years old. "And oddly enough," I concluded, rapidly calculating which year it was that Lily raped me behind the bushes on Hampstead Heath, "I didn't lose my virginity till I was twenty-six, either—and, may I add, to absolutely the wrong person!"

"It usually is." Denna sighed. "May I ask who?"

"A woman who became my wife for a few days."

Denna was clearly impressed, but Freddy, drunker than I by now, sleepily unmoved. It seemed the moment to leave. She walked me arm-in-arm to the front door, opening it to a high, sweet night. For an instant we might have been the only people in the world, stranded and moonlit on an eternal plateau.

"Norman, have you been always alone?"

"No," I said airily, "I build my bridges now and then."

A light kiss on my cheek. "I shall do your horoscope tomorrow, and find all the aspects of your fated sky."

I walked down the steps, thinking, Since *aspects* have been discussed, there are some of Lady D. that I see in Denna, or vice versa. If Lady D. hadn't been my mother, we might have become excellent friends. As it is, Denna is not, and that is what we've become. I apologize, Ahmin, if any of this seems unclear to you. I may be soused, but it's perfectly clear to me.

6th of February

That night I returned to my cabin bristling with elation, unable to sleep; and yielded at dawn to a very peculiar urge. Imagine the high mountains at cockcrow, first chilly light creeping over desert and canyon. Gliding mysteriously through a clump of balsam pines, the figure of an Arab woman, robed and veiled, reaches open country and kneels to face the great pale disk of the rising sun. While she prays, a crow flaps across the sky with a harsh, derisive squawk. Hearing the sound of a truck approaching, she rises, hurries back through the trees and disappears inside a redwood hutch just before some Indian workmen arrive.

I disrobed hastily, stuffed the old costume (which I hadn't worn since posing for Oum's photograph in a shadowy junk-room at Appleton) into a trunk; put a kettle of water on my stove for coffee; twiddled a knob of my radio, heard news of the Germans dropping bombs near the east coast of England

and hoped The House was safe; told myself this must really never happen again, then came out to issue orders for the day. One of the plumbers gave me an inquiring look, and for a moment I wondered if he could possibly have witnessed my *bal masqué*. Then I dismissed the thought, recognizing the look as one of simple incredulity—from time to time this whole project affects my artisans that way. In the daily round and common task I have often noticed that certain employees, merchants, so-called experts and practical people, regard my life as extravagant, even outlandish, which is only because they lack the imagination to live it. I once tried to explain to some bricklayers that the months go by like sullen drudges for me, there seems no end to the routine of building, clearing, watching, waiting . . . and the look of dumb amazement on their faces made me curiously sad.

8th of February

Denna has drawn the circle within a circle, and the twelve houses within the circles, dividing them up like spokes in a wheel. Suitably cryptic, dotted with various numbers and symbols, this coded map of my life is pinned to the wall of my cabin, above my narrow bed. Mercury, my planetary ruler, is the lord of speech and patron of voyages—but, Denna warns me, has notorious thievish tendencies. (When I ask her what I'm liable to steal, she merely shrugs.) Jupiter, in my eleventh house, means that I have many friends; but he's afflicted by Neptune, so it looks as if I lose most of them. Venus, in sextile to Neptune, endows me with a romantic nature, and Uranus in my seventh house has thoughtfully arranged a catastrophic marriage. In general my planets head for the signs of air and earth—"providing you, my dear, with high mental energy and almost infinite patience" —but *completely avoid* the signs of fire—"suggesting, I'm afraid, a lack of activity that might be called truly positive. Or, at the very least, a reluctance to do as much as you should." None of this really surprises, pleases, annoys or encourages me. The Lord giveth and the Lord taketh away, and as usual His right hand knoweth not what His left hand doeth. The mystery and the lesson lie elsewhere. Out of curiosity, Denna also charted Oum's horoscope, and found a similar absence of planets in the fiery signs—"which is rare in itself, Norman, and explains quite uncannily your creative rapport, your matching of temperaments." Who am I to disabuse her? The date, time and place of Oum's birth are of course my own fictions, supplied like other details because I found them likely, or piquant, or both. Our planetary coincidence merely confirms that if I hadn't invented her, she would have found it necessary to exist. So when I look at the circles, houses and symbols above my bed, I see yet another reflection of that teasing old conundrum about the chicken and the egg. And if, Ahmin, to lay the latter is my ultimate destiny, can I be reproached for meeting it with energy and patience?

1st of May

Yesterday Denna persuaded me to order an artificial lake. She wishes to design an Avenue of Statues leading to the shore—"highly expensive, both in terms of material outlay and my fee, Norman, but in time to come I can promise you that the result will be just as famous, and for not dissimilar reasons, as the wonders of Pompeii. Whatever they say about either of us after we've gone, we'll be remembered for the lewdly winking guides and the tourists eager to be shocked." I begin to see, with the skeleton of courtyard and atrium already formed, the bones of a domed and balconied tower rising, that I'll have a fantastic kingdom on my hands, a Monaco or Cockaigne of the old southwest. Although Oum has still not spoken since our reconciliation, I'm convinced *she's here,* biding her time—because, following her own example, everything threatens to go magnificently beyond my control.

Later. Corral being finished, goats started arriving after lunch. Freddy supervised the unloading from wagons; a shepherd he'd engaged for me—his uncle, small and rather dreary-looking old man with a switch and tattered eagle feathers in his hair—harried all seven hundred of them to their pasture. Collars tinkled as they leapt and baaed. My house—and, I believe, even Denna's projects—don't really interest Freddy. His sympathies lie elementally with animals, the earth, food, and of course copulation. When I pointed out my emergent tower, he merely nodded and said we should plan a cheese harvest for the autumn. Wanting to make him feel that the goats were a bond between us, I told him I was extremely happy that he'd inspired me to buy them. "I'm glad you're pleased," he said, and walked away, back to the station wagon, leaving me with the disconsolate sensation of being no more than a satisfied employer. On second thoughts, I reminded myself how reserved they are.

Part of their power, I knew, lay in keeping one wondering.

Even now, I could tell from his back that he was aware of my uncertainty. Obtuse or sophisticated, humble or proud? When Denna first saw him, he'd come to chop wood. She quickly found that she had fences to be mended and paths to be paved as well; and, after less than a decent interval, a bed to be shared. *There,* I decided, still watching his slow and graceful retreat, he dropped the sweetly aggravating pretense of being a servant, and revealed himself as master. As all the silent cunning dark ones do, he knew the only way to conquer clever, rich, masterful white women. . . . He turned back to stare at me now, and I gave him a pleasant nod.

Alone in my cabin at end of day I nipped at whisky, felt the blue twilight chill, heard distant baas, begged my mind to concentrate on things less of this world. So I stared at a sheet of blank paper, hoping for the return of my old companion and scourge, for lines to write me back in her favor. She had every reason, of course, to keep me waiting, and make me grovel. I dropped to my knees. Eventually, doors began to open of their own accord; and when Oum spoke, severe but compassionate, I felt the reassuring, exalted shiver of her embrace.

At dusk, in the shadow of King Atlas,
Silence approaches, then a song of bells.
The music tells me goats have found
Sweet cooling herbs in bitter crevices.
So, then. Tomorrow! Must I not search
For tenderness between two sticks
And joy in the whiteness of walls?

After this came a night of utter sleep, without dreams or longings, and no flicker of anxiety that extreme solitude might take its toll.

11th of October

Never a harsh word between us, throughout this glorious summer! When a cloud of curious silvery dust, which forms from time to time in this region, began rolling across my territory today, making everything dissolve and glimmer like a mirage, I was moved to climb the scaffolding of the tower and stand proudly on the furthest platform. With luck I'd be in residence by Christmas, and my mind leapt a century or so ahead, to a grand vision of travelers in a far future time coming here and finding the whole place a ruin—what manner of person, what Kubla Khan, would they think had decreed it? Then, through the swirling mists, I heard someone calling my name. It was my Indian shepherd, clambering up to inform me that CAPRICORN SEMISOFT would not, after all, go on the market from coast to coast this year. The cheese had been left to dry too long on the racks, and turned horribly rancid. As the old man confessed, his ridiculous feathers seemed to droop with disappointment; I came back to earth feeling the blow myself. Very pokerfaced and still, Freddy beckoned to me from the courtyard. He told me that the fault was his. When I wouldn't hear of it, he shook his head, blamed himself again, and offered me with the faintest of smiles a ring of silver and turquoise, explaining that it would ensure success next year, and from now on no harm could possibly come to me. The ring fitted beautifully on my little finger. I was moved; so, I think, was Freddy. I told him, rather to his surprise, that I would never forget this moment, that his unexpected gesture made the disaster worthwhile, and I even looked forward to drafting a letter to Parkinson and Parkinson, warning them to expect nothing at all for at least another year. However, Oum brushed the letter aside and rapped me gently over the knuckles with a couple of inimitable stanzas:

Say, when you closed your eyes
Was it to enter a palace of the interior,
Crossing the Hall of Hope
To reach the Gallery of Greatness
Which lies in the east wing of Forever?

Say, when you opened your eyes
Was it to a sigh and aching chill of rain,
A heart gone out like a fallen star?
O Hope, O Greatness, O Forever—
Are you alone on the Mountain of Pride?

7th of December

Alone in my hutch tonight, bedded with flu; indignant with the Japanese, who've just made war on this country for no apparent reason, and even more with a huge leak in the roof of my tower, provoked by a storm. Dreadful stains have disfigured the walls; waves of mud breaking over the balcony; no Christmas in my tower, but another month at least in this wretched hovel. Temperature 101.1; throat burning like the Sahara; one of those uncalled-for messages—"Toad's kiss"—buzzing in my ear when I wake after a doze; fugitive erection.

3rd of February, 1942

The colors of the spectrum were suspended against a violent sky; jagged clouds splintered into blue; tips of pines were caught in a streak of yellow and phantom stripes of red and green lay across the mountain snow. Freddy and I stood side by side looking at the rainbow, wondering at a landscape tinged with the weirdest unreality. The tower being almost finished *at last,* I was preparing to move into it. We'd made an expedition to various trading posts, buying rugs and pots and baskets, and returned in a downpour of rain. It stopped after I mixed martinis.

"Did you know the rainbow has two sexes?" Freddy asked.

I shook my head. "Never heard of such a thing."

"It joins the earth, which is a woman, to the sun, a man." Glanced at me, eyes dark and impenetrable as the stone from which they make pottery. "Such beautiful things should happen more often."

Very quietly, I asked why he thought it so beautiful.

"Two things look as if they are separate, then they join. Should happen more often," he repeated.

Now that is one bridge I simply must not build, I thought, resolved not to betray my feelings, stunned as I was by this remarkable declaration. Never again, after Scotty and Charlotte, would I attempt to pass through the straits of a marriage—that way lies only rough treatment from the whirlpool Charybdis and the rock Scylla! I remembered Denna's remark that my ruler Mercury has thievish tendencies. Was it a friendly warning? All the same, I couldn't help touching the ring that Freddy had given me, seeing it as another kind of warning. He didn't overlook my gesture, and nor did Oum, who whispered that she'd once told me having love is more important than making it.

At that moment the rainbow began to fade, then vanished.

"Is something the matter?" I heard Freddy ask.

"Snow's white again," I said. "And leaves are green. Furthermore, it's getting chilly."

He nodded; assumed the role of servant once more; said that if there was nothing more I needed from him, he would go. I was still thinking over Oum's remark as the station wagon drove away; and in retrospect, Freddy's remark about the rainbow seemed more ambiguous than I'd hoped and feared. In any case, nothing (as usual) had happened. But only a vulgar mind would consider the situation frustrating, I told myself later, sitting alone on the floor of my tower, admiring the rugs strewn around like brilliant laundry.

28th of June

Swimming nude in my lake, under a glistening blue sky, a blessed moment occurs when I stroke back to the shore and see—four hundred yards long, lined with sculptures of mottled volcanic stone, almost Egyptian in scale—the Avenue of Statues awaiting me. It's then I feel my will done and my kingdom come, more or less. The world outside is a desert island with rather more than two thousand million people, I believe, stranded on it; and from the reports that filter through, conditions are deteriorating. Frankly, I never go there—except to dine with Denna and Freddy, who live only four miles away in what I regard as a guaranteed neutral zone. My few necessary connections are made by employees, telephone, correspondence—as when I'm obliged to still the puling complaints of Parkinson and Parkinson, those ostriches with heads buried in the sands of finance and buttocks exposed to attacking Junkers, who will never understand that I sign check after check to achieve a nirvana in which *I don't have to look at anything I don't wish to.* My desires blend into oneness because oneness is something I own. All surroundings—discounting the firmament itself, which is really too far away to matter—have been submitted and passed for approval, or sent back; and since art can do what nature can't, I commission the rest. There are even strange, exciting moments when the island outside bows not only to my wishes but to my most demanding fantasies, and I enjoy a triumph so meaningless that it becomes, by a kind of double negative, profound.

This morning, for instance, a letter arrived from Lady D. My parent has become quite schoolgirlish since moving to the Antipodes with her great love, and I skipped a description of walking along a beach with my presumed father and exclaiming at a flight of wild swans. Then, "You'll be interested to know," she continued, "that I heard from Ellen—remember the maid Violet was so fond of?—who's still in Appleton, working on a farm and dodging the occasional bomb. She hopes the Japs don't get me and prays, if I ever return, that I won't be too appalled by the state of The House. The Government, which requisitioned it last year, has not only cut down our cedars for firewood but allowed the Clematis to die. (Parkinson and Parkinson have been informed.) Her most sensational news, however, is an item she read in one of those less reliable Sunday newspapers. A Norwegian patriot who escaped to London gave out the story of a "concentration camp" in the frozen north of his country, where the officer in charge—described in typical journalese as a handsome, ruthless blonde—goes by the name of *Violetta von Lichtwald.* So I assume that my poor, disturbed girl has returned to her original sex and bleached her hair, which was her best feature, for protective coloring. The newspaper, of course, identifies her as the Mad Major, and remarks that after the war she'll certainly be tried as a traitor or "war criminal," or both. With their usual heartless sensationalism, journalists have been trying to interview the few surviving Lightwoods, even poor old Aunt Hester—who (perhaps fortunately) lost her memory after being bombed, and lives in a hotel seeing no one except her spaniels—and dear Uncle Hector, who always liked you, and threatened to horsewhip the editor personally. I'm so glad *he* can take events in his stride. Anyway, knowing Violet as we do, my dear, it's to be feared she may have something to answer for—but granted that world events often divide a family, the price of victory is rather stiff if it includes putting one's own daughter in the dock. Maurice, however, is confident we'll be able to pull a string somewhere, and his dear loyalty, as ever, sustains me. Now I have a small favor to ask you. We run increasingly short of scotch, which I understand is still plentiful where you are. Please try to ship us a crate by American freighter. I believe they usually get through, and of course it's the quickest way across. A salute from the Blue to the San Juan mountains . . ."

Reflecting that the morning would be quite commonplace without the problem of Lady D. and her favorite tipple, I telephoned various shipping companies in San Francisco and was fobbed off, as expected, with evasive answers, false promises or astonished refusals. Finally I demanded to speak with the president of Oceana Lines, and pulled enough rank to bring the great man to the wire. It amazed me, I told him, that even a mildly unorthodox request was taken by bureaucrats as a sign of madness, or an impertinence, or a practical joke. This practice was slowing down the wheels of business, I continued, hardening the arteries of enterprise, and responsible for increased taxation, which is always the result of petrified thinking. Cautioning him not to let the pressure of world events distort his sense of proportion, I repeated my request for one of his vessels to carry whisky to my mother in Australia, and my willingness to pay through the nose. His reply was a sneering insult. Assuming from my voice that I was British, he thought I'd be better employed serving my country, or at least the great ally that was now going to save it as well as myself. "I have a weak heart," I said with dignity. "And Lady Dorothea, an artist and aristocrat revered and loved throughout the Empire, has not very long to live. However, I'm less appalled by your indifference to the last, painful year or two of a very great woman, than by your failure to jump at an interesting offer." His stunned silence could be heard across the hundreds of miles separating us. I prolonged it by mentioning various distinguished persons who were sending my mother little things that she needed—and, in a changed voice, the president informed me Lady D. had only to name her brand. Remembering that Old Heather was always served at Appleton, I hoped he could lay his hands on some; if not, we all had to make concessions nowadays. . . . Then we chatted pleasantly for a while, the magnate wishing to know what sort of operation I had going for me in these parts. I told him that CAPRICORN SEMISOFT would be launched in a few months, promised him an advance package, alluded casually to the Gran Chaco railway and, on the spur of the moment, to a chain of grocery stores in New Zealand. I had the impression that, though we'd never met, we parted good friends.

Later, lolling on my back in the water, under golden arrows aimed by the sun, my contentment subsided a little; an ache lapped at my heart; I felt the loneliness of Power, and an empty space that could be filled only, Ahmin, by *you*. Ready at last, eager and open, I wanted to cry out at the unfairness of Chance—for the jackboot strutting in your medina separated us now by blind, brute force. Even though Oum would have made a scene, for the top of St. Simeon's pillar is not yet scaled, she might have been persuaded, in her present mood, to agree to some kind of *menage à trois*. But all speculation seemed suddenly bitter and fruitless, the dice as usual were loaded against me, and I had no choice except somehow to go on, making the most of what was granted to me, steering my old course between elation and despair, clear sky and open sea. Tap tap tap. A bleating goat jolted me into reality. It sounded much too near, the corral being half a mile away—and when I turned towards the shore, I saw that one of the flock had escaped and was wandering down the Avenue of Statues. I returned to land and set off in pursuit as it frisked past a Navajo Oedipus embracing the thighs of a naked Sphinx with solid, reddish tresses, sniffed a great claw-like foot of the Three-Toed Sloth with an angel's face and paused for a bowel movement against the Ritualistic Orgy of the Titans. Then off it loped, God knows where.

Bellowing for the old shepherd without expecting an answer (he's so full of peyote and incompetence that I'd fire him, only he's Freddy's uncle), I carefully mopped up a detail of the orgy with a beach towel. Having always agreed with Denna that it's the masterpiece of a master stroke, I found myself once again lost in wonder at its vast, unprejudiced coital imagination. Each link in its chain, freely based on that monument to Tantric intercourse in the temple of Lakshmana, is so complex that whenever I browse among positions I find something new. Since a reporter from a national weekly sneaked in and denounced it as obscene, newspapers in the southwest have echoed his ridiculous attack and hinted with maddening untruth that my interest in the arts is a cover for licentiousness. I wrote strong letters of protest, giving all the historical evidence for regarding this orgy as an act of ritual purification, designed to unite one and all in Absolute Reality—but only the *Denver Outlook* printed me. "In time of war," was Denna's comment, "the Judeo-Christian-Puritan power group becomes more militant than ever. So they condemn us as Neros fiddling while Rome burns? I shall point out that fire is also an act of ritual purification, and suggest they get in it." No sooner had I settled myself in a favorite corner to enjoy more sun, and drowsed off with a St. Simeonish feeling that one could withdraw here forever, than I heard the goat baaing again. I opened my eyes to see it struggling in Eagle Feathers' arms. The shepherd stared at me with a patient, oafish grin, partly pride at having recaptured the animal, partly uncertainty as to whether my naked figure among the stone ones was real or the result of drugged hallucination. Dismissing him brusquely, I lay back again, felt the sun waning, and realized another day had almost gone. Time to wander back and prepare for dinner with Denna and her former *guru,* who'd just arrived from California.

"Jemadar is tired," Denna whispered as I entered the living room. "We shall dine earlier than usual, so that he can go to bed early." I saw a fairly stout little Asiatic personage gazing out the window, sipping a glass of orange juice. He had a mane of gray hair, wore a crimson robe and presented a flat puglike profile; but when he turned to greet me a smile of extraordinary charm transfigured his homely features and he looked younger than at first, forty-five perhaps. "Delighted to know you, Sir Lightwood, truly delighted." He took my arm at once and walked me back to the window. "Please look out here. Amazing! I am truly astonished by this landscape. Its form and colors are so infinitely varied and plentiful that they convey a feeling of total emptiness."

"Not to me," I said.

"Look again, please. We have rock, flowers, vegetation, snow, trees, mountains, valleys, sky, clouds, circles, semicircles, angles, cubes, articulations, curves, inflexibilities, blue, white, yellow, brown, pink and a thousand shades of green and gray. So much, and nothing at all. Completely empty. Amazing! Do you know why?"

"Well," I ventured, "there's nobody about."

He gave a deep chuckle, patted my hand. "Oh dear me, Sir Lightwood, how wrong you are." Then laughed quite immoderately, it seemed to me. "How completely wrong. But never mind."

"I *do* mind," I said rather huffily, and saw Denna give me a warning smile. Freddy, however, came up with a martini, looking pleased. "I hate riddles," I told Jemadar, "unless I can answer them."

"Quite right." He took my arm again, walking me away from the window. "I'll explain. The view is empty because it's so filled—*so* filled that we perceive at once how much *remains* to be filled. And the remaining emptiness simply overwhelms us. I am used to this, of course, which makes me all the more amazed."

He sat down, looking indeed quite stunned. Denna shot me a triumphant glance. "You see, Norman, how extraordinary he is!"

"Now, now, now." The sage wagged a finger at her. "I'm unhappy when she flatters me. Flattery, I must make clear, is a form of insult. I say something really too simple, hardly worth saying, because I am tired—but Denna takes it as profound, when it is *not* profound at all. Therefore the flattery is insulting. But never mind." Patted Denna's hand, demanded more juice, got up and returned to the window, resting his forehead against the glass. "Amazing. I am more amazed than ever. In the last two minutes things have changed; now blue is gray and yellow, brown, angles are curves and curves have become straight lines. All a trick of light, and yet—a moment ago things were *there* and now are *not*. So what shall we conclude? Which is reality, and which illusion? If things can be changed by a mere trick of light, which is itself not substantial, for light cannot be touched or felt, it is no more and no less than the absence of darkness—then we are obliged to ask, are we not, what *was* there, anyway, to be changed in the first place?"

"Nothing," I said. "Complete emptiness."

"How right you are." He came back, sat down beside me.

"And from what you so truly observe, we're obliged to conclude something even more amazing and overwhelming, something I'm tempted to call tremendous." His voice dropped low and his eyes became slightly glazed. "*Emptiness changes.*"

"Why don't you fill it?" Freddy came towards us. "Dinner's ready, Jemadar."

He was playing the role of servant, but with a veiled insolence; if Jemadar noticed, he gave no sign—on the contrary, beamed at his host and sat down eagerly to a delicious fish curry, cooked in his honor. "You wish to know where I come from," he remarked to me only a second before I started to ask this question, and I realized where Denna had learned to read thoughts. "I am mainly Persian," said Jemadar, without divulging the rest, "born in a small village on the Gulf of Oman, near the border of India." Demanded chutney, found it excellent, told me his father died, his mother abandoned him and as a child of seven he was adopted by dervishes, whose order he decided to join. "We did not, however, Sir Lightwood, whirl. Not all dervishes whirl." Sharp, admonitory nod. "We were simply Moslems who took extreme vows of mortification and chastity. The latter presented no problem, since we are only led into temptation by what has the power to tempt us, and no human being could ever break up my affair with the Supreme Being. Dear me no. Mortification, on the other hand, threatened to come between us and was responsible for our first and only quarrel. St. Francois de Sales remarked that when the body is overfed the spirit can't endure it, but when the body is underfed, *it* can't endure the spirit. At the age of sixteen I discovered how right he was—I emerged from

Ramadan with terrible feelings of guilt. Spending the hottest month of the year with an empty stomach and a burnt throat weakened my love for Him, just as a naughty debauch might have done for others." The dervishes were unsympathetic; Jemadar walked down to the sand dunes, listened to the silent, becalmed ocean and wondered bleakly what he should do; a wandering Buddhist monk passed by and explained that fasting or any other imposed penance was unnecessary, since daily life is mortifying enough. Jemadar decided to leave his village at once, and wander with the monk. His first experience of the world, beyond a cluster of mud huts, austere, gloomy devotees, fishermen and wild geese, amply confirmed his companion's view of it. Everywhere, and above all when they reached Bombay, he saw beggars dripping with sores, children deformed by hunger, old women dying in gutters. "Of course I had heard about such things, but now they became real to me. Or *were* they real? I had to find out." He supported himself by taking various menial jobs, and was finally employed as a servant in the household of a British major. "There is nothing more menial than that, Sir Lightwood, let me assure you. But I studied at night, learning new languages to read new wisdoms, and after seven years I found the total, unquenchable light for which I'd been searching. It came in a brief sentence by Kung-Sun-Lung, but it said more to me than many volumes."

He paused to sip water and Denna cut in, trembling with eagerness: *"The shadow of a flying bird never moves!"*

"Thank you," said Jemadar. "I began to meditate on this sentence, and I understood that the Evil I saw every day was in itself nothing—only a dark and smudged reflection of

Good, and it was Good that moved and soared into the highest realms—"

A chair scraped loudly against the floor. He broke off. Freddy had got up to offer us second helpings of curry. I was sure that he made the noise on purpose, because he was usually so quiet and graceful; Denna knew it too, for she gave a tense, quick smile. Wondering why he didn't like Jemadar, I complimented him on the curry and heaped my plate. The others refused. Jemadar waited politely for Freddy to sit down again, then explained that just at the time his way became clear, an English lady married to an American was staying in the major's house. Her wealthy husband died suddenly of a heart attack, Mrs. Fletcher collapsed with grief and much to everyone's discomfort Jemadar was the only person able to console her. He would never forget their first encounter in the garden, her pitiable bewildered figure huddled against the brilliance of tropical flowers. From noon till dusk they talked; the major and his wife tried to interrupt them, but Mrs. Fletcher shooed them away, and they retreated behind a window, watching furtively. At dinner she announced that the young man they treated almost as a slave was touched with sublime wisdom; out of gratitude and need she would take him back to her estate in Santa Barbara, California; next morning they left the house together, under the resentful eyes of the British Raj, to stay in a hotel while she made arrangements. Then, installed in her guest house and advertised to her friends, Jemadar began the series of lectures that people would drive a hundred miles to hear.

At the time of her father's death, Denna was in San Francisco. "I too drove down to Jemadar, asking for a private appointment, and presented him with my haunted, shattered ruins. My self-pity must have been really dreadful, I moaned for hours, calling myself a ghost, a wreck, a human junkyard—and at the end of it all he patted my hand, looking very cheerful. 'I'm so glad you're completely ruined; now you can start completely afresh,' he said, apologized for having to leave at once, asked me to come back in two days' time. . . ." Denna stood up, very sumptuous and glittering under a processional Mexican lantern made into a chandelier. "And here, as you see, I am."

Jemadar, whose eyes had begun to close, now opened them and announced he was sleepy. "We shall meet again," he promised me as Denna took him off to his room. With a deep sigh, Freddy poured brandy.

"Now what's the matter?" I asked. "What have you got against Jemadar?"

"He impresses you." Freddy shrugged. "You believe in him. I can tell."

"Don't *you* believe in him?"

Another shrug.

"Then what's the matter?"

"He impresses everybody. I wish he didn't."

Jealous of the wise man's influence over his wife, I supposed—a rather appealing and childlike point of view. I resolved to dismiss the matter tactfully. "Well, I don't suppose he'll be staying long."

"Who knows? The English lady died. She had two sons who didn't like Jemadar at all. They went to court because she left most of her money for him to go on speaking and living out there. Last week they won the case and threw him out." He sat down beside me on the wooden bench. "Now tell me why you were offended when I explained about the rainbow."

As if the bench had tipped me up, I shot to my feet. His hand pulled at my arm. "Please sit down. Tell me why you hardly speak to me any more. *You make me feel I don't matter.*"

I obeyed rather gingerly, but said nothing.

"Look at me. See how sad I am."

Dark as obsidian, eyes stared into my face. Obscurely baffled and pleased, aware of powerful, musky danger, I suddenly remembered that fiendish judge who accused me in the divorce court of contributing to the general decline of human decency. "How unfair!" I said aloud, and felt his hand tighten for a moment on my arm. Useless to explain that I seem to catalyze, without warning, waiters, actresses, young American married couples—but what am I to say to Freddy when he pleads with moist lips and quickened breath, even while his wife (my best friend) is engaged in conversation with her *guru*? I cannot attribute this remarkable situation to an instant of jealousy. After all, he brought up the rainbow long before Jemadar's arrival. . . . In a lightning flash, I wondered if he could also be jealous of *my* friendship with Denna, and in his own reserved but stubborn way plan a *liebestod* for all of us? If you think this far-fetched, remember that primitive schemes of revenge can be unexpectedly cunning, remember Corsicans!

"Yes, I am very sad," he said.

"You're wicked!" came Denna's voice. "Why do you needle the dear wise man?" she asked, returning to us, ruffling Freddy's hair with long, white fingers. "What has he ever done to you?"

"He takes you away from me," said Freddy promptly. "He makes me feel I don't matter." This wickedly persuasive gambit, his yearning eyes that moved so easily away from me and back to Denna, confirmed all my fears. No wonder, when she first saw him, she felt he had infinite possibilities! I shivered as she laid her cheek against his blue-black head. "No one, my love, could make me feel you don't matter." Then turned to me. "Forgive me, Norman, but I've got another suggestion. Isn't it fantastic that a man like Jemadar, a graduate *cum laude* in enlightenment and compassion, should be practically turned out on the street? Aren't we obliged to help?"

"I suppose so," I said, "if we can."

"*If?* Kuola's the perfect place for a foundation, and all we need—to begin with—is for you to build him a guest house."

After a moment, I ventured to express doubts. "Here? A centre of oriental wisdom in the wilds of New Mexico? Will anyone come? Is it practical?"

"Of course not." She seemed surprised. "That's why we must do it. If you simply want to be practical, I have a thousand simple suggestions. Drop bombs, my dear, support your local police or drive blind men to work."

"Or make goat cheese," said Freddy quietly.

Her hand stroked his cheek. "The times couldn't be more unfavorable, I agree, and no doubt we'll be exposed to further ridicule and attack. One takes all that for granted. I'll bring Jemadar to you in the morning, Norman, so if you change your mind, you can tell him yourself."

Weighing this challenge, and enjoying the still cool night, I sat in my car for a few minutes before starting the engine. As I turned around, my headlights swept across a darkened window in the house; I glimpsed nature imitating art, Denna and Freddy like human statuary on a bed, dark head between creamy thighs, before swerving wildly down the driveway.

29th of June (*4* A.M.)

Sleepless, I write it all down in the small hours, in the tower room reached by spiral staircase; arrive at the suspended present; pause; wonder if I should take a double sedative. *From this eyrie 6,069 feet above sea level, the thin clacking of a typewriter could be heard while the whole animal world (except for an occasional moaning coyote) slept. Stark whitewashed walls, barest of furnishings, a Navajo rug in subtly depressing shades of gray, a vertical slit of window to admit the dark—and his patient figure hunched over a worktable roughly carved out of unpolished cedarwood . . .*

30th of June

But having nothing more to say, I dozed off in my chair; then heard a servant calling my name—it was daylight again, past ten o'clock, and Denna had arrived with Jemadar. Clothes rumpled, back aching, I staggered down the staircase to greet them. "My dear, are you all right?" she asked. "Perhaps," I said, ordered coffee, and she left us alone.

After bowing gravely, Jemadar stood in silence, gazing out of my living room windows. He appeared to wince at the charming prospect of tiled fountain in mosquelike courtyard, archway that opened to a tantalizing intimation of my whole kingdom beyond and below. I thought I heard him sigh. Then he gave me a long, sympathetic look. "What can I do for you, Sir Lightwood?"

Naturally I was disconcerted, wondered if Denna hadn't mentioned her scheme, but led him to believe (for what reason, I couldn't imagine) that I wanted a personal interview. However, before I could say anything, "Don't be embarrassed to tell me you're doubtful of this idea for a foundation," Jemadar went on. "So am I."

"I thought you might agree with Denna that the disadvantages are somehow in our favor."

"If they were, they would not be disadvantages." Apparently not very interested in the subject I thought he'd come to discuss, Jemadar sat down and looked out of the window. "Forgive me. The verdict of Montesquieu on the Palace of Versailles keeps passing through my mind. *Everywhere, a great but impotent desire to accomplish great things . . .*" He smiled, with the air of someone paying a graceful compliment.

"I forgive you," I said. "It happens to suit me, which is all that matters."

"Dear Sir Lightwood, it is *not* all that matters. All that I saw here upon arriving depressed me unspeakably. I nearly remarked to Denna that I considered the case hopeless. Then, realizing that a mind capable of producing such a miscarriage might also contain the seed of a masterpiece, I took heart. At least one can say this whole thing is brilliantly foolish."

Though far from pleased, I wasn't angry. The man has a way of saying terrible, unkind things with an air of such sweetness and compassion that you are wounded without being hurt. Even more ghastly is the possibility that he might be speaking a measure of truth. "Please tell me what depresses you," I asked in a manner neither humble nor indignant, "in everything I've created here."

"Everything." He chuckled, then looked suddenly stern. "Possession, domination, self-delusion—that's what I see in all this enormous attempt to impose your own idea of yourself on the helpless natural world. And suppose your idea of yourself is wrong? Suppose you change, or imagine you do? My word!" Tck-tck-tcked. "What an expensive skin you'll be obliged to shed."

"But you have nothing against my taste as such? Even though you may not like what I've done, you admit I've done it well?"

"Now, now, now." Wagged a finger at me. "Stop fishing for compliments—I've already told you you're a brilliantly foolish person, what more do you want? Besides, we're not here to argue with each other. I don't attack or condemn what you've done, I only suggest to you what it means, or rather, how little it means."

"*How* little?" My coffee arrived and I offered some to Jemadar. He demanded fruit juice instead, and I graciously ordered it for him.

"So little that it cannot be described. We must place it under the microscope of a fable for a particle of a particle to show up." Jemadar's eyes grew twinkly. "The Buddha said *there is a path to walk on, there is walking being done, but there is no traveler. There are deeds being done, but no doer, and a blowing in the air, but no wind that does the blowing.* That is the truth of the world as the Buddha saw it. About you, Sir Lightwood, I think he would say—you travel, you do and you blow, and as a result there is *no* path, no deed and no wind!" Loud chuckle. "I'm trying to convey that your results seem even smaller when one considers the largeness of your efforts."

"And you have done so," I said. "You've told me that all is vanity—my tower, my courtyard, my Avenue, my goats—and frankly, I expected something more original."

"If you'd listened more carefully, you'd have heard it. Never mind." Patted my hand. "I told you all was *your* vanity, which is not the same thing. Dear me no. When we talk of vanity in the abstract, we mean any human endeavor that is finally empty and worthless, however impressive it may seem at the moment. That is not particularly important, for Time itself will take care of such vanity, including your own absurd tower, and so on. But personal vanity, Sir Lightwood—my word, how much more serious! You have so much of it, I fear, and so little time left to get rid of it. Who is going to cross all the walls and defenses you've built, before the end comes?" Deep sigh, clearly implying *nobody*. "The passage to your true self must be as dark and clammy, as blocked by false signs and alarms, as hindered by wicked booby-traps, as the way to a Pharaoh's tomb. Now I wonder, are you very busy this morning?" The touch of irony here didn't escape me. "Or could you spare me half an hour? I would like us to meditate together."

"Why?"

"I haven't the faintest idea. But I'd like to know *why* I haven't." Another affectionate, endearing smile. "Don't fidget like that. Don't move. Stay where you are, in that handsome chair. Your mind at this moment is like a public beach at high tide, and I want you at low tide, with all your seaweed and little fishes and shells and general rubbish removed. I want you fresh and empty, like a perfect white beach without footprints. So stop wriggling, please. Let your tide go out, by trying for once to sit quite silent and still."

Jemadar immediately looked at the floor. An impressive calm dropped over his face like a veil; his features became smooth and relaxed like someone in a dreamless sleep, yet I could see their inner waking alertness. For a while, I peeked at him. If he knew, he gave no sign. Then I began admiring my courtyard through the windows, wondering why mystics lacked esthetic sense. Having recently ordered some beautiful earthenware pots with long thin necks, I asked myself where I would place each one; and arranged six to my satisfaction before a bird swooped across. I couldn't see the bird itself, only the shadow—*the shadow doesn't move,* I remembered, and watched it moving but not moving until it seemed to go away. Reasoning to myself in Jemadar fashion that the bird moved because it was a bird, therefore substance, but the shadow remained still because it was only a shadow, therefore illusion, I posed the inevitable question: how much that we take for substance is no more than illusion? But I noticed my own shadow on the wall, and was distracted. Putting my hands to my ears, waggling fingers, I created the illusion of the shadow of a donkey that didn't exist. Next, with my hand and arm alone, made a nasty, menacing snake; the snake became lovely, *mudras* of an Indian dancer; and finally, with thumb pressed against palm, fingers flapping above it like a tent in the wind, an ostrich. So the time passed, until—discovering that at a certain angle I could get *two* shadows of my *one* arm, and if I clenched and nodded my fist the illusion was of a pair of dinosaurs preparing for combat—I realized that Jemadar was watching me.

"This game is exactly like life," I said. "For instance, I talked on the phone the other day with a shipping magnate I'd never met." Explaining how Lady D.'s whisky shortage brought this about, "don't you find it odd," I continued, "that by telling a fantastic lie I could transform myself in a stranger's mind from a complete madman to a respected member of society?"

"I find it more odd that you wished to tell a lie merely to transform yourself from something you are not into something else you are not."

One must admit he has an unexpected way of looking at things, with the cunning appeal of a court jester whose folly may occasionally bespeak wisdom. "Dear Sir Lightwood," he went on, "one leaves you alone for a few minutes and all you can do is amuse or frighten yourself with shadows. How well you prove that solitude with God leads to enlightenment, but solitude with self to consternation and the abyss."

As Jemadar spoke these words, the day was suddenly carried, the bell rung, the corner turned. . . . For a moment I thought I was about to faint; saw the sage looking actually puzzled. Only the obviousness of the conclusion, I knew a moment later, had blinded me to it. Jemadar, like the Object before my birth, *had been sent.* Since the St. Simeon idea occurred to me, more than five years ago, after that visit to the heart specialist in London, it has haunted me across oceans and continents, pursued me through jungles, the poem getting longer and longer and the end still far away. Oum scolds and encourages, yet I'm unable to leg it alone to the giddiest heights. Originally, if you remember, the mysterious command to begin was the word *anchorite* entering my mind, and I hurried to a public library hoping that the dictionary would provide a linguistic clue to this almost occult message. Instead, I was confused and disappointed. One thousand, one hundred and twenty-five lines and nearly $2,000,000 later, when I'm wondering how long this sublime groping can continue, the answer comes. *Inch'Allah!* Here, now, rescuing me from illusion, pulling me back to simple reality, stout and dusky, demanding more fruit juice with a sweet smile, stands the Word Incarnate!

"Dear Jemadar . . ." I kept my voice unnaturally light and calm. "You've convinced me that *I* am the most important reason for endowing your foundation here."

He chuckled. "I never intended to. And are you sure you're important, or even a reason?"

"I'm sure you're the only person in the world who could break me of my dreadful habits."

"No, Sir Lightwood. *You* are that person." Shook his head. "And the word *foundation* distresses me. It turns me into an institution, and like everyone who believes the Way is poetic, not official, I cannot allow that."

"Then let me simply build you a guest house. Just live on the premises, that's all I ask."

"I cannot be used as another excuse to satisfy your mania for building." Turned away, making for the door, and just as I was about to call for Denna to stop him, *he* stopped. "However . . ." he said. "As we drove up, I believe I noticed a log cabin."

"You can't be serious. I lived there like a squatter, for months, until this house was finished. There's hardly room to swing a cat."

"May I see the interior?"

Waiting in the hall, Denna glanced at me and smiled. "You look quite put out, my dear. I'm so glad he's persuaded you."

"He wants my old cabin," I said. "Please tell him I feel ashamed."

Jemadar, who'd already reached the front door, turned back for a moment. "Please tell him he should be ashamed of feeling ashamed."

As we walked along a path through the little forest, a stench drifted towards us.

"What is that?" asked Jemadar.

"Manure. We use the place for garden supplies."

He seemed interested. "I have a theory about manure, or rather about creating a new kind of it, which some day . . ." He broke off as I opened the door, and peered inside with a contented smile.

My hutch was now nothing but an armory of rakes, hoes, spades, sack after sack of overpowering fertilizer, some of it spilt on the moldering floor. A giant spider's web made a centerpiece for the window, and dead flies littered the sill.

"I find it by far the most attractive feature of your establishment," said Jemadar. "With all those trees surrounding it, there's practically no view at all."

11th of July

The cabin has now been cleaned and deodorized, and they begin painting it today; I gave an additional mischievous order for a few trees to be pruned nearby, so Jemadar will have a glimpse of my kingdom after all. Denna informed various newspapers that the sage will shortly be open to the public again, and this morning I found a reference in the *Southwest Herald* to the titled British millionaire-poet-recluse, a controversial patron of the arts who has now extended his philanthropy to the search for religious truth. I can't help feeling it gives a false impression of me, but Jemadar is amused and remarks that we shall both survive attempts to turn us into institutions.

On a second reading of the paragraph I noticed a final sentence in italics which I'd missed at first: *for a sidelight on Sir Norman, turn to Entertainment, p. 6.* This mysterious instruction filled me with panic. Obeying it instantly, I was confronted by a photograph of LILY VAIL, whose teasing smile, saucy wink and blond thatch headed a column of gossip reprinted from a Los Angeles paper. It appears that a film producer "discovered" my ex-wife in London last year, and Lily, Lady Lightwood—who will never remarry, I suspect, in order to retain that absurd title—makes the gallant war-torn island forget its cares and dangers while she sings and dances in a popular extravaganza called *Yours for the Asking!* According to the columnist, who recently saw the film, she has a universal message even though her accent's sometimes hard to understand. I found only a glancing allusion to myself, as Lily's former husband, "eccentric British peer who's built himself an Arabian Nights palace near Santa Fe and sees no one," which dismisses me quite curtly as a minor character but is preferable to being called a Moral Menace.

After the first shock, I felt no surprise at all, remembering that I'd had an intimation of the fiend's success when I left England; but my curiosity to see how she looked as a popular idol had to overcome my distaste for re-entering the outside world. In the meantime, I subscribed to all newspapers within three or four hundred miles of here, in case the film should be shown not more than a day's drive away, and so force me to a decision I dread.

27th of July

Small canopied bed, antique chest, local arts and crafts, Moorish café curtains, Japanese Buddha from the dining room at The House which I'd brought over with other Lightwood treasures—these and a few equally simple things having been arranged to my satisfaction in the cabin, Jemadar took up residence last night.

Beside a vase of wild roses I'd left a copy of Oum's poems, on the table by his bed; you can imagine my impatience for his verdict, and my disappointment when, after thanking me graciously for my kindness, he announced before retiring that he planned solitary meditation for perhaps a week. As I walked him to the cabin, he asked not to be disturbed, and for the plainest of meals—rice, vegetables, tea, fruit juice and so on—to be left outside the door twice a day. My reaction must have been noticeably unfavorable, for he gave me a sharp look and a sweet smile. "Dear Sir Lightwood, I should have warned you how important it will be for us not to talk to each other. Especially when we're together. Silence rather than speech elicits the deepest mutual responses."

With that he shut me out, door almost hitting my nose as he closed it. I stood in the little forest, gazing sadly at the light in his window. Almost immediately he lowered the curtains, abandoning me to a calm, enormous night.

4th of August

Four days of no word from the Word Incarnate, upon whose tray of food and blinded window I keep a watchful eye, hoping for a sign that the routine has broken. It fails to come. Then I noticed an advertisement in the *Denver Outlook* that Lily's film could be seen at the Cherry Creek Theatre. Rather to my surprise, I decided instantly to make the journey. It offered a prospect of adventure, like going behind the enemy lines. Next morning, after a shot of whisky, I set off in the Cadillac at dawn. The first two hundred miles or so were dangerously reassuring. Prepared to regard anybody or anything with suspicion, I rolled through the endless ranges and canyons of Colorado utterly ignored by the very occasional car or truck that passed. Then, in the heart of "dinosaur country," as they call this hinterland where ancient monsters used to prowl, a black sedan began hooting at me from the rear. Since the driver was clearly trying to attract my attention, I glanced in the mirror and was appalled to see Scotty, teeth bared in a grin of rage. I supposed he was either following me or trying to force me off the road for his own diabolical amusement, and though my heart leapt to my mouth I proceeded with dignity, at an even pace, hugging the white line in the middle; at last the thing zoomed past, on a blind corner, bellowing like a wild animal, dark smoke pouring from its exhaust. The driver wasn't Scotty after all, just some anonymous madman of the plains.

Stopping for lunch in a small shantylike town, I found people regarding me in the way I'd been prepared to regard *them*. Two middle-aged cowboys stared in furtive silence as I parked the Cadillac and entered the Silver Saddle restaurant; a sullen, indifferent waitress served me steak and potatoes, reacting very suspiciously to my request for wine, and finally bringing me a half-bottle of something sweet, icy and red. After paying the bill, I asked for the w.c., and a jerk of the cashier's thumb took me down a dark, sinister corridor. A door opened to a cell-like room where a young farmhand or yokel crouched on an open latrine; while I urinated into a stinking trough, I felt his eyes boring into me, and went stiff with alarm. My bladder, though unbelievably full, refused to empty itself at first; his eyes refused to look away; the scene froze into a ritual tableau, his cruel fascination, my anxious attempt to obtain relief . . . I realize it's hard to describe such moments without being accused of exaggeration, yet this is one I feel I've understated. Drained in every sense of the word, I emerged from that dungeon into space and air that had never seemed so wide and sweet.

Towards sunset, across the prairie, I saw my destination. A gray and smoky downtown huddled in the foothills of the Rockies, and at the corner of a block of buildings stood the Cherry Creek Theatre. There was no parking place on the street, so I left the Cadillac in a mean alley, full of garbage cans, walked round to the theatre entrance and met Lily perched on a hurdy-gurdy, blowing me a kiss from a crudely colored poster. I bought a ticket and a soft drink called Orangola because my throat was dusty, entered the bleak, almost empty auditorium to the tune of *Ole Man River* wheezing through a loudspeaker, and took a seat in the middle of the front row. The music stopped and a man wearing a tuxedo stepped in front of the spangled curtains to announce there was an unattended baby in the ladies' room. A woman shrieked, giggled and rushed out. The light changed to spectral green, the curtains twitched and parted, exposing a grayish screen, a newsreel of what I assumed to be current events began. With Orangola's sweet chemical taste on my tongue, I stared at an endless snowy plain, a burning city, heard the whine of swooping planes and the deep thud of bombs, and glimpsed a Nazi officer who reminded me of Violet before he fell out of a tank, dead as mutton. Next came tropical slaughter, grinning Japs with palm leaves in their helmets, rat-tat-tat of machine-guns in a steamy jungle. Then a battleship exploded in mid-ocean, the King and Queen of England shook hands with a bemused but cheerful family in the ruins of their Southampton home, mothers on a quayside fluttered tears, flags and handkerchiefs while a cheerful band struck up—and everything changed to a boxing match, huge black man with blood pouring out of his mouth before he toppled over and hundreds of spectators screamed applause, followed by a zoo at which a hippopotamus had just given birth. It was becoming difficult to keep one's bearings, but looking around at other people's faces, seeing them apparently calm, I felt comforted—if it was all right with them, why worry? When I looked back, Lily was walking down Piccadilly with a hurdy-gurdy and a monkey in a cap. Passing the Ritz, she actually burst into song. A policeman told her to move on but she wouldn't, stuck out her tongue, exactly the same as when I first saw her, bright and thin and mischievous; she winked at the gathering crowd and a handsome young man . . . I'm ashamed to admit that I can tell you no more, because something unexpected happened. *I dropped off*. Groggy from the long drive, dulled by the stale air, eyelids folded their tents; the rest was occasionally blinking awake and seeing Lily entertaining the troops, being kissed, laughing, weeping, on a train (!), at a beach. As if reassured that she wouldn't go away yet, I nodded and catnapped again. Later on I realized the audience was grumbling, presumably because it couldn't understand cockney. The rescued baby howled. A police siren screeched. Lights going up and a blare of music roused me at last, and I found myself sitting it out alone, sprawled in the front row beneath a blank screen. Feeling slightly ridiculous to have driven all this way only to fall asleep, I walked out through the peculiar desolation of a littered, empty theatre to a clear night and a full moon above the Rockies.

The alley lay in a silence that made my footsteps sound monstrous. As I approached the car, there was a violent metallic clatter. I saw the lid of a garbage can rolling towards me like a child's hoop, then the figure of a man. He lurched up to me, huge and unshaven; instinct warned me that he was armed, had spotted the Cadillac and waited to rob its returning owner. "I believe you're hungry," I said, reached into my pocket and offered him a dime. His face contorted with rage as he gave me a vicious, painful slap across the wrist.

"I didn't come here to be insulted," he said.

Aware that the person was not only drunk but desperate and mad, I apologized. "Is there any way I can help you?" I asked, wishing he hadn't placed himself between me and the car.

In reply he parodied my British accent, called me a few disagreeable names—jerk, fly-ball, fairy, etc.—and ordered me out of his way. I asked for permission to enter my car, but received only further threats and abuse. Sticking his face close to mine, he shook me furiously by the shoulders and inquired if I didn't know who he was. I apologized for my ignorance, which seemed to enrage him further. He glanced up at the full moon and shook me again.

"If I told you my name, would you believe it?"

"Try me."

"Alexander Graham Bell." Smile of infinite cunning twisted his mouth. "Do you believe it?"

"Of course."

"What a jerk you are." Shook me again. "It's not my name. But would you believe it if I said I was Jesse James?"

I searched his face for a clue, then reeled back from his breath. "I don't think so."

He let out a roar. "It's true! It's my name, you crazy British nellie."

"Then I believe it. Unfortunately I'm late for an engagement."

He grabbed me by the throat. "Listen, I'm tired of wandering around, tired of giving it to them in alleys for the price of a few drinks, telling them who I am when their minds are on something else. I'm tired of no one believing it!" Suddenly pushed me away. "You can't have it. You didn't believe it."

For a moment he seemed confused. I made a wild dash for my car and started the engine. The madman put his fist through a window, shattering the glass. "Listen, I'm Jesse James!" Clung to the door. "It's my birthday—ninety-seven today! Don't you want me to give it to you?"

Another ghastly string of abuse as I swerved away. A few lights came on in windows; a woman's voice called, "Quiet! Shut up!" Fifteen minutes later I sat in a dreary motel bedroom, shaking with fear, remembering all the lewd enemy faces that slant out of nowhere to haunt and menace my life.

Later. Exceptionally hideous nightmares—I remember dreaming that I woke up and saw a locustlike creature, about two feet long, brittle, shining, with wings and antennae, watching me beady-eyed before it rose in the air and flew off with a humming sound. I knew it had nested all night in my hair. I drove home like my pursuer in the black sedan, collecting three traffic tickets on the way from motorcycle cops looking like hell's outriders with their holsters, cruel mouths and jackboots. (And yet people like that man in the alley go free!) The cabin stood in a mellow shaft of light beyond the green of pines, its sanctuary so cool and perfect that I could have wept with gratitude. Reckless after this campaign of terror, I was prepared to interrupt Jemadar's retreat; but luckily cafe curtains were raised and through the open door I saw him sipping tea on the bed.

"Good evening, Sir Lightwood." No allusion to my absence and return. "Please sit down, catch your breath and tell me all about it."

Listening to my review of unspeakable encounters, he remained impassive most of the time, chuckled once or twice. "My word. It never rains but it pours."

"But what have I done to deserve it? How will it end?"

"I'd prefer to ask how it began." Glanced at the copy of

Oum on his bedside table. "By the way, I read some of your translations. Amazing! What a lucky woman. She reminds me of an actress playing a nun when the part of an elegant courtesan might be more suitable—but thanks to your gift of words she carries it off."

The comment jolted me, coming as it did from the horse's mouth, but even the thought of subtle, reconnoitering discussions with the Word Incarnate, to pick up useful spiritual tips, as it were, without giving the game away, couldn't excite me now. "Let's not talk about Oum," I said. "I want you to explain why they always pick on me."

Jemadar poured more tea. "Let us bear in mind that a so-called accident—be it death on a street or running into an old friend or new stranger—is never what it seems. It's *more* than it seems, you know. We cannot doubt that this unfortunate man, like a dream, was trying to tell you something."

"He was simply insulting me. They always do." *Hooting of an owl, panting kisses in the dark.* "It's never stopped since I was ten years old and our chauffeur, with his hand up my nanny's skirt, told her I was a filthy little bastard."

"My word. Why should he have said such a thing?"

"Well, I'm illegitimate. But usually there's no reason at all—they just smirk, blow raspberries, threaten to hit or denounce me or have me thrown in jail. Naturally I expected a certain amount of unpleasantness this time, so if the man in the alley was trying to tell me I should have stayed home, I agree with him."

Jemadar shook his head. "Since you are disturbed and indignant, we must conclude he said something with which you do *not* agree." Moment of deep thought. "It is never my intention to criticize, only to point out how a situation strikes me. So if I refer again to the landscape of self-delusion you've created here, please don't think me a scold. I mention it because this man in the alley was, in his own less successful way, *doing the same thing.*"

I stared at him. "Am I to believe you consider us both equally mad?"

"Dear me no." Patted my hand. "That word is much too vague. But how much kinder of you, and safer for you, if you'd said to this poor fellow, 'Eminent sir, I indeed suspected your true identity, but didn't like to say so in case you didn't wish it generally known. I am deeply honored to meet you at last. Happy birthday, dear Mr. Jesse James.' He recognized a kindred spirit, you see, and you might have returned the compliment."

Fighting back a desire to tweak the sage's nose, I gave him a calm annihilating look instead; unfortunately, he was gazing at the floor. "I know my alter ego, Jemadar. We've been extremely close for years. There's no connection, thank God, with that hideous maniac of last night." I felt my voice tremble. "Her name is Oum Salem."

Jemadar gave no sign of having heard or even listened. He appeared to sigh to himself, still gazing at the floor. The silence began to alarm me. "Let me put something to you in the simplest terms," his voice reached me, very low, as if soothing a child to sleep. "*We die to be born again.*" It was the second time, I noted, he'd referred to my death. "The cycle isn't over until the last life ends in union with the Supreme Being—something I know you desire, since you identify yourself (a little prematurely) with this woman who claims to have achieved it. In the meantime, each reincarnation is simply a stage in our long spiritual development, and if a life has been on the whole good, the next one will offer greater opportunities for goodness. If not, not." Dreadful, ominous pause. "So you see, there's always another chance to reap the fruits or the whirlwind."

Air went suddenly chill, froze into profound and futile terror, worse than the postcoital smoldering match my own wife drops on my naked tummy in the dark, worse than the man with tinted glasses sacking my bedroom at the Ritz, and the low toilet-paper threat from The Major! This dusky sage, my house guest whom I urgently beg for consolation, first tells me that an obscene tormentor is the other side of my psychic coin, then announces my imminent death and weighs my slender chances for the next time around. Buddha grins at me from the antique chest; trees rustle outside the window; and I hear an insinuating oriental voice that whispers, "*Are you listening? Let me tell you a story.* Imagine a young Englishman, born into the ruling class of his country—I know, from the Raj I once served in Bombay, what an inheritance of pride is there. . . . In spite of being so protected, so wealthy, so cultured, the young man is constantly abused by strangers, usually his social inferiors. . . . He runs from them everywhere, hides at last in a sanctuary of the most remarkable extravagance, which he builds himself. . . . The first moment he ventures outside, the strangers pursue him with threats and insults. . . . They tell him the voices of fear are the voices of desire, but he won't listen. . . . The tell him the longer he hides, the more angry they get, but he blames the voices, never himself. . . .

Always resists, never accepts. . . . But what will he do when the strangers climb over the walls? . . ."

After these frightful words, I heard and saw nothing. When the curtain rose again I lay on Jemadar's bed, aware of a spiced and oily aroma that lingered in the blankets. It was dark outside. He had left the room. The door was closed, almost certainly locked. I soon began to realize the extent of my danger. It was a great relief that in spite of my heart attack I was able to think clearly, carefully, logically. In the past, at awkward moments such as these, I've wondered *what they're after,* and it was always my money or my body or the help that I alone could give at a crisis. This time they wanted *everything.* An attempt had just been made on the life of my soul; a trickster from the East was trying to drive me insane by suggesting that the vulgar strangers were in league with each other, planning to take over my establishment here, then haunt and bully me down the corridors of Time. How uncannily right, with his primitive instinct, was Freddy! I felt a pang of remorse that I'd misjudged him, and thought him cunning the night of Jemadar's arrival. He was only fighting for his life, like me. The problem, I now saw, was how to get rid of my arch-enemy without offending Denna, whom he's made the innocent victim of his power. With a leaping thrill, I accepted the enormity of the odds against success. My only chance was to give nothing away, to play my cards with calm, immense secrecy, for I was frighteningly alone.

The door swung open. He to whom I gave bed, board and benefit of my patronage, who repayed my by disguising himself as the Word Incarnate *in order to take Oum away,* stood on the threshold with a glass of water in his hand. The smile that I used to think tender and affectionate was now a furtive leer, and the softness of his voice telling me a doctor was on the way couldn't disguise the serpent's hiss. When he stroked my forehead, I managed not to shrink from the touch of a scaly, reptilian hand; when he put the glass to my lips, saying he'd found the medicine in my bathroom, I took it and turned away so he wouldn't see me sniff the colorless liquid; when I found the smell was right, I smiled obediently up at him and drank, knowing he was much too clever to drug me quite so soon.

Difficult now. Doctor wished me to go to hospital but I refused, suspecting trick. They wish to stop me writing. Safer in tower. Fear attack if bathe in lake. Servants taste all food.

On the days when I make tremendous efforts, all seems well again. I realize that a secret duel is being fought between myself and the Power from the East; sometimes he gets the upper hand and I find it difficult to concentrate; then I rally, give orders, write to Parkinson and Parkinson, etc. This morning Denna paid me a visit. I could tell she knew something was wrong, sensed my danger, tried bravely and tactfully to behave as usual. She told me Jemadar is to give his first public lecture next Sunday, and a good attendance is expected. The Bluewater Inn has been booked solid and others will be staying in Santa Fe. When I explained that I couldn't possibly attend, she at once understood why. "But I can imagine the square in Kuola on Saturday night," I said, beginning to laugh, describing sleepy or drunken Indians squatted against walls, staring at rich women in search of truth.

For some reason she wasn't amused.

Heard laughter during night. Enormous turd on silver dish outside door this morning. No need to ask who sent.

A few minutes after the lecture began, I arrived in secret, concealing myself behind a piece of shrubbery. Since it was warm, Jemadar decided to speak in the open air, and chose a slope of land below the trees outside his cabin. About fifty people sat on folding chairs or blankets, rather like a picnic. He discussed the Mirror and the problem of keeping it clear. Otherwise, how can the beautiful and the ugly, the light and the heavy, be properly balanced and reflected? If we shake the Mirror, everything clouds. Then he quoted a Master who said that flying dragons ride the winds and serpents glide through a mist floating on the river; but take away the winds and the mist, and dragon and serpent, stripped of their elements, are no more alarming than earwigs. Afternoon light turned to dusk, blue sky became like glass, a pale moon rose; from my point of view, fine words buttered no parsnips. Finally he held my attention by announcing a plan for Gracious Manure. If we feed the earth only common refuse and shit, said the figure in the crimson robe, we have no right to complain when it offers us a bad smell in return. Therefore we must tempt it with more delicate remains, rose petals, peach blossom, the juice of limes, and it will reward us with a divine aroma. Thinking of North Africa, sun-baked dung flavored with kif-ends, henna-droppings, garlic and cinnamon, my nostrils quivered. Jemadar announced the formation of a Beauty Pile and asked for contributions on the spot; impulsively Denna snatched the rose she wore in her hair, tossed it to the ground and founded the Pile; others followed, emptying bottles of cologne, laying down strawberries; and snow glimmered on the tips of distant mountains.

When it was over, a man wearing a panama hat raised his hand, face terrible with anger. He wished to ask a question and his wife, who clearly doted on Jemadar, wished him not to; but he ignored the pleading fingers on his arm.

"There's a war going on," said the stranger loudly, "and our boys are being killed! Aren't you ashamed of yourself, talking about feeding the earth roses?"

Amid gasps of disapproval, the sage gave his sweetest smile. "Thank you, dear sir, for not asking a question but providing an answer. We feed the earth roses because too many others are feeding it blood."

I returned quickly to my tower, locking all doors. A fierce presentiment had me by the throat—Oum had allowed me to be caught in this glassy suspension between fever and trance (far worse, after all, than any previous panic or uncertainty) because it meant *the end of our journey.* The closing lines and finest jewels of *The Crowns of Seclusion* were about to be revealed. I prepared myself for what might come, and the vessel floated home at last to a strangely Blakean harbor—

Mountain air is pure and strange
A lonely Body's habits change

It does not even Feel the pin
That Pricks a finger's yielding skin

No Hurt cleaves through and no Blood flows
But silently a white Rose grows

Down in the cities of Alarm
They sharpen Blades to do me harm

They lay strong hands upon my Bloom
And lead me to a Darkened room . . .

This time will bitter Rue arise
Or winging Birds of Paradise?

Knowing my task had ended, there was scarcely time for the expected *postcoitus animal triste* sensation, for almost immediately—with a booming echo that seemed to shiver the tower—the great bell rang outside my main gates. I glanced at a clock and saw midnight; servants in bed, or a stupor somewhere, obviously; not a sound, even from the goats. Terrified, I went quickly downstairs, crossed the courtyard and directed a flashlight at the darkness ahead.

Freddy. I let him in at once, feeling I shouldn't, and knew that he'd been drinking. I begged him not to say a word until we reached the safety of my tower, and he made only a few vague guttural sounds, that might have been belches or his native language. He gazed round my sanctuary with a rather disturbing grin, noticed a bottle of brandy on the worktable, poured most of it into a pottery vase from Acoma, and took a swig. His speech was incoherent at first, but I gathered he'd had a quarrel with Denna, stemming from his alleged disrespect for Jemadar. You can imagine the conflict of emotions this aroused in me; I expressed them all, repeating my admiration for his wife, begging his forgiveness, praising him as human being and cook, and finally whispering that I myself was in unspeakable danger from the Orient.

To my astonishment, he swore to protect me and seized me in his arms. Though confused and exhausted, I'm sure I attempted to resist. I was kneeling at his feet, begging him to spare me, when Denna came into the room—or rather, when I became aware that she was standing in the doorway. Possibly she'd been there some time; my protests to Freddy were lengthy, because I didn't wish to hurt his feelings. Anyway, I got up and she held a long, icily composed stare. Unfortunately, Freddy lay down on the divan without a word and drifted into sleep. I tried to explain, but she seemed unconvinced.

"Don't crawl to *me* now, Norman. I've always known you wanted him."

"But I swear to you nothing has happened!"

"I'd respect you more if you had the courage to admit it."

"Nothing has happened!"

"I shall begin to despise you if you say that again." She went over to Freddy and tried to wake him. He finally opened his eyes, smiled, stroked her cheek. In a low voice she asked, "Are you coming back with me, or staying here?"

"Where?" He looked puzzled. "What happened?"

"NOTHING!" I said.

He glanced at me, then staggered to his feet. "You're in danger." Told Denna anxiously, "Norman wants me to save him."

She guided him out of the room. At the door she flashed me a last, contemptuous look. "Admit it now! Coward!"

I shouted another denial down the spiral staircase, but

was rewarded only by a mocking laugh and the echo of footsteps growing fainter. Shortly afterwards, all became clear. Denna knows I'm innocent, but is frightened of *my immense wealth.* She realizes I have the means to take Freddy away from her if I should wish. This explains her false friendliness from the start, her schemes to *bleed me dry.* Made me buy acres of land I didn't need. Extorted thousands from me to create her taunting Avenue. Put Freddy up to the idea of getting me in deeper with goats. Probably wrecked the cheese herself. Not Jemadar's victim but his ally!

Heavy breathing outside locked doors. Knobs turn. Whiff of dreadful spices. Power from East and his Delilah trying to enter.

Ask for help or complain? Should telephone Lady D. or God. Delay on line to Australia. Wish to speak to God please. Person to person. GEE OH DEE DEE. GOD. Claim no one listed of that name. Phone company on *their* side too. Try Western Union. Wish to cable GOD please. Fast rate. ORIENTAL IMPOSTOR CLAIMS REPRESENT YOU STOP ACCOMPANIED BY WOMAN WITH RED HAIR GOING UNDER NAME OF DENNA MARX STOP AWAIT INSTRUCTIONS

Hung up on me. What now? Oceana Lines might send boat.

Parkinson and Parkinson?

Try GOD again. Under different name? May be listed as ALLAH BRAHMA ALMIGHTY MARY SAVIOUR HOLY FATHER AUTHOR! No good. Advertising section in directory? Look under Yellow Pages for DESIGNERS GENERATORS ARCHITECTS PHYSICIANS PEST CONTROL

Our Lady of the Syringe. Tall, unknown Virgin with implements and halo. Quite intelligent. *May be on my side.*

In church. Sanctuary of vast mattress. Wearing white summer *djellabah* and bracelet on wrist! Many flowers on Altar. Charming young Priest. New Virgin with halo brings Extreme Unction in teapot. Warn her to admit no infidels from East. If God calls, tell Him to leave message. Feel *much* better.

Told Priest am ready for Ceremony any time he is. Demand perfume.

Still no word from God. Priest says we can't go ahead without Him. Feel *much* worse. Canceled all arrangements!

Our Lady of the Syringe. Holy Mother. *Definitely on my side.*

Allowed Bath today. Frankincense. Myrrh. Sandalwood. Given new striped *djellabah*. Demand henna.

Much better. Remind Priest best time for Exorcism is middle of night. My bed or his makes no difference. But stripes no good. Wish to wear white.

"*. . . And lead me to a Darkened room.*" How poignant that line of Oum's appears now!

First reactions, after consciousness returned and I discovered the nature of my location, were distinctly unfavorable. Demanding to see the manager, who called himself Doctor Taylor, with the intention of extracting a full public apology, I prepared myself for a difficult and painful scene. However, when he appeared at my bedside, I recognized him as the same personable young man that I'd mistaken for a priest and asked to perform some kind of ceremony. I therefore apologized to *him*. Moments of unusual fatigue and strain, I explained, had me at a slight disadvantage; the completion of Oum's masterpiece was one of them. He agreed, and talked with great charm and sympathy about creative tensions; asked a few questions—my background, parents, the events at Kuola culminating in Jemadar's arrival—and congratulated me on holding up so long; startled me by revealing that what I called a "moment" had lasted eight days, and suggested a long total rest, during which we might occasionally chat with each other. When he put it this way, it was like being invited to stay with him in the country, and I'd have felt ungracious to refuse.

After meeting a few of his other guests, I was encouraged by their generally contented attitude. They have minor complaints—room service could be improved, pool is sometimes underheated—but feel I will definitely enjoy my stay. Going abroad is difficult at the moment, anyway. In any place full of strangers in transit, be it an ocean liner or the Ritz, there are certain people one learns to avoid (the Sir Manfred Barrs and Mrs. Florence Lovejoys of this world), but I've made rewarding human contact with three congenial travelers. Mr. Jordan Ambrose, vice-president of a company that manufactures armaments, one day began to cry uncontrollably at a board meeting, even though profits were greater than ever. Mrs. Heaton Belmont VandeCarr

Gruber Mandelstam "Mopsy" Lord, a successful divorcée from the Jazz Age, grew depressed after her sixth millionaire husband refused to come home, and made shocking propositions on the telephone to rich young bachelors she'd never met. Sad, quiet Art, only son of Rear Admiral Howard Swicegood, wore a Ku Klux Klan hood over his face, stared at an imaginary window and waited for his dead mother to appear naked in a shower.

Unwinding together, we lie around like springs contented to be broken; the grounds are spacious and attractive, the food excellent, our private suites tolerably furnished in "international hotel" style. Mopsy Lord complains that Doctor Taylor asks too many personal questions, but I point out it's a fault on the right side, and shows that he cares. Like Jordan, she's signed in for the duration, because wartime conditions have rotted the stability of the male and she will no longer be pillaged, then abandoned; in preparation for a seventh, final and perfect marriage she left for three weeks to have her face lifted, returned smooth and a little tense with chin firmed and eyes depouched. Jordan awaits the end of hostilities because he cannot appear in public while bombs are dropped *with his name on them.* Art and I, however, agree privately that it's too easy to blame the war or society. We feel that our cases are timeless. For those around whose necks the gods have placed an Albatross, a pause that refreshes is the best cure. We remind Doctor Taylor of this when he pushes too hard, driven I suppose by insecurity to exaggerate his importance here.

This part of my letter remains undated, Ahmin, because time is no longer measured by the usual standards. All I can tell you, from this high estate that overlooks the rolling

Texas plains, is that when spring came, Jordan stopped weeping. At the end of summer, as leaves of oak and hickory began to turn, Mopsy Lord ordered a large, red telephone, sat in front of it, and felt at last no desire to dial a number and utter improprieties. About a week before Christmas, Art destroyed his hood. "I've waited eight months for Momma to take a shower," said the melancholy lad. "Now I guess she's never going to." As for myself, I celebrated a birthday by seeing if I could go to sleep without locking the doors of my suite. In a twilight of sedation (won from Mopsy at blackjack), deepened by secret martinis, the experiment succeeded. Early next morning, I was awakened by the telephone. The operator told me to hold the line for a long distance call from Australia.

After several false alarms and what sounded like the Pacific roaring in my ears, Lady D.'s voice came alternately very faint and very loud from the Antipodes. "Dearest NORMAN, happy BIRTHday." Before I could answer, "I have very SAD NEWS!" Pacific intervened. When it stopped, I asked her to begin again. "SAD NEWS!" her voice bellowed across the Equator. "My beloved MAURICE was KILLED last night."

Still dazed from my drugs, I asked who did it. The line growled and hissed again. ". . . ACCIDENT!" The operator broke in; Lady D., suddenly angry, told her to go to hell. ". . . driving up the MOUNTAINS after drinking a little TOO much of that EXCELLENT SCOTCH you sent . . . dark night . . . no MOON . . . sharp corner . . . FATAL DROP." A strange, total peace descended on the line. "YOU CAN IMAGINE I'M DEEPLY IN NEED OF COMFORT FROM MY VERY DEAR SON. I SHALL BE ARRIVING IN THREE DAYS' TIME, PLEASE BOOK ME A ROOM NEXT TO YOURS."

Stunned, I agreed to do so. Which is the moment to confess that, in my occasional letters to Lady D., I had failed to disclose many details of my present quarters, indicating that *San Angelo*—as it was called on the discreet, pale-gray notepaper heading—was some kind of luxury resort to which I'd treated myself after finishing *The Crowns of Seclusion.* I knew that my parent was sufficiently attuned by now to my whims and habitual restlessness not to find it odd that I abandoned my exciting establishment at Kuola so soon after moving into it. Staring at the phone, and dawn coming up through the windows, I had a momentary twinge of alarm—but then, after fearing the situation might be awkward, I decided that on the contrary it was all for the best. After reserving a suite with a really spectacular view, and ordering bouquets of flowers, I confided in Doctor Taylor. With his usual aplomb, he promised to handle everything. Who knows, he suggested, that when she got over the shock, she might not be grateful for a little help?

Lady D.-Day was a warm, clear morning, the air beautifully dry and pure. Mopsy, Jordan, Art and I played blackjack as usual by the pool; old Grace Hetherington II waded down the steps into the shallow end, then launched one of her paper boats. Suddenly nostalgic, Mopsy gazed at the little white vessel bobbing on the water. "Listen, kids, if we chartered a private yacht to cruise the friggin' Caribbean," her loud, fierce drawl echoed across the lawn with sprinklers playing, "we'd shell out less by the month than at this goddamned Ritz-Hatch." Strong, brown fingers took another card and stroked a thousand dollars' worth of chips. "How about that?" she said. Nobody answered. "The whole world's dragging its ass this morning." She took another card, laid down her hand. "Twenty-one. Your deal, Art." Scooped up her chips and opened a jewel case to take out a pill.

Jordan sighed. "We're rich enough to do anything, Mopsy, so it doesn't matter what we do."

"That's pretty negative thinking." She laid something small and green on her tongue, took two more cards. "Your lucky streak is showing, girl." Spread out a fan of cards. "Twenty. Beat it if you can." Nobody could. She added more chips to her pile. "But I'm so unlucky in love, you know."

A taxi pulled up outside the house, and a heavily veiled woman got out, all in black. Long, yellow cigarette waved vaguely in one hand. Having forewarned my friends about Lady D., I announced her arrival and hurried over to meet her. When she took me in her arms, I couldn't see her face through the dense widow's weeds; but her enveloping perfume came back like an old song.

"What a strange and sad reunion, my dear, after all these years."

I suggested that she come to sit by the pool for a few minutes. Other guests stared as she walked across the lawn, black veils fluttering in the breeze like the sails of a pirate galleon, probably marking her down as a new one with a taste for morbid masquerade. She commented favorably on our surroundings. "I can understand that you like it so well, Norman, that you hate to leave even to meet me at the airport." I invented some excuse about the car I ordered failing to arrive, and made a round of introductions. She sat down beside Mopsy. "I believe I met your third husband, in Rome, about a year before the war started. You *were* married to Toby VandeCarr, weren't you?"

"Son-of-a-bitch," said Mopsy, nodding.

Lady D. glanced towards the pool, where Grace still played with her boat. "That face looks familiar. Who is she?"

"Grace Hetherington," I said.

"Of course. Norman, dear, would you order me a scotch?"

The toy-factory heir, unfortunately, blew his regular noon whistle from a chaise-longue and ordered everyone to break for lunch. I knew that Lady D., behind her veils, gave me one of her most quizzical looks. "I think I understand," she remarked after a long pause, "why the taxi driver seemed apprehensive when I told him to bring me here. Shall we go up to my room, Norman, and have a little talk?"

In front of a triple mirror on the wall, surrounded by flowers, she slowly removed her veils. Three buddha faces were reflected back at me, no visible scars of time or grief. Faintest of smiles hovered at the corners of mouths. Six graceful hands lit cigarettes, and joss sticks of smoke curled across the mirrors. I sat on the large double bed with a quilted headboard, watching her watch me with the old, wary, unchanged composure. From somewhere inside her black she removed a silver hip flask; went into the bathroom; returned with scotch in tooth glasses.

"To us." Handed me one. "Now tell me how long you've been in this place."

"I'm not sure. About a year, I think."

"I always felt you should have come to Australia with Maurice and me." No flicker of surprise. "And what a shame poor Violet isn't here to complete our family reunion. Once again we shall have to make the best of things." She drank to absent friends and stubbed out her cigarette. "You look, I have to say, remarkably well. What was the reason, my dear, for putting yourself away like this?"

During my recital, she stretched out on the bed and lay on her back, absolutely rigid, hands folded across her breasts, eyes staring at the ceiling. When I finished, she raised one eyebrow; crooked a finger, wishing me to lie down at her side. Drafts of perfume were expelled with her quiet, steady breathing. For some reason I thought of Gracious Manure.

"Naturally I respect the oriental point of view." This startled me. She took my hand. "However, like certain wines, it doesn't travel well. What does Doctor Taylor have to suggest?"

"That I stay here. And continue to explore the problem with him."

Her nose wrinkled slightly. "He considers you have a problem? I find that a little facile of him."

"We've discussed several. My complex about being wealthy."

"Really, Norman. Either you want your millions or you don't. Besides, the way you've been spending, you're considerably less wealthy than you think." Closed her eyes. "I see no problem there."

"My obsession that all kinds of people are trying to rob, kill and insult me."

"But of course they are. The world is bound to pursue or resent a young man of your means and qualities. I see no problem there," said Lady D.

"My unhealthy identification with a poetess who never existed."

Eyes opened at once, very wide. "The young doctor has persuaded you of that?"

"No. I admitted it." And told in a whisper, as we continued to lie together, of my invented companion and scourge; of what the great man in Vienna said to me about Higher Masochism and unnatural worship of an impossible person; of my wild flight from her, across pampas and Andes; of our reconciliation in the mountains during a thunderstorm, and the temple to her charismatic power that I humbly erected.

During a long pause, the warm, black, fragrant creature at my side gripped my hand more tightly. "I admit there might be a problem there. I'll probably discuss it with the young man later. In the meantime, I beg you to tell *no one else*—we cannot have a story like that going the rounds. Far worse, in my opinion, to be humiliated in literary magazines than in the common courts or Sunday newspapers."

"Yes. My anal—"

"Norman, the time has come for you to comfort *me*." Sigh; head snuggled against my shoulder; lips kissed my hand. "Thank God we're together at this hour of uncertainty and loss. Divided we fall, my dear—hasn't that always been the case with you and me?"

Dusk came, all blue and silent beyond the windows. I was the first to wake; leaned on my elbow and scrutinized the ageless features, eyes closed and mouth slightly open. Hip flask gleamed on the bedside table; I found it still contained an inch or so, which I polished off; she stirred as I set down the glass, muttered something about her great love being gone and flicked open her eyes. They looked vague and glassy for a moment, then focused.

"A strange bed, and darkness outside." She smiled. "I couldn't imagine where I was until I saw your dear, happy face." Touched my cheek. "Happier now, I do believe, than before I dropped off."

"It's the old thrill of your simple, practical point of view. I'd forgotten how much I missed it."

"Then why don't you pack and order a taxi?" She stood up, unzipped her widow's weeds and revealed a black corset underneath them. "I'll soak these traveled bones in a bath first."

Half an hour later our bags were in the hall; I'd paid my bill and canceled Lady D.'s reservation. Heavily veiled again, she entered Doctor Taylor's office and asked his secretary to leave a message. "Just say how sorry I am to have missed him, and thank him from me for all his kindness to my son."

The secretary pressed a buzzer on her desk. "But I'm sure he'd like a word with you, Lady Lightwood."

"And of course I would adore a word with him, as I've explained already." She turned away. "Alas, we're pressed for time." A door opened, and she waved a black glove quite skittishly at Doctor Taylor. "Forgive us, dear man, for abandoning you. I wish I could have seen more of your charming place, but I'll certainly recommend it to everyone I know." A last, almost flirtatious wave. "Goodby, goodby. Norman, is our luggage all aboard?"

Doctor Taylor followed us through the hall, calling out to me that I was making a mistake. "You mustn't take it so personally," said Lady D. over her shoulder. "But all he needed to cure him was his mother."

Mopsy, Jordan and Art stood wistfully by the taxi. In a gruff voice, Mopsy said she'd miss me at the blackjack table and Jordan made the touching joke that he felt like crying. With a poignantly hopeful expression, Art asked Lady D. if he might see her face.

"How sweet." She chucked him under the chin. "But what do you expect to find?" I reflected that there might have been grave complications for Art if Lady D. had stayed very long. She turned to the others and felt sure we'd all meet again. "Here or somewhere else," she said, and hopped into the taxi. They waved from the terrace as we drove away.

Ribbon of endless highway across the desert plain; twinkling lights of a city ahead. Lady D. touched my arm. "Norman, are we by any chance being followed?"

"Of course not."

"You feel no twinge of danger or alarm?"

"How absurd you are."

"I'm so proud of my boy. Shall we stop off in Kuola, and see that all is well there?" I nodded. She reached inside her black and produced another silver flask. "The last of your excellent scotch, I fear." Drank from the stopper and passed it to me. "By the way, that fatal crate arrived with a rather strange little note. Some man with 'President' typed below his name signed himself 'Yours Compassionately.' I had the feeling he was sorry for me without knowing why."

Swigging, I explained to Lady D. the legend I'd created of her great fame and imminent death. Behind the mask of veils she began to giggle, almost like a schoolgirl; then silence, and her black glove fastened lightly on my arm. "Yet another of life's grim ironies, my dear. If your clever trick hadn't worked, there would probably have been no scotch to drink that night, and no last appointment in the Blue Mountains for Maurice. But let's not think or talk about it."

Sprinkle of rain now against the windows; we skirted the edge of a brief, nervous desert shower. As the glass misted, it seemed to me that our journey began very slightly to blur. We drank, dozed, woke up to exchange memories of the old life. Cut off from her great love, Lady D. compared herself to an uprooted tree, and said that she would like, as soon as the terrible war ended, to return to her native earth. She longed for our fifty-three drafty rooms; she would take up her brushes again in the studio, watch roses grow and golden leaves drift to the autumn ground. "I ask no more, for I have seen too much. Believe it or not, my dear little Norman, I am sixty-seven, have lived through many wars and those intervals, when angry giants pause for breath, laughingly called peace. I have seen nations, kings and comets fall, waltz yield to tango, and tango to jitterbug, the humble dray replaced by the Rolls-Royce and the zeppelin by the Stuka—which reminds me of poor Violet; we must in due course unite to save her. . . ." A sigh interrupted her in mid-flight. "Anyway, all I want now is to live out my remaining forty or fifty years, with the flesh of my flesh that is left to me, in the English countryside."

Dinner in San Antonio, at an almost empty hutch of a restaurant near the station; a train or two rattled by, but Lady D. remarked there was still another hour to wait before we boarded ours. At such moments I suspected her of planning things in advance, then dismissed this reflex of an ancient fear. With her, after all, I had always been safe. We left the restaurant hand in hand to explore the Spanish town, and she flitted through the archways of Alamo Plaza like a mysterious duenna. Next morning I followed her sable figure, cool and quick under dazzling sunlight, off the train at Lamy; sniffed piñon in the air; gazed at cliffs of orange lava and saw sleepy amazement in an old Navajo's face as she pressed dollar bills into his hand and ordered an immediate taxi.

All seemed in order at my establishment. Naturally I'd arranged to pay the servants during my absence, but I confided to Lady D. my fears of finding them drunk, the place filthy and neglected, or even Jemadar enthroned and refusing to admit me at the gates. She merely pressed my arm. "Are you forgetting that if there's any trouble, *I* am here?" Perhaps a warning had been flashed. Fountain played in my courtyard, my staff actually recognized me, even Eagle Feathers displayed an affectionate idiot grin—which faded when I asked about the cheese this year. It had turned out well, but since I wasn't there, they had no idea what to do with it, and gave it all away. In the workroom of my tower, table and papers were untouched; I gathered up *The Crowns of Seclusion,* added it to a suitcase. Then we strolled down to the Avenue of Statues, where Lady D. lifted a veil to inspect the Ritualistic Orgy. "Yes, I can understand you'll be sad to leave this place. I felt a pang at saying goodby to my Australian home. However, the important thing is never to sell. In this world, who knows when one might want to come back?"

As I led her along the path to Jemadar's cabin, I glimpsed the door half-open and the sage on his bed, sipping tea. Nothing, it seemed, had happened. He greeted me with a sweet smile but no surprise, made no allusion to my absence and return or to the figure at my side. "Good afternoon, Sir Lightwood. Please sit down. Tea? A cookie, perhaps?"

I introduced Lady D. She inclined her head gracefully, and sat close beside him on the bed. For a moment, neither spoke. Jemadar handed her a cup of tea. She took it, and handed it to me, adjusted a veil, more impenetrable than ever.

"Appearances oblige me to conclude," said Jemadar softly, "that you are in mourning." She gave a brief nod. "I am deeply sorry."

"Yes, so am I." Touched his hand with a black glove. "But please don't fell obliged to console me. My son is the only person who can do that."

Jemadar gazed at her, or what he could see of her, with evident admiration. "Amazing!" Glanced at the copy of Oum still on his bedside table. Held out a plate of cookies to me. "May I say that your remarkable mother reminds me of a certain household in Bombay?"

Lady D.'s fingers tapped impatiently inside their glove. "I have never been in Bombay."

"We cannot be sure of that," said Jemadar.

"If you're implying that I've lived before, you take the argument—quite unfairly, in my opinion—into the realm of special pleading."

He seemed puzzled. "Dear lady, I'm not sure that I understand you."

"You hardly know me." Sigh. "I only meant that you introduced obscure religious beliefs into a simple discussion of where I have or have not been." Got up and stood beside me, resting a hand on my shoulder. "They all do it, of course. But I refused to be intimidated."

"Truly amazing," said Jemadar.

Since they were not getting on too well, I decided to change the subject. "Last time we met, Jemadar, I was tired and slightly irritable. If I offended you, I'd like to apologize."

"I cannot accept an apology." He smiled sweetly again. "It presupposes guilt, and I do not accept your guilt. Or your innocence," he added quickly. "Just before you arrived I was remembering a helpful thought from the mind of Chuang Tzu. *The legs of a duck are short,* said this Master, *and they cannot be lengthened without making the rest of the duck very uncomfortable. The legs of a crane are long, and* they *cannot be shortened without making the crane equally uncomfortable.* There, in a nutshell, we have it. A duck is a duck, a crane is a crane, and who would blame the one or defend the other?"

"Quite right," said Lady D. in a more approving tone. "We must take each other for what we are, to put it more practically." Tap on my shoulder. "Norman, dear, we're pressed for time." Inclined her head again toward the sage. "I so enjoyed our little talk. Since we won't be returning, I'm sure I can speak for my son in offering you the run of the house here. Frankly, you'd be doing *us* a favor—by keeping an eye on the servants, you know, and running the baths, so that if ever we come back for a night or two, we won't be plagued by rusty water or chill, unwelcoming fireplaces. Feel free, of course, to invite your friends to stay." By now she'd opened her bag and taken out a checkbook. "Let me leave you a little something for emergencies." Scribbled a signature and handed Jemadar the check.

He looked at it, then bit into another cookie. "Forgive me, dear lady. It is not enough."

"Norman, does twenty thousand dollars seem niggardly to you?"

"Not enough," Jemadar repeated with his mouth full. "Please don't ask me what it's not enough *for*. That introduces obscure practical considerations into a simple metaphysical problem. Which is why I shan't even remind you of all the comforts and conveniences I would be giving up here. I am not asking for more for myself. I am merely asking for more."

After a moment, Lady D. observed to me: "Their minds are so devious." Then turned back to Jemadar. "All the same, one has a right to know where one's money is going."

"Ask them in any place where they are poor and wounded, therefore wish to eat, or feel less pain."

"Then we're discussing charity. Why didn't you say so?" She tore up the check, wrote another and placed it in a pocket of his robe. "I never stoop to argue about *that*." Took my arm, hurried me out of the cabin and along the path. "The only way to deal with them," she murmured, "is to call their bluff."

I glanced back. Jemadar sat calmly on his bed, sipping tea again. The crimson robe dwindled to a sharp dot of color. Somewhere in the air floated a rich, delicate aroma.

"How much did you give him?" I asked.

"More. One dollar more. Now, have we other outstanding accounts before we leave?"

Half an hour later, we stand together in front of the Spider Goddess. Denna was speaking on the telephone when we arrived; Freddy, after I introduced him to the figure at my side, withdrew silently to mix martinis. I hadn't really wished to come here, but Lady D. pointed out that to slink away without a word could create an impression of guilt. "And if *you* won't look them in the eye, *I* certainly will. This couple took advantage of you: the woman exploited your wealth and the man, your romantic innocence." She gives the painting a last, casual glance and moves away. "In her art, at least, she's not afraid to bare her soul."

Now Denna, red hair bunched up on her head, spots of paint decorating her jeans and shirt, arrives eager and barefoot. "So sorry to have kept you waiting. Chicago was on the phone to tell me my show there has been attacked—for the usual reasons, of course." Kisses me on the cheek. "Let me say at once how I appreciate this visit. A single crisis cannot divide people like you and I. We have to go beyond differences to our essential closeness."

"Or vice versa," murmurs Lady D. in my ear, just before I introduce her to Denna, who smiles briefly and takes me aside at once, walking me over to the bay windows. Beyond them, a touch of ghostliness appears; caravan of white dust clouds floats above the valley and begins to climb the mountain slopes.

"Now tell me your plans. Are you back home? Why is *she* here?"

"We're leaving later today. That's all I know."

"You must be exaggerating. Leaving for where?"

"I haven't asked her yet."

"But shouldn't you? And why is she got up like the angel of death?"

"My presumed father died last week. You mustn't think, on account of her costume and sometimes outspoken manner, that Lady D. is in any way sinister. Eccentric, yes, and a bit of a show-off, too. But she's just rescued me from the total void of my life. Oum's work was finished, every thread of human connection snapped—the hour of desperation struck for both of us, and brought us together again."

"A woman who did what she did, in her own bed, to her own son—and you can still say, Mother knows best?"

Muffled laughter at the far end of the room makes us both look round. Veil lifted, martini glass in hand, yellow cigarette dangling from mouth, Lady D. whispers something in Freddy's ear. His handsome mask relaxes, more completely than I've ever seen, with amusement. I remark that they seem to be getting on very well, but Denna hurries over to them, linking her arm in Freddy's.

"Now what have I missed?"

He stares at her, enigmatic again. "Nothing important."

"Time presses, Norman dear." Lady D. lowers her veil again and nods to Denna. "Such a charming visit. I love your house and admire your work." Freddy makes a point of seeing us to the door. He and Lady D. exchange a silent goodby, in which I detect a note of conspiracy. So does Denna, who hovers in the background with a slightly forced smile. "Though we've hardly spoken," she whispers to me, "I feel that I know your mother. Please get in touch if there's anything I can do to help." With a last wave to Freddy, Lady D. enters our taxi. We leave through the tunnel of overhanging trees.

"Tell me what you said to him."

"As you know, my dear, I believe in taking the bull by the horns. So I explained that I knew everything, and couldn't understand why his little wife made such a fuss—if she truly believes Ritualistic Orgies are all they're cracked up to be, why didn't she join in and try her hand at some Absolute Reality that night, instead of creating such a conventional scene?"

"Was he struck by the force of your argument?"

"Well, he wanted us both to stay." Lays her head on my shoulder. "In any case, he's no longer frightened of that strangely bourgeois woman. I gave him a stick to beat her with. Not that I wish her any harm, of course, but as I've told you before the only time I ever interfere is when I see people intimidated." As if to bear this out, she doesn't ask what Denna and I talked about, but admires the scenery as we start slowly down the winding mountain road.

Ciudad Juarez-Vera Cruz
20th of June, 1943

For the first time since Lady D.'s arrival, events strike me as a little too much out of the ordinary. When I examine them one by one, there's nothing I can put an alarmed finger on; all, if you accept the premises, seems logical and just; though I'm no longer frightened by anything I see, and no insult or threat has come my way, I begin to suspect *things I don't see, words I don't hear,* the *absence* of any specific warning in the air. Can you imagine what a delicious but appalling sense of terror this instills? Naturally I keep it to myself, like smuggled goods, since *she* remains calm, veiled, black, thoughtful, affectionate, nerveless, utterly in command.

As the long, uncomfortable journey began, a consciousness of hours and days returned. I knew the time, the date, the temperature (91 degrees); then looked out of the train window, saw miles of empty desert in the harsh and poignant Mexican light, was crushed by what seemed an infinity of dust, sand, stones, donkeys, filth and the occasional solitary person vegetating in a kind of helpless, stupid grandeur. No phantom voice this time to whisper *Ah God, dear God, that night when two dark eyes* or other teasing verses —but instead this figure sitting opposite me, intently reading *The Crowns of Seclusion* while I continued my letter, and two mounds of stiff pages, read and unread, formed like an hourglass at her side.

Still dazed but apprehensive, no longer sure whether anything was for better or for worse, I felt her glance upon me while I wrote and imagined her faint, inquiring smile.

"You know, my dear, you never told me what he looked like. Can't you make him real for me?"

After thinking it over, I knew that I'd totally forgotten. I could remember, of course, every detail of our encounter; could find my way blindfolded to that house; could draw a picture of mattress, lantern, shuttered window, tiled floor, stripped body with open arms; could feel or smell breath, skin, musk, sweat, laugh, growl, bite, and all resulting splendors; but couldn't, even when I closed my eyes, summon any part of the magic face.

"Was he tall?"

"Quite tall."

"Eyes?"

"Dark, I think."

"What about his mouth?"

"A charming smile."

"Nice strong hands, I suppose?"

"Very."

"If you'd rather not, I understand."

We sat in a public compartment, since there were no private ones; at night it became a Pullman. A steward with grimy fingernails tipped up our seats, converted them to narrow, coffin-like beds with rough, prickly blankets, then drew a kind of hairshirt curtain across the compartment. Slipping off her weeds, Lady D. lay down on her bunk with a bottle of Mexican brandy and pages of my huge poem; I dozed off at last, only to be woken by the sound of a whistle blowing shrilly at nothing—the train had stopped, like an animal sensing hidden danger, in the middle of a plain dotted with motionless silhouettes of cactus.

"Don't fidget, Norman. Nothing is wrong. So much of what seems mysterious in these countries is just incompetence."

After a brief, cool wait in the terminal of Mexico City at dusk, the usual gloomy vista of gray-roofed courtyard, barred gates, drifts of smoke across naked, spectral lights, we boarded another reluctant express. During the night I awoke with the sensation of being lowered down a sheer, precipitous mountainside, and in the morning found it confirmed. Looming wall behind, dense tropic lowlands beneath, and we slid towards flowers bursting into scarlet and purple, glittering foliage that clawed against the windows. Air grew soft and steamy, a Negro came up with bottles of urine-green liquid on a dirty tray, I sniffed familiar sweet and sour mixtures, felt my heart lurch and polished off Lady D.'s brandy. She continued to read, unbothered by mosquitos, which could find no dent in her armor of mourning.

In a hotel

Train parked in a field of hibiscus and palm; we had arrived at Vera Cruz. My spirits rose when nothing I saw looked quite real. Appearances had the improvised, theatrical tone of a sultry climate, atmosphere too lazy to be confusing, buildings too light and casual to last—it affected even Lady D., who paused to pluck a yellow rose from ramblers pushing through the barrier, and stuck it in her veil beside an ear.

Taxi drove us to the vivid, ramshackle town, narrow streets with houses painted in fading seashell colors, coral, sand and summer blue. The balcony of my bedroom overlooks a Plaza with tiled benches and an elaborate fountain that hardly even drips with water. Sweet, ridiculous music comes from somewhere, cascade of harp and tap-dance of xylophone. I remove this letter from its strongbox; paper clip falls off immediately and pages scatter to the floor, settling there in a disorder of years, places, fantastic humiliations. I fasten them back together, then search my so-called youth to find, Ahmin, how I described you at our first and only encounter, in 1936. . . . Serious omission! Hair, eyes, nose, cheekbones, mouth, etc.—*where are they?* Unreachable as a ship on the horizon. You know that dreadful sound of a bell ringing forever throughout an empty house?

Below, in a glare of sunlight on the Plaza, I notice a tall and boyishly slim figure in a faded red T-shirt and belted workman's trousers—the material called chino, I believe. He stoops over the fountain to splash his face with cooling water from its wretched little jet. Not Mexican, which is probably why his presence intrigues me. I put on dark glasses to see more clearly. Rusty hair, a pale and perhaps freckled skin, eyes no doubt blue, wears "sneakers"—as I finish the inventory, he glances up without appearing to observe me, moves on, crosses the street in front of this hotel. Usually I'm quick to respond to an exotic person in a setting that contradicts him; now, by some odd reversal, the opposite arouses me. I withdraw at once in confusion, and lie on the bed. A minute later, someone tries my door from the outside. Knob turns, door slowly opens, my throat goes dry—and Lady D. enters, carrying a small mountain of papers.

She's changed her costume, which is still black but less dazzlingly so: simple short-sleeved dress with a large bow above the buttocks, little and rather girlish one in her hair. The result might be described as versatile, equally correct for a cocktail party or mourning. She lays *The Crowns of Seclusion* on top of a chest, sits on the edge of my bed and gives me one of her slow, ironic, third-degree looks. It seems the moment to ask her what she thinks she's up to. Several years ago, I point out, a mulatto sea captain dumped me without explanation in Costa Rica. No comparison intended, but why has she led me, so peremptory and mysterious, to this remote tropical port?

"I just wanted you to feel at home."

"I'm sure it's my own fault, but I've lost my bearings."

"Don't we all, my dear, from time to time? It's very confusing to stay too long in one place. I found that out for myself, by myself, during those lonely years at The House, and was only put back on my feet when Maurice swept me off them." Takes my hand. "Equatorially speaking, we've drawn up alongside the heart of your beloved Sahara. Since it happens to be inaccessible at the moment, I racked my brains—as so often in these troubled times—for the best and most practical substitute. Only one shadow, Norman, has ever fallen between us. You've always suspected—*feared*, I suppose, would be the better word—that in some obscure way I disapproved of you. But I'm a less conventional woman than you think. How can I convince my son that I'm no ordinary mother except by taking his hand, leading him like a horse to water, and begging him, on my knees if necessary, to drink?"

As I listened, bewilderment gave way to understanding, shock to reverence; old, almost atavistic sensation returned of being patted and cuddled, lifted up from cold staircase and tenderly placed in a warm and noble bed. Fatigued, queasy and confused as I was, I could recognize blindness falling away at last, could silently marvel at the mind of this extraordinary, tragic and patient woman, could receive, through the touch of her hand and the sound of her voice, a transfusion of the sane hard-headed strength I'd always lacked. Only hoped it wasn't too late. Let me confess, too, that I've misjudged a few people in my life—but if Lady D. was my most drastic error, can I really be blamed? Remember the nanny who poisoned me against her, and the famous professor in Vienna who listened to my tale, then glibly catalogued me as Case 43!

She moved away now, walked to the threshold of the balcony. "I once remarked that all I wanted was for my children to lead their own lives." Lit a cigarette. "Violet, at least, has done so—and though the reckoning may come from a cruel and prejudiced world, I shall do my best to save the poor dear girl from it." Wisp of smoke curled towards me. "Now it's *your* turn. I read your poem, all of it, and found it quite charming in its way—but shouldn't a boy *live* a little before he settles for mere wisdom, solitude, dedication, and the desert of the inner life?" Pointed a steady finger at the Plaza below. "Night will soon fall. Down there, around the corner from that picturesque square, there's an odd little street that leads to the waterfront and other points of interest. I happen to be pleasantly tired; I shall eat a light supper, take to my bed and sleep at last, if I can stop thinking of Maurice. So why don't you go out and amuse yourself this evening?"

Then the door closed, leaving me alone with an echo of smoke and perfume in the late, heady afternoon.

In a small room with no view

Dawn, I should imagine. Atmosphere misty and suspended, anyway. Might have been seriously discouraged if I hadn't, at this very odd and annoying moment, scrounged around and come up with a nasty stub of black pencil and, believe it or not, *three large paper bags*. Folded and tore them into manageable octavo strips, upon which I shall scribble until the situation improves.

It began with taking Lady D.'s advice and setting out a little before dusk. My only departure from her itinerary was to arrive at the waterfront first, by a somewhat roundabout route. There was no reason for this, except that quirk of obstinacy in my nature which demands the illusion of free will. I found a long, breezy, cobbled stretch of quay, appealing in a mildly raffish way: Negroes stripped to the waist as they unloaded a freighter, a woman with a black eye shouting abuse at two sailors, the remains of a pair of yellow shorts, understandably abandoned, on the bench where I chose to sit. Strum of guitar from a boat on the bright, restless water; stink of shellfish from the row of vendors' stalls. As darkness crept up, figures hardened into silhouettes, poignant reminder of another waterfront on the far side of the Equator.

Some time later, after a dinner of fish soup and insolent pink wine, I turned into the little street off the square: moody sailors' hotels, with an impression of faces behind each narrow, darkened window, bodies stirring on the shadowed balconies. I pushed at a shuttered swing door and found myself the only customer in a dimly lit bar with a hideous oleograph of the Virgin Mary above the counter. A wave of surprise, disappointment and relief broke over me, which I disguised by giving the barman a curt nod, sitting down at a table and ordering a glass of beer. One glance was enough to show that the place lacked everything except ugliness—view of brownish, peeling walls, rough wooden tables and chairs, spidery fan, Our Lady garish but mournful between rows of bottles. From the hip pocket of my trousers I removed a Tauchnitz edition of *The Strange Case of Miss Annie Spragge* by Louis Bromfield, typical reading matter stocked in the lobbies of remote foreign hotels. Towards the end of Chapter One a few Scandinavian seamen arrived and sat at the bar, ignoring me. Whores followed. Barman switched on a radio, filling the warm room with sad and brassy popular music. Cantina door swung open again, another whore surveyed the scene, grimaced and slouched away. All of this struck me as unpromising.

When I entered the bar next door, the only difference was no music playing. Ignored again, I ordered a beer, sat down at a table, felt prickles of sweat on my forehead. Cantina door swung open. The young man I'd seen at the fountain in the square came in; noticed me, but gave no sign; sat on a stool at the counter; smiled faintly to himself; whistled snatches of a tune and seemed, unlike myself, completely at ease. I judged him American, twenty years old, a country boy of quite good family. He wasn't particularly handsome, but sturdy, cheerful and open, the opposite in every way of a person like Scotty. Let me admit, Ahmin, that he reminded me of *you*. If you think this odd, remember that *I* can't remember clearly what you look like. When I wondered what he was doing here, every possible explanation seemed a little shady, which was disconcerting—but couldn't he have been equally uncertain about the immaculate though perspiring Englishman watching him from a table in the corner? My thoughts were interrupted as a large whore came up and informed me she was available for fifty pesos. When I declined, she laughed, drank the rest of my beer and flounced off, well pleased with herself.

Back with my speculations, I decided the young man was most probably a deserter. My sympathy for him increased. I ordered another beer, put a cigarette in my mouth, reached for a match and was forestalled by an already lighted one appearing under my nose. He lit his own cigarette after mine, then turned casually away. Cantina door swung closed.

When I returned to the first bar, I noticed him sitting at the counter, still by himself, cheerfully disassociated from his surroundings, untroubled by the merciless radio at his ear. I stood next to him to order my beer, received no acknowledgment, impulsively changed my order to two and handed him a bottle. He nodded his thanks and showed no surprise. Wind taken out of my sails, to use one of Nanny Gray's favorite expressions, I could think of nothing to say—or, rather, shout—and retreated to a table. Sat for a while, drooping and becalmed, had *pulque* spilt all over my shirt by a passing whore, who merely laughed, but determined not to *give in* and didn't budge. However, when I looked up after this interruption, he had gone.

The shock went straight to my bladder. At the back of the room I found a listing door, gave it a shove and entered a dark, stifling, unspeakable latrine. My relief at discovering him there was followed by dread that he might suspect me of following him. Hoping to dispel his fears, I chose a trough some distance away from him and stood staring at the wall in nauseated silence. After what seemed a decent interval, I said that I guessed he was an American. He made an offhand sound that I took for assent, so I inquired his name.

A curious hesitation followed. Then, almost reluctantly: "Ned."

"A very short name."

No answer. He moved towards the door.

"My own is somewhat longer."

"Maybe so. But this place smells terrible and I'm getting out of it."

When I emerged, he was sitting at the other end of the bar, near the cantina door. This time he recognized me and accepted my offer of another beer in the same manner. As he drank from the bottle, his eyes watched me with a mocking but, I thought, genial amusement.

"Tell me your long name."

"Norman Charles Evelyn Lightwood."

"Jesus Christ. What kind of a name is that?"

"Lightwood is the family name. My presumed father was Charles Evelyn. My grandfather was Norman Charles Maurice. And so on and so on. Our names have always kept within a rather tight little circle."

"Why?"

"Perhaps, if you're wellborn, it's considered vulgar to show off by calling yourself Hugo or Vernon." I felt myself warming up. "Take the famous Cecil family. After three hundred years, most of the men are still Robert. Or think of all those kings of England called Henry and George. Quite frankly, *I'd* feel better off without Evelyn."

"Who wouldn't?" said Ned. Looked at me with the same mocking expression. "So what are you—some kind of earl, or count?"

"We don't have counts over there. My rank, I'm afraid, is the lowest. I'm just a baronet, which entitles me to call myself, though I never do, Sir Norman Charles Evelyn Lightwood, Bart."

"How about a castle to go with all that?"

"It's not really a castle, only a house with fifty-three rooms. I built a kind of castle in New Mexico recently. But I'm not living in either one at present, as you see."

"Come off it."

"Though I admit it's odd to run into me here, everything I've told you is true."

"Jesus Christ. They ought to lock you up."

I found this reaction, for various reasons, unattractive. "You shouldn't resent someone just because he's out of the ordinary."

He smiled broadly. All the strength and openness of his

face came back, and I realized I'd misjudged him. It was a case of simple wonder a little crudely expressed, and he couldn't be blamed for it. He gave me a light punch on the shoulder, then rocked on his heels, whistling to himself.

"May I ask where you come from, Ned?"

He hesitated again. "Yuma, Arizona. We only got six rooms."

"And how did you get here?"

"Hitched." He slid off the stool. "You'd better not stay here," he said.

"Why?"

"Anything could happen."

My absence of fear was exhilarating. "I doubt it. I've been totally ignored, except by you."

Shook his head. "They've got your number. They know there's a rich nut in town, waiting to be rolled."

I knew it too, of course, but since Lady D. had advised me to take the greedy, cunning world for granted and shown how perfect grandeur could cast out fear, I asked Ned with a kind of amused weariness what he thought I should do. Two minutes later we walked together through the town, under a sliver of golden moon; beyond the little street of bars and hotels, all was empty and silent. Our footsteps echoed along the quay; lights nodded on boats at anchor; I followed him through narrow, unfamiliar streets, past dark houses, almost expecting to see a beggarwoman crouched against a wall. At last we came to a heavy door, set in a thick, blind facade. He turned a key in a rusty lock. We entered a courtyard, climbed some unlighted stairs; he whispered to me that everyone was asleep and unlocked another door. When he switched on a lamp I saw a bare little room with a bedstead, a low easy chair with faded serape thrown across it, a trunk with flaked blue paint, a stone floor cracked across the middle and shutters blocking out the window. Air felt stale and warm, with the ancient, unavoidable, plaintive, far-off residuum of dung.

"Sit down." Ned indicated the chair, opened the trunk, took out a bottle of tequila and two clouded glasses. After he'd poured me a drink, he sat on the bed and stared at me with a bright, wondering smile. "Question," he said. "What kind of a person do you think I am?"

"You're an enigma."

Smile vanished. "You calling me ignorant?"

"No. The word was *enigma*. It means *mystery*."

"Jesus Christ, *you're* the mystery." Smiled again. Whistled for a moment. "What are you doing, hanging around bars like that? Giving lectures on British families and castles?"

"It's the first time I've been there. We only arrived this morning."

"Who's 'we'?"

"My recently widowed mother, Lady D."

"Now I've heard everything. But go on. I like to hear you talk. You're out of your Chinese mind, but I like it. Say your name again, all of it."

"Sir Norman Charles Evelyn Lightwood."

"There was more last time."

"I forgot the Bart. But let's get back to the enigma," I said. "It answers to the name of Ned, was born in Arizona but resides in Vera Cruz, for reasons undisclosed. Apart from obvious personal charm, the rest is hidden."

He didn't answer but came over and refilled my glass, whistling, then returned to the bed and sat smiling at me.

For the first time, his smile struck me as a little oafish, possibly simple-minded. I had a brief, thrilling fantasy that he might be a kind of primitive genius, a Rimbaud, appearing coarse and cloddish when he was secretly dazed with occult rages and visions. . . . *"Better relax,"* his voice cut through, and I looked up with a start to find simplicity and smile had disappeared. "Instead of shooting off your mouth," and the voice itself sounded harsh, "why don't you offer me thirty dollars?"

Certain that I'd misheard, I reached for the tequila bottle and poured myself another glass. "Answers to the name of Ned," I said. "Let's get back to the enigma."

"There isn't one. Do you want it for thirty dollars?"

Instinct warned me not to call his bluff. I didn't know why he was lying, trying to behave like Scotty or the man from Denver, and the combination of wine, beer, tequila and heat, to say nothing of recent events, had dulled my usual quickness; but the sight of his face, wearing its pathetic mask of ruthless indifference, aroused my immediate compassion. I opened my wallet, which was full of Mexican and American bills, and gave him the equivalent of a hundred dollars.

"There you are, my dear Ned. I'm going back to my hotel now."

I turned calmly towards the door, then gasped with pain. Seizing my arm, he twisted it more cruelly than he realized, gave me a shove and landed me back in the chair.

"Have another drink."

I shook my head. He poured it for me. "If you insist," I said, and drank it. He stood right over me, buckle of his belt on a level with my face. "What's your game?" he said, and I knew it was beginning to work.

"Not to make you do anything you don't want."

"Why?"

"I'm only human."

"Well, that's your problem." He smiled and became as he truly was, very young, welcoming, eager. "You've asked for it, you've paid for it and it's got your name on it."

What followed, at the time, felt like ignominy, the rack, and bestial pain. It couldn't have been, of course. For I remember Ned whispering that I'd given his life meaning, and I fell asleep in his arms, —ing* Lady D., hearing a clock strike in the distance and not wanting to know the time.

Now, almost at end of last strip of paper bag, I reach an interval in this puzzling episode. Reluctantly I assume that poor Ned, some time before dawn, fled from me; the room appears to have been completely stripped; I wish he hadn't taken all my clothes as well as his own. The loss of my wallet may also be inconvenient. A little while ago I noticed stains of somebody's blood, dried and brownish, on the sheets. I don't feel as well as I usually do, my mouth is swollen and peculiar bruises show here and there. Naturally this room is without a telephone, the shutters are padlocked and I've already tried the door. All the same, limbo is less disconcerting than I expected. I shall remain in it for the moment, without fear or cigarettes, recalling how often one is obliged to make the best of things.

* Part of word illegible. (*Lady D.*)

Postscript

I AM not a writer, only a woman, a widow and a mother. For many years I have hesitated to offer these pages to that multitude of strangers known as the reading public. Not only personal reasons but the laws of libel gave me pause. Time, however, in its wise and kind-cruel way, has taken care of all my problems. All members of the Lightwood family, with the only known exception of myself, have come to worms and dust; and Miss Lily Vail, that once famous star of stage and screen, has written to me from the isle of Ibiza, where she has settled down with a local admirer, to boast that she's never minded what anyone said about her. Perhaps I have waited too long, for those curiously innocent, carefree decades of the 30's and 40's, during which Norman's candle flickered all too briefly, seem very distant now. The very dramatic change in my own life does not bring them any nearer. For here in Nanga-Jobo, the daily round and common task—be it an outbreak of hookworm among our dear Bantus, or the local witch-doctor and his deluded followers trying to wreck our laboratory again—

occupy most of my waking moments. For twenty years now, at the end of every eventful day, I have usually found it more relaxing to watch a sunset spill over jungle of bamboo and gum tree, than to muse on the past of family and friends.

It may be wondered what led me to become a voluntary helper to the famous Doctor Wilhelm Brod, whose service to humanity is so great that I shall not attempt to describe it. The answer is that for years, without realizing it, I had been asking myself, *"Why?"* Some people are satisfied with wealth, health, desirability, an interest in and talent for the arts. I needed more, which is why I came to share, in my humble but vigorous way, the Doctor's burden. To watch the lot of our less fortunate brothers as we slowly but surely improve it is to remain eternally young, because it satisfies that most important sense of all—Wonder. Obstinate and primitive they may be, but they *are* my brothers, and one day I am convinced they will agree. The reader must forgive me for occasionally intruding my own life, but I believe it to be of considerable interest.

To return to Norman. Doctor Brod has read his letter, of course, and found it quite distasteful. However, he agrees that it displays a certain literary talent, misguidedly put to use as that may be. I regard this as the highest praise, since a man of his fundamental purity and humane preoccupations could not be expected to respond with great enthusiasm to a life so different, and to a temperament that must strike him as a little erratic. He even warned me that certain people might consider it foolhardy of a mother to allow such a portrait of herself to appear in print. That, with all due respect, is easily disposed of. Norman's account of me is not only unflattering, but unrecognizable. By this, I do not mean simply that I have changed. (I hear you ask, Does anyone *really* change? Forgive me if I refuse to enter those deep and treacherous waters.) A sensitive reader, particularly if he happens to be a woman, will soon realize that Norman's perception of what we call reality was not always just. It would be petty of me to suggest that he exaggerated or lied—*de mortuis*, etc.—but I feel obliged to point out that my son, in his attitude toward the weaker sex, was governed by rather special considerations. I believe I am as tolerant as the next woman, but it is useless to close one's eyes—Michelangelo, Proust and two or three others notwithstanding—to the facts of life.

To return. The last sections of Norman's letter are not dated, but we may conclude that it ends on the 28th of July, 1943. We arrived in Vera Cruz on the morning of the 27th, and it seems improbable that he survived beyond noon of the following day. The causes of death were almost too numerous to mention. They certainly included heart failure, which I incline to regard as the *coup de grace*. (He seems to have been unaware of this, but his heart had given him trouble since the age of ten, when Miss Gray—under the influence of alcohol—behaved in a somewhat thoughtless manner.) I believe, however, that my son could have survived *if he had wished to*. What sustained me, after the first shock, was to discover from those final pages that Norman left this world with a good grace and high humor—feeling, as it were, that he'd had his say. Pessimists will no doubt emphasize the irony of a person who was always fearing and imagining the worst, who at last conquered fear (with his mother's help) and who could not then recognize the worst when it finally arrived. That is their own affair. I prefer to stress that Norman, in his last moments, kept his unique sense of humor and his basic faith in the goodness of humanity—blind, on this particular occasion, though that faith may have been. Doctor Brod agrees with me on this, and pointed out after reading the letter that at least Norman believed (wrongly but admirably) that he'd found a friend. I refer to the young man referred to as Ned.

On the morning of July 28th, I was not unduly concerned to discover that my son had been out all night. He was, after all, thirty-three years old. Only when he failed to return, or get in touch with me, after two more days did I feel mildly uneasy. By the end of the third afternoon I had to face the fact that he'd met with some misfortune. (The only other possibility was that he'd run away, and obviously I dismissed it.) I donned my full mourning and began to make inquiries from sailors and barmen. A few remembered someone answering to my son's description, but that was all. I suspected them of holding back, fearing a brush with the law, and since some of the sailors were German, of allowing the international situation to harden their hearts. As a woman, a widow and a British national, I began to feel helpless. Reluctantly I reported the matter to the police, who struck me as lazy and casual, but promised to make an investigation.

I piece together the next events from what was reported to me. The only element of them that might be called firsthand is my own agony. Next day, the resident of an apartment house in the poorest, most remote quarter of the town detected an odd smell coming from behind a locked door.

The reason she hadn't noticed it sooner, since she passed that door every day, was the general prevalence of smells in her neighborhood. The woman, a local prostitute, good-hearted so far as I could judge, decided—with another member of the sisterhood—to break down the door. The *senoritas* found, in the little room beyond, my dead and naked son lying on a bed. Strips of brown paper covered with writing they couldn't understand were at his side. His body bore marks that suggested physical attack. To those of us fortunate enough to reside in more civilized communities, it may seem surprising that the *senoritas* decided not to go to the police. Mysterious ends being not uncommon, alas, in the underworld of Mrs. Warren's profession, they too were frightened of a brush with the law. Instead, they reported their find to a mutual friend, and this *senor,* who happened to be their landlord as well, took steps to dispose of the body in secret. It was therefore placed in a sack, weighted with stones and rolled into the Gulf of Mexico at night. Needless to say, this somewhat amateurish device failed. The sack burst and the body floated to the surface next morning, where it was sighted by a local *grande dame,* owner of a villa on the seafront, as she began her usual early stroll along the beach before the sun rose too high. I was asked to identify it and take it away.

I should like to mention, though I cannot describe, the expression on Norman's face. At some point ecstasy must have overcome terror, for in all the years I had known my son, I never saw him look happier.

Naturally I wished to return to England with him, and arrange for a quiet, simple funeral; his condition, to say nothing of a time of war, made my task not altogether easy;

however, the Esperanto of money broke down all barriers, and the captain of a Portuguese freighter agreed to take us on board for a sum on which he could have retired for life. Our journey back to the war-torn island I hadn't seen for years was, as can be imagined, long, rough and dangerous. I couldn't help reflecting how different it was from any return that either of us could have planned. Once again, I shall not dwell on my agony. My first act upon arrival in London was to ask Parkinson and Parkinson to make all arrangements. They informed me that Norman had deposited a will in their office safe shortly after his divorce from Lily Vail, and we consulted it to see if he had any personal views on his final rites. (The disposition of his fortune, incidentally, included twenty thousand pounds to the Arab youth, Ahmin; the same amount to found a Society for the Identification of Mysterious Objects, which I shall touch on later; a fairly generous bequest to myself, if I survived him and the rest to Violet, provided she did not marry.) Since he asked to be buried wearing the *djellabah* of Oum Salem, I made immediate inquiries, and though having it shipped from the establishment at Kuola involved yet another postponement, I wished to respect all his whims.

So, during a slight drizzle on a chilly autumn day, Norman Charles Evelyn Lightwood, eleventh and last baronet, was laid to rest, in the faded robe of his beloved though non-existent poetess, in the family vault at Appleton-on-Waveney. He lies between his Aunt Beatrice and his Uncle Hector. After the ceremony, attended only by myself and our faithful Ellen, I walked up to look at The House. It was still occupied by civil servants, of course, and I didn't wish to add to my grief by seeing what havoc they might have wrought inside. The sight of our favorite walks, of my studio, the lawn where the Object fell, the cedars chopped down and the great Clematis no more, was melancholy enough.

Wartime conditions made it impossible for me to think of tracing the Arab youth; so, unfortunately, did peace at last. Since Norman never recorded his full name, and left no description by which he could have been identified, that task remained undone. I took it upon myself, however, to try to publish *The Crowns of Seclusion*. Although no firm displayed any interest in it, I had five hundred copies printed at my own expense when paper restrictions eased some time after the war. Only one magazine reviewed it, not very favorably, the critic's opinion being that Oum was essentially a miniaturist, unable to avoid a certain monotony when she attempted the larger forms. At least, I reflected, Norman did not live to endure this—though if he had, can it be said who, in fact, would have had the last laugh?

Factually speaking, I have reached the end of Norman's story. For the rest, I dare say that some people will be disappointed at my refusal to make clear what, in his letter, is true or untrue. I take this stand for various reasons. Sometimes I do not know. Sometimes I don't quite remember. If I deny certain things, shall I not be accused of trying to "clear" myself, or "blame" Norman? And finally, who can say what is truth and what, illusion? I advise readers to bear in mind, all the same, that certain things related in the letter will strike them as immediately improbable, or fantastic; at these moments, the old adages not to judge by first impressions and that appearances are deceptive may come in useful.

Another warning. The idea that my son—and even, by association, myself—should be considered, from a social or psychoanalytical point of view, as either "representative" figures or curios will bear little fruit. As Norman's admired William Blake remarked, to generalize is to be an idiot. I suppose that both our lives have momentarily touched on such abstractions as the silver spoon and the ivory tower, motherhood, bastardy, orientalism, and various other phenomena of our times; but one remark of Norman's at least I wholly agree with—*what are we, except what we know and what happens to us?* That, in my opinion, is finely said.

Which brings me to the Object. I wish publicly to confirm that it *did* fall and I shot it. In his unquestioning acceptance of this little memento from the sky, Norman was—as in certain other ways—ahead of his time. Today, with flying saucers constantly zooming around us, it seems a mild enough occurrence. Since endowing the Society for the Identification of Mysterious Objects, as he requested, I have received several thousand eyewitness accounts of falling animals, wheels, pig iron, blood, damp hay and so on. Quite a few land hereabouts; the dark continent seems especially to attract them. Last week, for instance, while taking an evening stroll in the jungle, I was startled by an unfamiliar sound, aimed my gun and then lowered it when I saw only a harmless fall of fish. To those who may still scoff, I remark that Doctor Brod's station is a hundred miles from the ocean, and seventy-six from the nearest river. Moreover, they were fish completely unknown in these parts—hake, as a matter of fact, a species of cod found only in the North Atlantic and the Baltic Sea, and therefore never could have swum, walked or flown a distance of more than two thousand miles. To judge from the flurry, there must have been a large pailful heading in my direction. I managed to retrieve three, brought them to Doctor Brod, who confirms this conclusion, and have kept them pickled in jars in my bedroom, as a constant reminder—not that I need it—that there are more things in heaven and earth than are dreamt of in most philosophies.

Now I shall be bold enough to relate a few things that occurred, principally to myself, after my son was laid to rest. Feeling homeless and abandoned, I drove to London and engaged a suite at the Ritz Hotel. The blackout, the air raids and the petty food restrictions were disagreeable reminders of changing times, but I managed not to be depressed by them. One day I took a walk down Bond Street, remarking its loss of elegance and charm and the rubble taken sadly for granted. Ignoring the hawkers, street entertainers, cripples and dwarfs blowing trumpets and so on, my eye was caught by a Rolls-Royce parked outside the shell of a building. It seemed vaguely familiar. A glance at the license plate identified it as the vehicle that once belonged to my cousin Beatrice. A female hand in a long, black glove, diamonds glittering on the suede, extended from the window, the fingers crooking and beckoning. A small boy was buying some kind of toy from a pavement vendor immediately outside, and I deduced that glove, diamonds and hand belonged to his mother, who wished him to hurry up. Then the lady herself, wearing a broad-brimmed hat, leaned out and called, "My God, come along, will you, you little horror?" A moment later she saw me approaching, and waved. "Well, if it isn't old Dotty!"

So I came upon Lily Vail, the star of stage and screen. "Well, Miss Lily," I said, polite but reserved, and she offered to give me a lift back to my hotel. The child was ordered to sit up front, next to the chauffeur, and I took my place in the sumptuous rear, beside the irrepressible ex-wife of my dead son. Naturally I was somewhat moved, above all to find myself in the Rolls that held such intimate memories for me. But I refrained from letting Lily know the particular car she'd bought, and said merely that I'd had no idea she had married again and was the mother of a little boy.

"I haven't, and it's not mine," she informed me. "It's *his,*" by which I understood her to mean the film producer who launched her career. Quite openly she told me they'd lived together for two years; he was married, but his wife got hit by a bomb in one of the first air raids, and remained in the twilight of coma. Under the circumstances, a divorce would have seemed in bad taste. I thought to myself that everything else certainly *was* in bad taste, particularly the way Lily referred to her lover and benefactor. She affected to be unable to pronounce his name, because it was Roumanian and had seven syllables. She used the phrase, "sexual magnetism of the tremendously ugly," and expressed sorrow but not surprise over Norman. She never could understand, she told me, the fascination of the upper class with the gutter. "I know opposites are supposed to attract, but everything that's opposite isn't necessarily attractive." Then she playfully ruffled my hair. "You're looking wonderful for seventy, Dotty, I must say. Tell me your secret—I may need it one day."

I replied that I was sorry to disappoint her, but I would be sixty-eight next month, ate and drank what I liked, and despised all rejuvenation methods, whether involving surgery or mere night creams. I implied that youth was an internal matter and thought she looked very well, considering. Indeed, beneath the inappropriate finery, including her hair, bleached even lighter and worn pompadour style, the little face looked pert and childlike as ever. I was sure she'd have a great success as Peter Pan, which she was on her way to rehearse. "It's really a sinister, dirty play," she said. "I'm hoping to get that across." A wink and a nudge followed as we drew up outside the Ritz. Standing in the colonnade, I watched the Rolls drive away down Piccadilly, past hotels and ruins.

Not long after this I decided—to the astonishment of everyone I knew, including myself—to buy a public house. It was the first sign of dissatisfaction stirring within me, like a weevil in the depths of a tree; painting was not enough, for in these times to convey, however exquisitely, the orangeness of an orange, left me feeling too "special" and cut-off. The protests of loyal but somewhat old-fashioned friends, such as the Hon. Dorothy Fielding and the senior Parkinson—touchingly shocked at the idea of a distinguished widow pumping beer—only made me realize that my circle of acquaintances was in need of broadening. I discovered a charming place on the Embankment, near Chelsea, with a classic Edwardian interior of tinted mirrors and art nouveau chandeliers, wasting away through slipshod management. When I bought it, the press was kind enough to notice the fact; oddly enough, I at once attracted a large and somewhat raffish bohemian crowd. Those who lived in London from February, 1944, to the end of the war, and who enjoyed an evening of steady drinking, good conversation and unexpected romantic encounters, no doubt remember *The Port of Call* as a kind of landmark. It was vastly crowded, except for the weeks when business declined after a raid from the police, and gave me the interesting sensation of putting my finger, as it were, on the pulse of the times. The habitués nicknamed me Mother Lightwood, a mark of affection, not disrespect. I was invited to many lively and unusual parties, often given by young men rejected as unfit for military service, in spite of all their efforts, and eking out a living in the chorus line of a musical comedy. On these occasions I saw Lily Vail from time to time. She had reached the peak of her popularity but had to be assisted home.

If, considering my background and present connection with Doctor Brod, a few conventional eyebrows are raised at this account of my earlier activities, my answer is ready. It so happens that as I wrote the above paragraph, the Doctor himself entered my little room. I could tell from his expression that something extraordinary had happened, though he was trying to appear calm. You may have guessed. He had just been awarded a Nobel Prize. I asked him if a mention of my *Port of Call* period in this postscript might be undesirable, and I quote his reply: "Your life has been so extraordinary that one surprise more or less can make little difference."

With the fall of Berlin, my thoughts naturally turned to Violet. Since the privileges of rank counted for less than they used to, my request for an interview with the Home Secretary was somewhat curtly dismissed. I also wrote to the director of the Secret Service, reminding him that we'd met in Paris in 1935, and offering to foot the bill for an agent to be specially assigned to "Operation Violet," as I called it—in other words, a mission to discover the whereabouts of my daughter. He lacked even the courtesy to answer. I record this as historical fact, in no spirit of complaint. Nevertheless, it was a disheartening experience for a mother wondering if her daughter might be trapped in a blazing German bunker. Helpless, I was reduced to scanning newspaper photographs of slain or captured Nazis, and was relieved not to find Violet among them. In the meantime, I *was* able to evict the Government from The House at Appleton-on-Waveney. I returned there for a rest, but the place felt lonely without my children, too large for a single widow. I passed sad weeks engaging servants and itemizing the damage, which was unbelievable; then I changed my mind—these were restless days—and put the whole thing up for sale. It would make an excellent school or prison, I thought, and was eventually proved right. Faced with my suit for repairs, the Government offered to buy it instead, and it is now a home for delinquent girls under the age of twenty-one. Interestingly enough, Lightwoods have always been lucky with property. In his letter, Norman fails to mention that we owned the village as well as The House. Years later, when an aircraft company wished to build a new plant there, I sold it all. About the same time, a rich yield of pitchblende was discovered in the mountain slopes above the goat corral at Kuola. This rare mineral, the source of uranium and radium, made the land infinitely more valuable. I sold it too, over the protests of Denna Marx, who wished to preserve her Avenue. Naturally I was sympathetic, and felt a qualm over the destruction of this unusual work, but there was nothing I could do. Besides, I had more important things on my mind. A fraction of my now alarming fortune was enough to build Doctor Brod a new laboratory, clear a stretch of jungle to build a new native village and ensure the life of his station for another twenty years. All this reminds me of that little poem which compares life to a game of whist. "*. . . From unseen sources The Cards are shuffled and The Hands are dealt.*"

But I anticipate. Three years passed with no news of Violet, which in one sense was good—at least she wasn't under arrest—and in another, less so—was she dead or alive? Once again I draw attention to my agony, and pass over it. The summer of 1948 found me in Monte Carlo, and as I went aboard the yacht of King Farouk for a party, I wondered whether I was beginning to drift. During the evening, I noticed an Egyptian lady staring at me in a rather odd way. Since she wore the traditional garb of Islam, with a heavy veil across the lower part of her face, I couldn't see much of her, and since she spoke no English, we couldn't converse. I gathered she was there to chaperone a favorite niece of the monarch, of whom she was said to disapprove. Be that as it may, I was surprised to receive through an interpreter an invitation to proceed to her villa in Luxor by private plane the next day. My first instinct, hardly knowing the woman, was to refuse politely; but in my present situation I felt like a leaf in the wind, and decided to flutter where it blew. Rumors had reached me of the habits of Egyptian ladies, the result of their feudal seclusion, and I can say without immodesty that at seventy-three I looked a slim and quite provocative forty-four; it was a relief, therefore, to discover that my hostess had the lesser eccentricity of disliking loneliness, and extending hospitality to whoever happened to be in her neighborhood when she felt an attack of it coming on. I would be simply one of a mixed group.

The villa lay south of the village itself, on the east and more verdant bank of the Nile, screened by immense banana plants and guarded by two sandstone figures, each more than sixty feet high, representing Gods of the Dead. I walked straight to the terrace to drink my fill of an incredibly beautiful sunset. The sun dropped low and golden over the west bank, with its desolate hills surrounding the Valley of the Kings, and the moon rose high and silver over the east, above my head. Feluccas with their tall masts glided along the swift, wide river, an ibis or two waded in the shallows, and a group of *fellahin* still toiled devotedly in the nearby beanfields. While I gazed at this magical scene, reflecting how little had changed here over the centuries, imagine my surprise at hearing a female voice whisper in my ear: "*Sprechen zie Deutsch?*"

My hostess, a veiled and enigmatic shadow in the fading light, had come up behind me. I informed her calmly that I could speak only English, French, Italian, Spanish and a smattering of Gaelic. In a heavy Teutonic accent, the Egyptian lady told me that English would do, and her name was Ilse von Knoop. "I'm afraid," said I, "that means nothing to me." Then, in a flash, I realized this wasn't true, and remembered Norman telling me that Violet had telephoned a powerful friend in Berlin before finally leaving her native shore. "Forgive me," I corrected myself. "You knew my daughter." She nodded, laying a hand on my arm, and told me that arrangements could be made for me to see her soon. Naturally I was overjoyed to learn that my dear girl was safe, and begged von Knoop for further details. Swearing me to secrecy, reminding me this house party was a "blind" so that we could have a few words together without arousing suspicion and warning me that from now on I would be watched, my hostess told me of Violet's escape to Lisbon, where she lay hidden for several months; of her removal to a "clinic," in a country and of a nature she couldn't reveal, where "work" (also not specified) had to be done on her; and of her recent arrival in Cairo, which contained a few influential people sympathetic to her defeated cause. At that moment, other guests appeared on the terrace. I managed to exclaim, most convincingly, on the loveliness of our surroundings.

The next few days, as can be imagined, were like a dream. I accompanied the other guests on sight-seeing trips to the splendors of Pharaonic Egypt, but tombs, temples, pylons and wall-paintings passed before my eyes in a meaningless blur. At last my mysterious and formidable hostess told me that everything was in order, and I left for Cairo in her private plane. A chauffeured limousine met me at the airport, and drove me smoothly and silently to Ma'adi, an outlying suburb on the banks of the Nile. The chauffeur was Arab, but with pale blue eyes that watched me coldly in the driving mirror. Ma'adi itself reminded me a little of Biarritz, with handsome turn-of-the-century villas, flowering trees, enclosed courtyards and a scent of jasmine in the air. I remarked that most of the inhabitants, walking dogs or watering trees on the street, were somewhat westernized women. Quite a few wore slacks. We stopped outside a gate in a high wall. I stepped out of the car, smiled at my chauffeur, who did not respond, and rang a bell. After some while, an Egyptian houseboy approached through the patio. Hounds barked from within the house. As instructed, I murmured "*Agarthi,*" not without the feeling of being asked to play a rather childish and old-fashioned game. The boy admitted me, I followed him into the house and was left to wait in a large living room furnished with English Victorian pieces. Light filtered sparsely through louvered shutters. The atmosphere reminded me a little of a London club for gentlemen only.

You know the sensation that someone you cannot see is watching you? I had it now. A pair of eyes, I knew, was on me. Lighting a cigarette, I strolled over to a piano I noticed in the corner and strummed a few bars of Chopin. Then, from the shadowy opposite end of the room, a young man stepped forward. He was deeply suntanned, with wavy black hair, wore riding boots and carried a whip. A black Labrador retriever walked by his side. Naturally I stopped playing and said, "Good afternoon."

"It's Vi," replied the young man gruffly.

And we embraced. My girl looked extremely well, though entirely changed. In spite of the male attire, I would never have recognized her. Instinct told me that the situation—to borrow an American phrase from Norman's letter—had to be played by ear; but as I saw that plastic surgery had performed probably its greatest miracle on her, I couldn't help inquiring, in a tactful manner, whether the work stopped at her face. This was a mistake. She drew away abruptly, asking what kind of person I took her for. I apologized, pleading slight nervousness and shock. We embraced again, and all was well. She snapped her fingers and a deliciously shy local creature tripped forward to be introduced. Farah, Violet's friend and companion, was not given to talking, but seemed sweet and devoted enough, indeed even more attentive and obedient than the dog. I was reminded of those stories in newspapers about G.I.'s stationed in Japan after the war, and how womanhood there was a revelation to them. Further intimate details of this reunion must be passed over. I will record only that Violet was unwilling to talk about her experiences, and that curiosity once again pushed me too far. "Have I, as your mother, the right to ask," I said quietly, "exactly what you *did*?" She began to glare, and veins stood out on her forehead. "Is there anything," I continued, "of which you feel . . . ashamed?"

Her reply, I must admit, had dignity. "Shame is for the victors, mother. Nothing can strip the vanquished of their pride."

Later, we drove out to the Pyramids for cocktails. As we sat on the terrace of a cafe and gazed at the fantastic monuments, I asked if she'd heard about Norman. She answered that she wasn't interested. I felt she ought to know, anyway, and at the end of my account she remarked: "Poor little bastard." I then revealed the considerable sum he'd left her in his will. She said arrangements could be made for it to be deposited in Switzerland.

It may be asked how I dare to tell all this, since Violet is now the only "war criminal" and the only British "traitor" officially unaccounted for, *non grata* on both sides in the climate of peace. I shall no doubt be criticized for not turning her in. Both challenges are easily met. Setting aside the fact that in betraying my daughter I would certainly have lost my life—unimportant, if the cause were just—it may be thought that I faced a simple dilemma of love versus duty. Not at all. I faced no dilemma of any kind, since my outlook has always included the belief that two wrongs do not make a right. As for Violet's own security, she and Farah now live in a very different part of the world, as the result of a serious quarrel with von Knoop. I always visit them on my annual holiday, and am of course expert in giving people "the slip." My girl has become rather stout in middle age (and was once mistaken for my older brother); but it has somehow released her essentially sunny nature. She relishes the open air, and is a brilliant markswoman and huntress.

To satisfy those with a literal turn of mind, I must add that no pressure can be brought on me by any government or world organization to divulge my daughter's whereabouts. I have let it privately be known that she is, in a personal sense, all I have. The world, I predict, will not accept this part of my story, preferring to believe that I am "covering up" for Norman's sake. If by any chance an investigation is rashly ordered, I have dealt with such things before.

To conclude. Since my energy and youthful appearance continue unabated in spite of my somewhat venerable age, I asked Doctor Brod recently—on the principle that a gift horse should always be looked in the mouth—to perform a thorough check-up. The resulting X-Rays amazed even him, since they showed that my tissues and organs belonged to a woman of perhaps forty-six. Once again I have no comment, except that a life without fear is the best answer to Time's winged chariot. It is all very well to be as young as one feels, but more important to feel as young as medical science confirms that one is.

The journalists who wish to write my biography, the film companies eager to dramatize my life, will no doubt be disappointed with these unassuming explanations. Which is why I continue to decline all their offers. I find them too interested in my alleged sensational aspects, too indifferent to my inner self. Nothing displeases me more than to be told I'm a legend. It implies that I cannot be verified.

Allow me, then, to insist again that I remain above all a mother, whose resourceful exploits should not disguise a retiring and contemplative nature. I have watched a daughter make port after a difficult crossing, and now wish a dear, lost son to speak for himself at last.

"Lady D."
Wanga-Jobo, Africa.